THE STORY OF SARAH

Book Four

THE NEW LIFE SERIES

BY **LOUISE BOUCK**

ACKNOWLEDGEMENTS

It is important to say thank you to all the people who have cheered me on. A special thank you goes to those who have given unfailing prayer support. I give a big thank you to my husband, Dale Bouck, my first editor, who also managed to keep my computer running in spite of the monsoons. Thank you to my family members that suffered through reading very rough drafts. A big thank you hug goes to R.J. Dick. He was the first to want to read "The Story of Ben Slater" and to Brenda Dick who read "The Story of Sarah" to RJ when he was very ill. An appreciative mention goes to Donna Shaw, who wholeheartedly helped me to keep Sarah's feet on the right path.

I also want to mention Maureen Burge, my current editor. She has been enthusiastic and encourages me to keep up the pace of converting the series to paperbacks. Thanks Maureen.

Enduring Thanks goes to Ray Shaw for his time and patient repetition with new technology until I got it. Without him my stories would just be files in my computer. And, what would any of us do without the public libraries and the wonderful people that work there?

Copyright
Registration Number TXu 1-942-208
Register of Copyrights, United States of America
Effective date of Registration August 18, 2014
Copyright Claimant Louise Irene Bouck
Content Title, The Story of Sarah
Title of Work: The New Life Series, book 4
Of 4,5,6,7
ISBN 978-1-943984-13-8 EBook
ISBN 978-1-943984-03-9 Paperback
Volume one
Hisgivenstories LIB Productions

DEDICATION

This is dedicated to Jesus, and my family, those gone before me, those with me now and those to come and all my brothers and sisters in Christ.

✝

TABLE OF CONTENTS

INTRODUCTION

This is book four in "The New Life Series." The Christian fiction in this series is written to offer the reader a wholesome entertainment, starting back in a simpler but not easier time. Their example of spiritual strength and "never quit" attitude is refreshing and inspiring. The adventurers follow the trail to a new land and challenges they never imagined.

In book one "More Than Survival", follow Benjamin Slater as he copes with the wild isolation of the new frontier and the lessons of self-preservation. He experiences the pain of loss and joys of accomplishment. He travels "Life's Many Journeys," in book two and learns to appreciate The Land's Heritage," in book three.

In Book four, you will find out "The Story of Sarah"

As you read the books, Ben develops into a man of physical and spiritual strength. His problem solving mind is challenged many times.

When Sarah, his sister returns to him, they are finally "Together," in book five. You will find out how her life affected the Indians that took her and how they became "The Blue Stone People" in book six.

A change of scene takes you to the camp of the Sentu and three survivors enter the story, in book seven "Teewahpanyee the Boy, Two Feathers the Man," Willow and Water Bug bring new strength and young blood to an old people. In book eight, with Willow at his side he becomes leader of "The People of The Lion". They are chosen by the Lion of Judah to be rescuers, and are rewarded in book nine, by being allowed to discover "The Lion's Den."

In book ten, the land that Ben Slater's father chose has miraculously remained with the family as time has gone by and generations were born. In a day beyond today, the series skips to the final times after the rapture. A new heroine stands up bravely to the soldiers of the anti-Christ. She finds Ben's Bible, Mary Slater's journals and the gift of faith. Emily spreads the word and struggles to survive the time of tribulation as she finally realizes that this is "Just the Beginning" for those who believe.

PROLOGUE

The story of Sarah is the fourth book in "The New Life Series". It takes the reader from the simple thoughts of a young girl, to the stirring challenges of a forming new nation in turmoil. She struggles between two worlds, held in each by love. Through her, the people of the Winahatah are saved from annihilation and spiritually reborn.

THE STORY OF SARAH
CHARACTER LIST

Sarah, nearing nine years old, blond, blue eyes and thin, she had to learn to live with a people whose ways and language were foreign. Their gods were not the God of her father. She became Brave Sparrow.

Chief Rising Eagle, head of the Winahatah. A man filled with hate for the white man and with the power to send his warriors to kill them.

Yellowbird, wife of Chief Rising Eagle

Dark Wolf, son of Chief Rising Eagle and a leader, he became Sarah's adoptive father and head of the Winahatah People.

Moonflower, wife of Dark Wolf, kind and gentle, she taught Sarah to live as one of the people.

Singing Lark, a healer and wife of the shaman, she became Sarah's mentor.

Talking Mountain, the shaman of the people, led by his belief in the unseen, he works at his magic and dances to provide favor with his gods.

Blue Stone, Brave Sparrow's friend

Growling Bear, top hunter, gruff and strong willed

Sharp Knife, a young hunter, warrior and friend.

Roaring Water, husband of Morning Dove

Morning Dove, closest friend of Moonflower

Sleeping Bear, Blue Stone's father

Dancing Willow, Blue Stone's mother

Rising Sun, a woman with a sharp tongue

Corn Silk thought Sarah had done something to her baby to make him cry.

Singing Wind, Blue Stone's brother, a flute maker and herd guardian

Gray Cloud, a flute player and herd guardian

Night Hawk, scout, hunter and warrior

Snow Star, Moonflower's second natural born daughter

Running Deer, promised to Blue Stone

Falling Stones, Brave Sparrow's first patient, a hunter and

warrior

Red Squirrel, wife of Falling Stones

Bending Grass, a young boy with potential

Fire Grass, Sharp Knife's mother

Sweet Grass, apprentice to Brave Sparrow

Mary Parker, pioneer wife, stolen by Growling Bear

Adam, Mary Parker's two year old son.

Jedadiah Jones, adopted big brother of Benjamin Slater

Benjamin Slater, Sarah's Brother

Beth, survivor of the wagon train raid

Joshua, Mary Parker's oldest son

Chemanshaw, the name of another people

THE STORY OF SARAH
CHAPTER ONE
TAKEN BY DARK WOLF

In the village of The Winahatah, the scout rode into camp stirring a cloud of dust as he pulled his horse up short and bounded to the ground near the Chief's tent. Running Fox was well respected and trusted by Chief Rising Eagle. The flap opened before Running Fox reached it.

"You have news?" He asked.

"Yes, my Chief. They come,"

"Dark Wolf, gather my warriors." The respected son of the Chief took only a few steps from the tent, before he was met by some of his best warriors. They anticipated battle and had watched for the scout's return.

As more men gathered, the heart of the village filled with people. All the tents emptied and women stood with grim faces, near their cooking fires, holding babies and controlling youngsters, looking in the direction of their men, gathered in a brief meeting just outside the chief's tent. They understood what this meant. Soon their men would leave. Some might not return alive. Others could come back wounded.

"Growling Bear, as always you will lead. Wait in the big rocks. Attack just beyond where the wagon trail curves near. Growling Bear's reply was a simple nod.

"Running Fox, from there you will be able to return or send news."

"Yes, I am ready."

"Go now and prepare to leave at daybreak."

The men scattered, hurrying to their tents. Some stepped inside, out of sight, to hold their wives close and hug their children. It was not their way to show affection in front of others. Dark Wolf explained to his wife, Moonflower, what was happening.

"A wagon train comes. Prepare food and water bags for the days that I will be away." In each tent, other wives were doing similar chores.

Horses were brought from the herd and decorated with war paint. Symbols of victory and spirit protection symbols were added by Talking Mountain, the shaman and then each horse was tied near their owner's tent. They were fed hand-picked wild grain and given waterproof baskets filled from the lake. These were each man's favored warhorses, swift and strong, ready for the morning. Weapons were checked and readied by the men. Women did not touch them. It was thought that the woman's hand might bring the displeasure of the war god's. Each tent was quiet, as the sky grew dark.

They all understood that if they didn't protect their hunting grounds, more white men would come and the buffalo would no longer roam the prairie lands near their village, providing the food and shelter that they counted on for their very lives.

*****

It was the beginning of a new life. Everyone was excited and enthusiastic. They couldn't wait to get underway. Thirty-one covered wagons were packed and ready. Some were badly overloaded. The wagon master smiled, showing a missing tooth. Dark, sun-creased skin and a gray beard surrounded his wise brown eyes. As he carefully rode through the din he nodded to folks encouraging them to get up on their wagons. The congested area surrounding the wagons was crowded with people and a dog here and there, trying to avoid the stomp of a horse's foot and nervously wagging and barking at the same time. The air held the sounds of loud voices trying to convey last messages. A baby was crying, frightened by the unusual energy packed environment. Horses jerked and were hard to handle, stomping, eager to be moving. Women held lace hankies, dabbing at their eyes as they clung to those they loved.

He knew that necessity would soon cause much of the unneeded belongings to be hesitantly left on the edge of the trail. This was a once in a lifetime thing. Families were saying good-bye to loved ones. Most of them would never see each other again.

For now, he would give them time to deal with their deep emotions. He gently urged families to climb into their places on their wagons. Last hugs and kisses had been given and tears streamed down the faces of both those leaving and left behind. Sarah's Grandfather held her tight for one more moment before he handed her up to the waiting arms of his son, Josiah Slater. She breathed deeply memorizing the smell of his pipe and wool sweater mixed with his English after-shave and the dust in the air.

Sarah's mother steadied her with a hand as she moved inside the wagon to a spot that had been prepared for her on top of their folded bedding. Her rag doll and a drawing slate with chalk waited to entertain her.

As soon as she saw the slate, a gift from her Grandmother, she remembered her tight hug and her advice to always learn as much as she could and to memorize the Holy Bible, a little every day. I'll remember her and miss her. I understand why she didn't come this morning. In all this confusion, you can't say much. Our quiet talk in the kitchen was best. She always got up so early. She had bread rising on the cupboard near the stove and coffee made for the grownups before we left. We have a box of her wonderful oatmeal cookies in here somewhere. I can smell them. It is strange that I am thinking about all the scents this morning. A single tear made its way down her cheek and she rubbed it away. She promised she would take good care of Smudge.

My sweet kitty, she couldn't come. Grandmother said she would probably jump out of the back of the wagon and get lost in the prairie. She said she would write us all a letter and tell me how she is doing but we have to write the first time so she can get our new address.

As the wagon master shouted and waved his hat, the first wagon pulled out, heading west along a barely visible trail. Cheers filled the air and encouraged the pioneers as one by one the wagons took their assigned position. Arms ached from waving but still they continued, until the people left behind were mere dots on the landscape.

The wagon train was well underway before the wagon master rode slowly by each wagon asking if everyone was alright and if they had any questions. His comments were simply intended to calm and reassure the new adventurers.

The mid-morning air smelled sweet. The wheels of the wagons crushed the grass as they rolled along. This was all new to everyone on the trail, with the exception of the trail boss and a few hands that rode along in case of trouble.

All, too soon they would be in Indian Territory. If the wagon train was discovered, their guns and knowledge would be needed. Most of the wagons held families. He guessed that less than half would be capable of effective defense, if the train came under attack. Two more men had been added the very morning they left.

They had traveled slowly for what seemed like a lifetime to the people of the train, sleeping at night under or in their wagon in the cold wind, pounding rain, or heat. They endured the constant bouncing and bumping of the wheels as they traveled on the dirt trail. It felt like all the insects in the world were intent on making them miserable both day and night.

Sarah's father, Josiah Slater and his wife Mary rode up front. Her brother, Benjamin, often walked or rode on the back of the wagon. Once in a while he rode on Dart Away, the beautiful black stallion that had won races enough to pay for the wagon and supplies they needed for this opportunity to find land for a good farm. Dart Away was the only luxury the family had allowed themselves. They couldn't part with him.

Today, Ben rode on the back of the wagon, watching the tall prairie grass reach for the soles of his bare feet. His pants had gotten short during the winter months and now seemed even shorter. His blond hair was bleached almost white by the sun. It reached beyond his shirt collar. He hoped his mother would not notice. She would insist on cutting it again. He shaded his bright blue eyes with his hand as he watched a hawk circle high above the prairie. Ben would be sixteen in the fall. He longed for the day when his parents would acknowledge that he was a man. He thought of himself as full grown. He didn't know it, but he looked older. The harsh sun had burned his skin into a dark tan, setting smile and frown lines in his handsome face.

Josiah watched the soil as they traveled along.

"Good soil and a reliable water source is what we need, Mary. The grass is taller and greener in this area. Look way over there. See that line of trees. That has to be a river. Tomorrow at first light, I will take Dart Away, and check out that area. We will be stopping soon. You and Benjamin should break camp when the others do and keep our wagon in line until I come back."

"Josiah, I am concerned for you. The wagon master said we should stay together."

"It is something I must do." He was firm about it and she left it at that. She had been taught to be meek, but that did not mean that she was weak. She prepared their meal and he read from the Bible as they had each night on the trail. Many people from the wagons gathered around sitting on the grass to listen to the reading.

He left quietly the next morning and was still gone when Mary and Benjamin hitched up their team and stirred the campfire one last time, making sure it was out.

As they traveled along, Mary kept watching in the direction Josiah had gone.

Finally a smile broke across her face as he came into view. Ben hopped down and his father took the reins. The exchange of drivers took only a moment.

Ben gave Dart Away a drink and rubbed his beautiful coat with a burlap bag walking with him until he had cooled down. Even now after the long ride he pranced with energy. This horse was special, lean, long legged and strong.

Ben could hear his father talking excitedly.

"Mary, it is beautiful. The river is a good one, big enough that it runs all year long. On the other side there is a high bluff that we can snuggle our cabin against and it will be out of the wind. The trees are huge virgin oak and pines and the ground is good. The grass is thick, tall and dark green. Mary, this is it! I'm sure of it!"

When Josiah described the wide river and suggested they pull out of line and discuss what he had seen, Mary's heart lurched with fear. She didn't want to leave the other wagons. The vast, open prairie was intimidating.

Pulling out of line from the other wagons, he prayed.

"Heavenly Father," he began. "We look to you for protection and guidance. I have heard the warning of the wagon master, and yet I feel that it would be foolish of us to ride past all this good earth to stop somewhere less desirable. We are considering setting up camp at the river over there. I rode over there and checked it out this morning. The ground is rich and the river looks like it runs year around. You are our provision. We thank you and trust in you. We ask your blessings on our plan."

"Amen," they all said together. Sarah's father had headed their team of horses to a tiny line of trees, just visible, far in the distance. Mary was frightened. This didn't feel right to her. This wasn't how she had pictured it at all. She thought she would have neighbors, someone to help when it was time for the baby to come. Father, please change his mind. Please change his mind.

"Josiah, have you lost sight of the authority of those who have been placed here to lead us?" Father God, is this his plan? Or is it really yours? She prayed silently.

Just then the sun weathered wagon train scout rode over to check on them.

"Is something wrong?"

"No Gus, we are fine. We have decided to stop. The ground is good in this area and that's a river over there."

"This is Indian territory," Gus said. "It isn't safe for you folks to leave the wagon train yet. Don't stay out here alone."

"That's a risk we are willing to take. We have prayed about it and it feels right. Tell all the people on the wagons that we will pray for them and ask them to do the same for us."

"Alright then, but we will miss you, and the reading of the Bible each night. It turned the people on this train into one big family. Folks on this train get along better than any I have seen. Be safe, and always stay alert," he said as he turned his horse back to the moving wagons and rode away, preparing to report to the Wagon Master.

It took Josiah Slater, longer than he thought it would, to reach the trees, as the single wagon traveled cautiously through the unmarked, long prairie grass.

"We will pull up under that huge oak up ahead," Sarah's father, announced.

The whole family was excited especially Benjamin, Sarah's brother.

"I can't wait to be off this wagon. I want to explore this land that will be our home."

"Me too," Sarah giggled excitedly. "I will race you to the edge of the river."

*****

Growling Bear had the men settled in behind the rocks making their camp as comfortable as possible for the long wait. Running Fox had returned to the Chief twice reporting the slow progress of the wagon train.

The warriors were gone and the women were left in the village wondered how long they would have to wait. They cared for the children and talked together, as a strange hush had settled on the camp, unlike anything they had ever experienced.

"Oh, we have been through wars before, with other tribes attacking our hunting parties. Remember the tribe from the north that swept into camp at dawn leaving death and destruction. Women grabbed their babies running and screaming to hide in the trees. When it was over, blood stained the ground and tents of our people," said Singing Lark, wife of the Shaman.

"Yes we remember. Those that were left alive moved our village, roaming until they found this beautiful little lake and settled here, said Moonflower."

"That was many summers ago. But now, more and more of the white men come. At summer council the chiefs told stories of white soldiers that entered villages and killed every man, woman and child. What kind of warrior kills women and children?" The old woman asked.

"Chief Walking Cloud of the Chemanshaw told of their people having been friendly to white families that had entered their area. They had shared food and their campfires, but the Gods were angry with them and a strange new illness had come, making red spots and high fevers. Stinging Snake, their medicine man, had prayed and danced, but the Gods would not listen. Many died, both young and old."

Moonflower frowned.

"Yes, that illness took my Raven. I miss her everyday"

"White men bring evil spirits, we must stop them from coming before we all die." The old woman that had made that declaration stood abruptly and shuffled to her tent, jerking the flap shut behind her.

"She still mourns her husband and son. They both died at the hands of the white men." The small group of women all murmured sympathetically.

*****

"I wonder why they have left the others," said Dark Wolf. If they are ill, we will leave them alone, but if they are planning to settle there we must stop them. Leaping Deer and Night Hawk come with me. You speak their tongue. The rest of you will wait until Growling Bear gives you the signal to attack."

Staying behind a gentle roll in the land so they would not be observed, the three warriors headed for the river.

Once they entered the shade of the trees, their horses were allowed to drink and rest as they enjoyed the sweet grass growing near the water. Studying the angle that the wagon approached the river, they decided they should move down, closer to the biggest oak tree visible.

"They seem to be heading right for that huge oak. That's good. There is plenty of cover all along there."

The wagon neared, and the three waiting warriors could hear its squeaks and creaks. Still they waited and stayed hidden, trying to discern if the wagon held sickness, or settlers.

As predicted, the wagon stopped in the shade of the oldest oak. Mary could see the refreshing blue moving water peeking between the bushes.

"I think those are raspberry bushes," she said, thrilled to imagine the wonderful jams and pies she could make from the berries when they were ripe.

"We are home!" Sarah's father shouted loudly. That announcement triggered an immediate action and the sound of swiftly running horses breaking a path through the brush softened the sound of the arrow's twang as it hit with a strong thud in Josiah's chest. He had pulled his rifle from beneath his seat intending to check the area for dangerous animals. His finger jerked its trigger and a single shot rang out, as he fell. The startled team yanked the wagon forward, dropping the left wheels into a deep trench made by runoff from the prairie. The wagon shuddered and turned on its side.

Benjamin jumped free and ran for cover, chased by Leaping Deer, who shot an arrow that sliced through the flesh of his shoulder. Panicking, Benjamin ran recklessly, tripping and landing in the thorn bushes hitting his head on a rock. He lay still as consciousness slipped away.

Sarah had been seated in the center of the wagon. She screamed as the wagon tipped, and a heavy, wooden box of dishes and pans slammed into her shoulder.

A moment later, as she was trying to crawl out of the back of the wagon, strong, rough hands pulled her up and out. She looked into a face painted red, white and black, with braided hair as black as coal.

He lifted her up in front of him on his horse. It too was painted with symbols.

He is taking me away! She thought, feeling terror, join the distress and physical pain, she turned and screamed, scratching his arm, squirming, and kicking hard, to get free as he held her tightly against his bare chest.

When she tried to bite him, he pushed her face away from his arm laughing, as if she were a fly. Nothing she could do was enough to affect his resolve to take her.

As they galloped away, she could hear shouting and whoops from the attackers at the wagon.

He held her tightly against his chest as she twisted and tried to wiggle free, while all the time, crying, kicking and screaming for her mother and father to help her. Sarah was spared the sight of her parents lying on the grass. She worried what had happened to them and Benjamin.

Sarah was young, just short of nine years old but already, a strong growing faith in God's power filled her heart. She prayed and thanked Him for being with her.

"God help me! Take me back to my mother and father and Ben. If they were hurt, please heal them. Watch over all of us." She repeated those words and other prayers over and over in her mind as they rode across the prairie at a steady pace. She could hear horses behind her and hoped that it was her family. She saw smoke from something burning in the distance as they finally crossed the wagon trail. They continued on until it seemed they would never stop. The horses were lathered and tired.

"My father would never use a horse this long without a break," she said. "Your horse needs water and rest." He ignored her. She didn't know that he could not understand her. They slowed to a walk as they moved across the prairie grass into the edge of the huge rock area. Just as the sun was setting, they stopped at last.

She looked around as she was lifted down, hoping to see Ben and her parents on the horses that followed. All she saw was two other men with their faces painted. They led her father's workhorses with large rolls of her family's bedding, clothes and other things on their backs that she recognized from their wagon.

Dart Away, her father's beautiful riding horse was unburdened and led on a long rope.

Dark Wolf, her captor had been leading him the entire time. The horses rested and were given a drink from large covered pots stashed in the rocks.

They didn't tie me, she thought, but I can tell they are watching me closely. I wonder what they are saying. I can't understand them. The man that grabbed me seems quite pleased with himself.

He handed a water bag to her so that she could drink and then a small piece of deer jerky to chew as he motioned for her to sit and eat.

It was growing cold, as the night wind brought strange sounds. She huddled close to a huge gray rock that radiated warmth from the day's heat. She wrapped her skinny arms around her knees and with her eyes squeezed tightly shut; she waited for what would happen next.

In spite of her efforts to stop them, tears began to form little streaks on her cheeks in the coating of trail dust on her skin. She was afraid, cold, and tired. Now that they had stopped to rest she was more aware of the pain in her shoulder. In the fading light, she lifted the thin sleeve of her dress to see that a large, dark, bruised, bump had formed.

"Girl, do not cry now, sleep," said Night Hawk. He was the one with the blanket roll. He took it down, pulling out a quilt her mother had made. He gently wrapped it around her.

"Soon you will have a new mother. Now sleep."

"But I don't want a new mother! I want my real mother," Sarah wailed.

"Girl, be quiet. Sleep!" he ordered, as he gently pressed her down on the grass.

A soft strip of leather was tied to her ankle and then fastened to the belt of the man that had plucked her from the wagon. He laid his head on the edge of her quilt and wrapped a fur around his shoulders. He was soon asleep, snoring.

Sarah's thoughts bounced from wondering about her family, to thinking of how she had been treated. She realized that the men had spoken to each other but she had not understood what they said. At least one of them talks so I can understand him, she thought.

Actually, she could sense that they did not intend to harm her. They had fed her and given her a blanket when they saw that she was cold. Then she remembered the one man saying she would soon have a new mother. I wonder what he meant. She tried hard to be brave.

It was very dark without a fire. It wouldn't be daylight for many hours. She asked God to bring her family soon. During the night she dreamed of the sounds of the raid, the wagon tipping and the hands of the man pulling her out and onto his horse. Her scream woke the camp as she shook with sobs. Dark Wolf's hands held her shoulders causing pain. It jolted her fully awake. Her face was wet with tears again and her shoulder throbbed. Worst of all her dream had renewed the terror of the day before.

Her tether was released. Still wrapped in the quilt; she was once again lifted onto the horse in front of Dark Wolf.

Now awake, the raiding party moved out. They moved at a slow easy walk, beside the boulders. The soft rhythm of the horse's movement, the warmth of the chest behind her and the arm around her, although imprisoning, secured her and after a while, Sarah was lulled into a more comfortable state.

Entering a forest, they stopped by a spring to water the horses and rest. The trees were large and dense in every direction. She was grateful for the shade. Sarah was not used to riding at all. Her legs and bottom were so sore she could barely walk behind a bush to relieve herself. Her tender skin had been in direct contact with the horse's hair and she was raw.

One thing that was an exception was that the man that she rode with had noticed her discomfort and after a few comments from the others, he had coated her legs with grease.

Again on the horses, they rode slowly through the trees. This time he made sure that she sat on the quilt. They rode beside a high bluff.

CHAPTER TWO
A NEW MOTHER

When the horses stepped out of the trees, Sarah saw a sparkling small lake partially rimmed with cattails and willow trees. On the far side of it was a large Indian camp with many tents.

They stopped in front of one of the larger tents, and Sarah was lifted down into the waiting arms of a woman that took her gently and protectively.

"My wife has a new daughter now," he said proudly. "The white man's sickness took many lives. Now you will have this girl to help. She is not our Raven, but she will grow. Teach her well so she is useful in a man's tent. She has a strong spirit. Watch she does not run away."

Sarah wondered what he had said. Her eyes followed him as he nudged his horse and walked it to the next tent. It was the largest tent, and not far away. He dismounted and disappeared inside. The black stallion, Dart Away, stood nervously beside his mount. The new surroundings made him uncomfortable.

Dark Wolf was glad that his raid had yielded the one thing that the Chief had wanted most.

The sister of the Chief, Moonflower, mourned the death of Raven, her 8-year-old daughter, from measles. He had captured a girl that would grow to learn their ways. Her pale skin would soon darken in the sun, but her blond hair and blue eyes would always mark her as being of different blood. Dark Wolf loved Moonflower. She was his wife and he shared her sorrow. He thought of Raven, their beautiful daughter as he entered the tent and greeted Chief Rising Eagle, his father and Yellow Bird, his mother.

Dark Wolf had conducted the raid with success and had added a girl to the Chief's family. He had also brought back a fine riding horse, one worthy of the Chief's praise. He fully expected the Chief to take the horse as his due, but because he was so pleased with the news of the girl child for his sister, he gave the horse to Dark Wolf after seeing it and praising its quality. The other four horses were healthy, and very large and strong. They were released by Leaping Deer and Night Hawk into the guarded herd that grazed near the village. They would belong to everyone and next spring perhaps they would add their strength and stamina to the bloodlines of the herd.

*****

Moonflower carried the girl into their tent and placed her on the furs.

As she pulled the blanket from around her, it dragged against Sarah's injured shoulder. She winced and pulled back. The woman tenderly examined the injured shoulder. She pulled the girl's dress off over her head and checked the rest of her. She clacked her tongue when she saw the raw skin on the child's legs and bottom, and the many smaller bruises and scrapes on her body, caused by the tipping wagon.

"You are a skinny girl. You need to eat" she said, handing the child a cake of pounded smoked meat, grain, fat and berries, lightly sweetened with honey, resembling a bumpy cookie, it was travel food, tasty and rich. It appealed to Sarah. She nibbled the new food and decided that she would eat some of it while she was sponged with sweet smelling oil from top to bottom. Her hair was also oiled and then brushed, braided and tied with a strip of leather. Moonflower gently covered the little girl's shoulder with a poultice of mashed cool clover leaves, and crushed cambium layer of cooked willow bark all added to bear grease, held on by a strip of cloth. It cooled the ache deep inside.

Over her head was pulled what looked to Sarah like a shirt made of very soft tan leather. It was tied at her tiny waist with another strip of leather. She had to admit that she felt a lot cleaner and smelled good, too. The woman talked as she smoothed a mint and clover salve on the chafed areas. Sarah just listened, hoping to make sense of some of it. She couldn't.

Moonflower took her hand and slowly led her out of the tent. Sarah's mouth dropped open in awe. It was like walking into a different world.

Although nothing was immediately threatening, everything was frightening.

Sarah was on her way to be presented to the Chief. If he accepted her, a special celebration would soon be held in her honor and a name given to her.

Moonflower was sure that her brother would accept the child. He knew how much she had missed her own daughter and how many other children had been lost in the past year from the sickness of the white man.

Moonflower remembered that at first the various villages had tried to welcome the white men as friends. They had traded with them and held special celebrations in their honor. But as more and more white people came, they began to act like they owned the land. Then soldiers and disease followed.

Moonflower stopped at the door to the Chief's tent. She scratched on the edge of the flap, waiting permission to enter.

When the flap was raised, Moonflower guided Sarah gently in beside a frail looking woman with gray hair, and a colorfully beaded dress. This was Yellow Bird, wife of the Chief.

He was an older looking man with long braids that blended from white at the top to gray in the middle and black at the tips. They were adorned with bone beads and shells. He sat on the floor near the fire. Sarah looked about, curious to see everything. She identified beds made of furs and a fire pit with a pot of soup cooking. On the floor she saw many covered baskets. Strings of dried foods and herbs hung above her. Other bundles looked like dried weeds. She liked the scent in the tent.

The Chief sat with his legs crossed in the center of a large dark brown hide. He was leaning against a woven willow backrest. His skin was dark and his face had many deep lines and wrinkles from years spent in the sun and wind. His eyes flashed a look of disdain as they met Sarah's, for just an instant, before he concealed his feelings. Her ever-observant eyes caught it.

This is a good day, he thought, deliberately changing his mind to a more optimistic attitude. My son has returned safely from a successful raid and has brought back horses, blankets and this girl child. He studied her. She is thin, but seems healthy enough. Her hair is the color of straw. I like black hair. Moonflower's daughter, Raven, had black hair and dark brown eyes. She was lovely.

He remembered the little girl peeking in at the flap of his tent and if he allowed it, she would enter and crawl into his lap. He had loved Raven. He missed her. This child could never take her place, but she might be able to soften his sister's pain. He looked at his sister's face as she eagerly waited for his decision.

"You may keep her, if the spirits accept her." Moonflower left in high spirits and one step closer to being allowed to keep this precious girl.

Talking Mountain, shaman of the people, had seen the child arrive. He knew what would be expected of him.

Later when he was ready, he crossed the village to the Chief's tent and scratched for admittance.

"Yellow Bird, I need to speak with Chief Rising Eagle. Where is he?"

"He is there." She pointed with her chin, indicating the knoll where he often sat thinking.

"Yes, I see him. Thank you, Yellow Bird."

Talking Mountain approached the small hill with respect. "Come, my friend. Have you decided when you will have the ceremony?"

Talking Mountain settled beside him and spoke softly. "It must be late this afternoon, before the evening meal."

"I will have the communal fire prepared. Is there anything else?"

"Yes my Chief. The fire should be long and low. It will go as you wish. One more thing, when Dark Wolf, Moonflower and the child are seated at the fire with you, and Yellow Bird, you must all sit on the west side of the fire, with the camp and the setting sun at your back."

"Why is that important?"

"I cannot tell you now, but you will see at the meeting."

Back in their tent, Dark Wolf spoke, trying to comfort Moonflower, telling her that she should not worry.

"It is up to the spirits. If they will allow it, she will stay, whether the people want it or not. They will have to accept her, if the spirits do."

"Dark Wolf, I want so much to keep her. She needs me and I need her."

"I know. Please trust me. I brought her to you and I feel the spirits will see that it is good."

Even before the communal fire was lit, Dark Wolf had asked Moonflower to place their furs on the west side of the fire. Yellow Bird had been asked to do the same. Singing Lark and the other women followed their example, placing their sitting pads or blankets in the appropriate positions according to status in the tribe.

Talking Mountain waited in his tent until everyone was seated. Moonflower and Dark Wolf placed Sarah between Chief Rising Eagle and Dark Wolf, a definite position of honor. She tried to maneuver her way back to Moonflower, but Dark Wolf firmly placed his hand on her head, pushing down. Indicating she must stay where she was placed. The child looked down at her hands frowning and pouting, near tears, not wanting to be there. She had no idea that this gathering was about her. It would determine her fate. If Talking Mountain had made a mistake in judgment this could end very badly.

Chief Rising Eagle rose, standing near the fire. It had been deliberately built long and low, as the shaman had requested so that all those seated could see activity on any side.

"My people, you are all aware of the reason we are here. A white child has been brought into our camp. My son, Dark Wolf and his wife Moonflower, ask that the girl be allowed to remain. Stories from the Summer Council have all of us uncomfortable about her presence. I believe that it is best to rely on the wisdom of the ancient ones. Their spirits watch over us and are here as I speak."

Talking Mountain had slipped into the circle of firelight, without distracting anyone. He seemed to simply appear. Chief Rising Eagle sat back down making a display of touching the child's hair as he took his seat. This was an accepted symbol of affection used from Grandfather, to

Grandchild. This simple act sent a ripple of reaction around the circle.

Talking Mountain gave a subtle signal and the drums started softly. His helpers were well trained and sometimes their work was to enhance the ceremony of the shaman, but not become a noticed part of it. As he strutted around the entire circle, it was apparent that his garb and appearance was different than it had ever been before. His fringed cape had been blackened with grease and ash. His legs were bare and painted white with a paste of grease and crushed chalkstone. White bars marched across his face as if no other features were evident. More white bars decorated the backs of his hands and tops of his bare feet. He looked like he belonged to the other world, and at the moment he did. The drums grew louder and his face became a magnified sneer, while red palms turned down and striped fingers became claws. He whirled and feigned attacking the area near the girl. She shrieked and sobbed with fear attempting to slide back, away from the horrible wraith in front of her. Once again he plunged forward as she screamed. He could not have asked for a better reaction from the child.

"The spirits that surround her are angry," he announced loudly.

It was all Moonflower could do to stay in her place. She wanted to pull the child to her lap and cover her with arms of protection but she knew that Dark Wolf would be furious if she moved at all. He held the sobbing child in place.

Talking Mountain occasionally bent and tossed dust into the air as he chanted and danced. He was sweating profusely from the heat of the fire, the weight of the heavy hide that covered most of him and the exertion of the dance.

Suddenly he stopped and raised his arms high, shouting.

"Spirits of all the ancient ones, protectors of our people, counselors of our wise Chief Rising Eagle, fierce warriors of our legends, surround this white girl child and force the evil spirits of the white men to leave her and to leave our village. Fill her with strength, courage, intelligence and health! We beckon you to do it now!" As he said the word now, he folded his body into a low crouch. Everyone was staring at the girl as he backhanded an abundance of fine powder into the coals. A dense black cloud rose from the fire and spread over the gathering. The smell was noxious causing everyone to cover his or her nose and mouth.

Then the gentle breeze from the west brushed the air clean and moved the cloud out of the village where it disappeared. Awe and silence followed. Talking Mountain jumped up with a flourish of his cape replacing it on his shoulders, inside out. It had been coated pure white inside and he smiled broadly.

"The bad spirits are gone!" He announced. "They will not return. The girl can stay!" He gently reached for her hand and she drew back, but as he continued to offer his painted wiggling fingers and smile from his clown like face, she smiled back and took his hand. He slowly led her around the fire for all to see.

"The people have a new child in their village. Let us rejoice with a feast and naming ceremony tonight." The applause and laughter filled the air as Moonflower received the child and wrapped her arms around the little girl, pulling her close. Tears slid down Moonflower's face as she rested her cheek on Sarah's blond hair. There was much to do. They would prepare a naming feast. This was usually done for infants, but tonight it was for her new daughter. She wondered what name the Chief would choose.

After that ceremony, "Sarah" would be gone and a new person would be entered into the tribe, or so they thought.

Everyone would call her by the name given her by the Chief. Sarah was completely unaware of the reason for the preparations. She was taken back to the tent of Moonflower and laid on the furs and with motions, told to sleep and it was easy to obey, for she was exhausted by the events of the past three days. She slept until Moonflower woke her. She wiped her face with a cool wet cloth and gave her a drink of water.

"Come now, they are ready. When Chief Rising Eagle signals, you must stand before him. Say nothing. Just stand and listen. Do you understand?" She really didn't, not a word of it, but she walked beside Moonflower, to the common area outside.

A large fire was burning in the center of the clearing. People sat all around it. In some places, people were sitting in a row behind others. The village numbered more than one hundred tents of families.

The Chief stood inside the circle. Moonflower could feel the eyes of her people turning toward her, as she brought Sarah to a space saved for them beside Dark Wolf. Sarah sat down looking at her dusty bare feet. She didn't want to meet the eyes of all these strange people. She was surprised to recognize the man beside her as the one whose horse had carried her to this camp. He was no longer wearing the red, black and white paint. He had bathed in the lake, removing the paint, dust and sweat of the raid. His hair was oiled and freshly braided. He smells a lot better now, she thought to herself. He has the same oil on his hair that she put on me.

The Chief had begun to speak. The people were quiet as they listened. She couldn't understand him. He was telling a story in the language of the Winahatah people.

"Our warriors have been brave and they have stopped the wagon train." The people cheered.

"They brought back many big horses, blankets, and food, but most importantly they brought back many rifles and bullets to stop the white people from taking our hunting ground!" The people cheered loudly.

Then he turned toward his son,

"Dark Wolf brought back a fine mount. He will bring speed to many foals. He brought back four workhorses, bigger and stronger than any we had. They will add strength and stamina to our herd. He brought back warm blankets to protect against the coming winter, and a rifle!" The people cheered for each acquisition. The Chief waited for total silence.

"My son, Dark Wolf, has brought back a girl child. The spirits have accepted her as one of our people; she will live with him and Moonflower. Their tent is empty. Their hearts weep for their only child that is gone to the spirit world."

He sat down next to the medicine man, Talking Mountain.

Soft murmurings were heard but no one cheered. They feel as I do, he thought. Now we have whites in our own camp! The ceremony started. Brightly colored costumes and feathered headdresses danced gaily by. Sarah had never seen such a spectacle.

When the music and the drums stopped, the dancers returned to their seats. The medicine man spoke with authority.

"The spirits have taken all evil away from our people. They inhabit the black smoke," he said, as he pointed, reminding the people of the ceremony earlier in the afternoon. The people's cheer was followed by a dramatic silence.

He made a loud announcement.

"The spirits accepted the girl child." This time nearly everyone cheered and stood dancing in their places as the drums beat and flutes carried the sound of joy to the lake and forest beyond.

The Chief slowly stood and the people grew quiet with anticipation. He beckoned to Sarah. She realized that he wanted her to come forward but she froze in fear. Moonflower had to pick her up, set her on her feet and push her forward. Sarah stood before the old Chief, for all to see; a sad, frightened, white child, with hair the color of straw, and eyes as blue as summer skies. She was visibly shaking so hard she could barely stand.

He looked around at his people, and with a wide smile, he said,

"Her name is Brave Sparrow." The people laughed and applauded.

Once again the people cheered. Moonflower came up beside her and held her hand.

"Brave Sparrow, you are my daughter now."

Many women came up close to look at the new child and say her name. They touched her hair or face and smiled at Moonflower. They wanted to share in her happiness.

Some in the village strongly disapproved. They did not come forward to congratulate Moonflower. She was aware of their feelings. Sarah wished that she could understand what was being said.

Sarah was beginning to have a small understanding of what had taken place. All that was in her rebelled! She did not want this new Indian mother. She wanted her real mother. She promised herself that as soon as Moonflower looked the other way she would run away and find her mother and father. Why hadn't they come to get her yet she wondered, as tears escaped her eyes?

"Hey you're not a brave sparrow," yelled a boy. "You are a crying sparrow." He taunted as he and his friends laughed and pointed at her.

"Go away," said Moonflower. She was glad that the child could not understand them.

"She is going to have something to eat now."

Food was the last thing that Sarah wanted. Her stomach ached and her head ached from crying and she just wanted to get away from all these strange people. Moonflower seemed to understand, and picked up a few delicious bites of meat and small cakes from the feast, placing them on a hand carved wooden plate. She led Brave Sparrow back to the tent and motioned for her to eat, saying the word for each food. She brought her a cup of cool water and said the word for water when she handed it to her. Sarah drank it all. She hadn't realized how thirsty she had been. She took a few bites to please Moonflower, who seemed concerned. She is a nice lady, thought Sarah. My Mother will thank her when she comes, for taking care of me.

CHAPTER THREE
BRAVE SPARROW

After Sarah had eaten, Moonflower gathered the little girl onto her cozy lap, and began to hum. Because she was small, Moonflower guessed her age at six or maybe seven. She stroked her hair and rocked her gently until she slept. Moonflower felt tears escape her own eyes as she felt the warmth of a child in her lap again. She knew that she had been given a precious gift at someone else's tragic expense. Her heart ached for the mother that had lost this sweet little girl.

"I promise I will raise her well and she will be a good woman. She will have a heart full of love and her mouth will laugh. She will see the beauty in the spring flowers and learn their benefits as food and medicine. She will see the bounty in the time of the falling leaves, and not know hunger. Her hands will learn skills, which will make her husband proud. A great warrior will choose her and he will love her and treat her well. She will have many children to hold as I hold her now. This I promise to you, mother of this girl." Although her words were silent, this was a promise that Moonflower would work hard to keep. They echoed in her heart all the days of her life.

Moonflower made a soft bed of furs next to hers and laid Sarah on them. She would need many things before winter. Moonflower would receive gifts after the feast, furs and hides that could be used for clothing, and beads to use for decorating them. Moonflower proudly returned to the feast, laughing and joking with the other women. For the first time, in a long time she felt like dancing.

Each woman had brought the very best that she could as a gift. They liked Moonflower and besides it would be good to have Dark Wolf see that they were kind and generous to his wife. He was son of the Chief.

"We will be going down to the field to pull the weeds tomorrow. You should bring Brave Sparrow so she can start to learn how we do things," said Morning Dove.

"Yes, I will, said Moonflower. I want her to learn all that she can. She must learn the wild flowers and how we use them and how to read the seasons, how to weave baskets and rugs and she must learn our language and to speak correctly and with respect."

"It will take time, but she will learn."

"Did you see the look on Growling Bear's face when he finally came back?" Something made him very angry. He looked like he was wearing war paint, without any!" said Singing Lark. They all laughed, enjoying the joke. Singing Lark, wife of the medicine man, had a way of finding out details of stories that people were not anxious to share.

As the women bent and pulled weeds from the corn field, they gossiped.

By morning when they reassembled in the field to work, Singing Lark had found out that during the raid on the single wagon, by Dark Wolf; Growling Bear had led the attack on the wagon train. He had captured a young woman from the wagon train and was bringing her back.

While the raiding party slept she had cut her ropes and escaped into the tall prairie grass with his knife. The warriors looked for her but couldn't find her.

Growling Bear's wife had died with the same sickness that killed Raven. He wanted a woman to care for his tent, to cook and sew. He had taken her to be a slave wife.

"Talking Mountain said that Growling Bear was furious because he left his knife at his waist where she could reach it. He is lucky that she didn't kill him with it!"

"I have never thought it right to bring their kind to live with us," Said Rising Sun. They are not like us and never can be, no matter how hard we try to teach them."

"How would you know, Rising Sun?" asked Moonflower. "Have you lived with one?"

"Oh, I am sorry Moonflower I didn't mean anything, I'm sure that the youngster will learn to do something…"

Rising Sun was mother of two sons, both big and strong. She was too proud and often used a sharp tongue to cut down the other women. Moonflower wisely didn't rise to the bait. She didn't want to argue.

"Let's work faster so we can finish before it gets too hot," she said. Other children had come with their mothers to help prepare the field for the planting. They stared at Brave Sparrow and tried to talk to her but she didn't understand. Moonflower showed her how to use a stick to pry up the weeds but she wasn't very strong and the weeds usually broke off. She tried again and again.

Finally Moonflower thought it best if she sat in the grass by a baby to shoo the flies away. Moonflower put a large leaf in her hand and showed her how she could use it as a fan.

When Sarah leaned over the baby to take a close look at it, the baby laughed at her. Sarah enjoyed babies. She thought of the doll her mother had made for her. It had been in the wagon and she longed for her mother. A tear slid down her cheek. She peeked at the baby again and once more it laughed.

"You are like a big doll. You have big eyes though, and can laugh," she said. At the sound of Sarah's strange words and sad expression on her face, the baby scrunched up its face and let out a howl.

All the women looked at Sarah.

"I didn't do anything," she said.

The baby's mother came running and scooped him up, pushing Sarah out of the way.

"Stay away from my baby," she said. Sarah didn't understand the words but her tone and actions let Sarah know that she thought that Sarah had done something to him.

Moonflower was furious with Corn Silk. Words were exchanged and everyone was uncomfortable. Moonflower gathered all the children on a blanket under a tree and gave them water and a treat made of pounded berries mixed with nuts, honey and starch from roots. She gave Sarah an extra-large piece. She was trying to show her that she knew that Sarah had done nothing wrong. The treat was delicious and soon all the children had finished.

They began to play, as children will if left to their own methods. They found ways to communicate. Moonflower's heart lifted when she looked over to see Brave Sparrow smiling. Some of the other children had drifted back to the field and were trying their best to help. One little boy had fallen asleep on the blanket with his thumb in his mouth.

Sarah sat there for a while but soon became bored. She wanted to help, but wasn't strong enough to dig up the long roots. She knew she could pick up the small pieces left behind by larger hands. Mother always asked me to do that. She said that each small piece of root could grow into a weed if not carried out of the garden, she remembered. So she began in the row behind Moonflower, taking care to not leave even the tiniest piece behind.

When her hands held so many that they started to drop, she ran to the edge and put them down, coming back to continue again, where she had left off. It wasn't long before others noticed that Moonflower's part of the field was free of any sign of roots. They praised Brave Sparrow, and soon set their own children to doing what she was.

It was early afternoon before the women finished. They were tired and dust stuck to their sweaty bodies. They stretched their aching backs, knowing that they would be back in the field working hard again the next day, planting the corn.

When they returned to camp their husbands had not yet returned. A hunting party had left the camp at dawn. They were certain to return with fresh meat for the evening meal.

"Let's go down to the water and swim. We could all use a good wash," said Singing Lark, wife of the shaman. "The water will feel good and I feel dirty after pulling weeds all morning." As they headed for the water, the women behaved like children. Freed from chores for the moment, they laughed and teased each other.

Once near the water they all stripped themselves and the children, placing their clothes near the edge of the water. Splashing and playing games made bath time fun. They stayed behind the screen of low willow branches just in case the men would return before they were finished.

By the time children could walk, they were taught to swim. In times past, the people traveled with the seasons and crossing rivers was much easier and safer if everyone knew how to swim. Now that they stayed in one place and planted crops it wasn't as necessary, but swimming was still a skill of the people.

Moonflower watched as Brave Sparrow timidly tiptoed on the edge of the lake.

"All in time, Moonflower, she will learn in time." Morning Dove assured her.

Refreshed by the water the women returned to their tents with their clean children to feed them and put them down for a nap.

The mothers cherished the time, as an opportunity to sit quietly and rest. They would talk and sew or work on their favorite craft. Morning Dove sat down in the shade of an oak tree beside Moonflower, bringing arms full of fresh long stemmed grass that she had just gathered.

"Don't let Rising Sun, bother you. She often speaks without concern for other's feelings. Most of us think that Brave Sparrow is a worthy addition to our people."

"I try hard not to argue with her, but she does make me so angry sometimes. What are you making," asked Moonflower?

"I saw small hands busy gathering this morning, but they had no basket to carry things. I thought Brave Sparrow should have her own basket, so she can carry it when we work. She can use it when berry season is here."

"You are so thoughtful Morning Dove. You are like a sister to me. You always know what to say or do to make me feel better." They sat together enjoying each other's company.

Moonflower picked up first one piece of leather and then another.

"I think this will make a nice long dress for winter. There is enough. That piece will make some trousers to keep the wind off her skinny legs. She will need a heavy coat. She gets cold easily. I noticed that she had pulled two of the bed furs over her last night."

"I have a wolf fur that you can use to make a warm coat. I am not using it and it will be nice for her."

"You are generous Morning Dove. You have given me so many things already. But perhaps we can trade."

Moonflower rushed to her tent to return with an elk hide that had been expertly worked. It was very soft.

"This is wonderful, but will Dark Wolf mind if you give it to me?"

"Why should he? It is a trade, to get his daughter a warm coat."

Morning Dove took the elk hide to her tent and returned with the wolf skin.

"You did a wonderful job on that elk skin. I can make a new shirt for Roaring Water. He needs a new one."

"This wolf fur is heavy. They must have found him in the fall."

"Yes it has an undercoat. Roaring Water says that's the best time to hunt them."

"Look the hunters are coming back and they have a big deer." "That's going to turn this evening into another feast. We have some things left from last night's celebration. All we need to do is put it on over the community fire."

Morning Dove's experienced hands were fast. She had nearly finished weaving the small utility basket.

"It is not very pretty, but I will finish it after we get the deer cooking. Then she can use it tomorrow." She said, holding the basket up for Moonflower to see.

"It is beautiful, like all the baskets you make, Morning Dove. It looks finished to me. What else do you need to do to it?"

"You will see," She answered, cleaning up the scraps and brushing the loose bits of grass from her skirt.

Morning Dove hurried back to her tent, where she got out dark brown strings of leather and the sharp bone needle she used to sew leather clothing. It was strong. She placed them in the little basket and hurried out to help with the fire.

Several women brought armloads of branches to keep the fire going. Morning Dove thought it would be a good treat if she cooked some of her wild apples. She washed them and dumped them into her biggest kettle. She picked out any stems or leaves and covered the apples with water. This was set back from the fire. It didn't need to be hurried. The deer would take until nearly dark to roast.

She wondered which hunter had actually gotten the deer. It was an honor, to have your husband provide the meat, but it meant more work for his wife. She was expected to process the hide, even though her husband might already have promised it to one of the other hunters.

Moonflower peeked into the tent.

"Brave Sparrow, wake up. Come out in the cool air. It is hot inside the tent." Sarah was already awake but she had quickly shut her eyes when she heard someone coming. She didn't want to come out. She didn't want to know these people or their ways. She was remembering the Chief's first glance at her, and the baby's mother pushing her aside. They don't like me. She thought. She was already learning their words. Some of the things people said about her were not very nice.

"Brave Sparrow, get up now." The voice was insistent. Sarah crawled to the door and stood up without looking at the woman's face. She knew that Moonflower was not pleased with her pretending.

"We will have a good meal. The hunters are back with a deer." She pointed at the deer hanging over the big fire. If you are hungry now, you can eat this." She pushed a piece of jerky into Sarah's hand.

"Water is here," she pointed. She had filled the cup and it stood on a rock beside her. "I will be working under that big tree. Come over if you want to help." Moonflower motioned for her to follow and then went back to the shade of the tree and sat down. She was watching to see what Brave Sparrow would do. She kept her head down so that the girl would not know that she was being watched. After a few bites of the hard meat and half the water, Sarah decided she wanted to see what the women were doing. Moonflower had cut out the dress and now was sewing it together. I wonder what she is making, thought Sarah.

"I am making you a long dress, with sleeves, so you will be comfortable this winter. Come see." She motioned for Sarah to come sit by her in the grass.

The girl's mind was full of thoughts but she didn't think that Moonflower would want to hear that she didn't intend to be here long. If that is for me, I don't think I will be staying long enough to wear a warm outfit. She assured herself that any day; someone would come to get her. The leather is very soft, thought Sarah, as she touched it.

"You can tell me which piece of leather you like better for your trousers, the dark one or the one that matches the dress." Moonflower held up a piece of leather to Sarah's waist, and let it hang down.

"You are making me trousers or a skirt, too?"

"You will need trousers. It gets cold here in the winter. We will roll the sides of the tents down and dry grass will be made into bundles and put between the walls for insulation. The outside is weighted with dirt and stones so the wind cannot come in." Sarah touched the leather and smiled, wondering what Moonflower had said.

"You can look through the beads in that basket and pick out twenty blue ones." Moonflower handed the basket to the girl and picked up one blue bead to show her and tucked it into a pouch.

"Put them here in this little pouch." Sarah stirred the beautiful beads with her finger and then picked out two yellow ones and put them in the pouch.

"You like yellow," said Moonflower. "Next I will need sixteen green ones." She showed her a green bead and put it into the pouch.

"What are you going to do with all those beautiful beads?"

"Beads," Brave Sparrow, "say beads. We will use them to decorate your dress. You will need to learn to sew before you can decorate with beads. Look here is Morning Dove. Be sure you speak to her courteously."

"Hello Brave Sparrow. Did you sleep well after working so hard in the field this morning?"

"Morning Dove," Sarah carefully said her name.

"Yes, I am Morning Dove. That was very good! She learns quickly. I have a small gift for you. I hope that you like it." Morning Dove handed the basket to Brave Sparrow. It was just the right size to hang comfortably on her arm, and on the side was stitched in dark brown leather, a branch with a bird on it.

"Thank you, it is very beautiful." Sarah said with a smile.

"This is a sparrow, so everyone that sees that basket will know that it belongs to you."

"I think she just said thank you. Basket, say Basket"

"Tomorrow we will be planting corn in the field you can put the seeds in here, and when it is berry time, you can pick them and carry them back in your basket."

She made this just for me. I wish I could say thank you in their words Sarah thought.

"Brave Sparrow, all the women have their own baskets."

"I would like to learn how to make one," said Sarah smiling. "Would you teach me?" Sarah motioned with her hands.

"I would love to show her how to weave and she can learn words as we work. I have no daughter to teach. My large son is not interested in baskets unless they hold food," she said, and the women laughed.

With the corn planted neatly in rows, after a quick wash in the lake, the women returned to the shade tree with their crafts.

"I am almost nine years old. I will be at Thanksgiving. My brother's birthday is in October. He is going to be sixteen. He is very tall. He is almost as tall as my father."

"I wonder what she is saying," said Morning Dove.

"Brave Sparrow, it is not good for a woman to tell what she knows unless she is asked. You must learn to say only what is needed. Women should work hard and speak little," Moonflower sternly instructed.

"She seems to think that we will learn her words, too," said Morning Dove.

Although Sarah couldn't comprehend Moonflower's words, she felt the sting of correction from her tone as surely as if she had been slapped. She ran into the tent and threw herself on the furs. If I can't say what I want, I just won't say anything at all! She thought. They will be sorry for yelling at me. I can talk about my brother if I want to! He will come get me soon and I won't have to learn their dumb words! She stormed inside.

It grew hotter. The sides of the tent had been let down for night and they had not been rolled up in the morning. Moonflower ignored the child's tantrum and continued to work. Morning Dove raised her chin to indicate the direction of the tent.

"That one will be very hot soon. She will come back out." The two women laughed together and continued working. "You will have to be very patient with her. She has much to learn and a strong will."

"Yes I have seen it already, but she is young and she will learn."

Sarah was becoming very uncomfortable. She was thirsty and hot. She peeked out to see if anyone was watching. No one seemed to be. She took a step out and then another. No head turned in her direction. I could slip down to the water and they wouldn't know where I was. I could run away and they would never find me! Her thoughts were still thunderclouds. She saw the cup of water on the stone and inched to it. She gulped it down. It was warm from the sun and not refreshing.

Moonflower did not acknowledge Sarah as she came near and sat down in the grass.

"Stand I want to measure you." She said finally. Sarah was quick to respond to the hand motion. She knew that she had behaved badly. She looked at the leather dress. It seemed very big and long. Moonflower turned to Morning Dove and asked what she thought.

"It will be good for winter and in the spring if you need to, you can shorten it."

"I think I will put the sleeves in tomorrow." Moonflower stood and walked away, taking her sewing with her.

Sarah was left under the tree with Morning Dove. She inched closer.

"What are you making? May I watch?"

"Come watch, but wouldn't you rather make something too? This is a simple mat to sit on." She indicated the one she had brought with her to cover the grass. "Anyone can make one. Let's go gather some grass for you, so you can start." Morning Dove liked the little girl and tried to make it as pleasant for her as possible.

She took her hand and led her to a patch of the tall grass that she had been using.

"This tall green grass is best. It is strong and bends easily." She tried to demonstrate the meaning of her words, repeating them and showing her what she meant. Before they returned to the shade Sarah had learned the word for grass, and what green was and what dry meant. She understood that it was strong and bent easily.

"Dry grass will work too but it is good to soak it for a day before you start." They returned to the shade, dropping their armloads of grass in a pile. Morning Dove was amazed at the speed at which the girl learned. She picked up a small bunch and helped her get the first row started.

"See, like this. Turn your wrist and then lift it up so the new piece will slide under your fingers."

"You are doing well. Keep working. I will come back. I have a chore to do." Morning Dove nodded approval and smiled. Her work was left where she had been sitting so that Brave Sparrow would understand that she planned to return. Sarah felt a rush of affection for the woman. Even the slightest smile was appreciated. Sarah wished that Moonflower would come back to see what she was doing.

When Morning Dove returned, it was not to sit down but just to collect her work.

"It is time to prepare the evening meal. The men will return to camp soon. Pick up your work now and bring it back when you see me here working." Sarah proudly carried the small strip of woven grass. She didn't think she should take the bundle of loose grass inside. It would probably make a mess, but she did want to take her weaving inside. The tent was large but held many things. The only place she could think to put it was under the bed fur that she slept on. She carefully smoothed it out and replaced the fur.

CHAPTER FOUR
LEARNING NEW SKILLS AND BLUE STONE

It was hot inside. Moonflower had not rolled up the sides again. She decided she would surprise her by doing it. She had noticed that some of the other tents nearby were rolled up and the door flap was tied open so the breeze could blow through. She lifted one section a few inches, but it was a lot heavier than she thought. She couldn't hold it up, roll it and then tie it there. She just wasn't strong enough. Another pair of small hands lifted with her, and reached for the cord and tied it as Sarah held it up. Sarah smiled and walked to the next section and with two girls lifting and rolling, it was much easier.

"It is very hot inside. It is good to let the evening air in to cool it before sleep."

"Hot," questioned Sarah?

"Yes, hot."

"Thank you for helping me. I am Sarah," she said tapping her chest.

"Who are you?"

"My name is Blue Stone," the girl said, touching her heart. "I must go now to help my mother. If you work under the tree tomorrow, I will join you." She smiled and pointed at the big oak as she walked away. Sarah felt happy inside. I think I am going to have a friend. Blue Stone, Blue Stone, Blue Stone." She said, saying it three times. She is pretty. Sarah didn't understand what the name meant. It was just sounds she was trying to remember. It was nice of her to help me. She was deep in her thoughts as Moonflower walked up.

"Brave Sparrow, it is good that you have raised the sides of the tent. We will sleep well tonight." She smiled and patted the rolled up leather. Brave Sparrow smiled back.

She turned to the small cooking fire in front of the tent and stirred a big pot.

"What are you cooking?" asked Sarah as she peered into the pot.

"Can you tell me what is cooking?" asked Moonflower. Sarah picked up the big wooden spoon and cautiously stirred the pot.

It is rabbit thought Sarah. She energetically hopped three times to let Moonflower see that she knew what it was.

"It smells good." Moonflower chuckled at the behavior. "Rabbit," she said it over and over until Sarah said it correctly in the language of the people.

"I saw you working with Morning Dove this afternoon. What are you making?" asked Moonflower. Brave Sparrow recognized the name Morning Dove and felt eager to show Moonflower what she was learning.

"She is teaching me how to weave a mat to sit on." Sarah hurried to get her small piece of work.

"It is good. You will enjoy using it this winter, when the ground grows cold." Moonflower nodded her head and smiled her approval.

The men had returned from their scouting trip and were walking to their separate families. Dark Wolf sat down heavily on his mat near the fire. Moonflower handed him a large cup of water.

"You are tired. Did someone see the buffalo herd today?"

"They come from the west but are still far away. The earth is dark with them. We will have plenty of meat for winter and hides to use. I wish to make our tent larger before winter. We will be leaving before the sun rises tomorrow. You and the girl will come. You will be needed and she can watch and learn." Moonflower nodded.

She was hoping that she would not have to go this time; many of the other's would go. She wanted to stay and teach Brave Sparrow other things.

As soon as they had eaten a small pack was brought out and filled with the few things they would need for the next week, as they camped on the prairie and processed the buffalo meat and hides.

They would ride horses to the spot chosen for their camp, near the hunt, but they would have to walk back. The horses would be used to transport the heavy bundles of dried meat and hides. Sarah wasn't sure what was going to happen in the morning but she knew that they were going somewhere. Moonflower packed travel cakes and some jerky. She also baked a batch of crackers, made from dried roots, pounded into a type of flour and mixed with grease and a little water. She added herbs and salt and spread small dabs of the dough on greased hot rocks near the fire. Sarah was glad to nibble the first one done. It was delicious.

As she finished Moonflower told her to go to sleep because she would be up before the sun. She was getting used to her bed, but it was still warm inside and she was nervous about the coming trip. How would her family find her if she was gone?

It was then that she remembered Psalm 33 v 12-13 NIV. "From heaven the Lord looks down and sees all mankind: from his dwelling place he watches all who live on earth." He will direct them, she thought. She felt better. Thank you Jesus for watching over me, she prayed.

Sarah was still sleepy when she was lifted onto the horse in front of Moonflower. They rode all morning and then in the distance she could see what looked like a brown cloud of dust drifting across the prairie grass.

"That is the buffalo," said Moonflower. "Buffalo." She said the word slowly so that Brave Sparrow could learn it. "They are many. We will make camp soon." Dark Wolf rode over and indicated for her to set up camp near a cluster of tall trees ahead.

"There is water over there. See how tall the trees are. They cannot grow tall without water. They will provide shade and the wood we will need for the fires," she said.

Sarah noticed that it was Moonflower that directed the others where they would put their things. It seemed to Sarah that they were arranged in nearly the same pattern as they were back at the main camp.

Once again Blue Stone was on the far side of the camp. She was away from Sarah and away from the water. Sarah wondered why the families were arranged that way.

"Moonflower why is Blue Stone always on the other side of camp?" Moonflower understood that the girl was asking something about her new friend Blue Stone but wasn't sure what.

"No, you stay with me and help. Blue Stone must stay there and help her mother. You should always conduct yourself with care. You are daughter to the son of the Chief." She would repeat this often, until the girl was a grown woman. "That is a very important position." Moonflower was laying out their sleeping furs. On top of hers lay the small piece of weaving.

"You can practice on your mat when I am busy."

"Now we must start a fire. Go gather dry wood. Brave Sparrow, go get wood. Do not wander far." She held up a dry branch to be sure that Brave Sparrow understood what was expected. Moonflower was pulling packs and bundles from the horses they had been leading. Still Sarah saw no tent. She wondered about that, but since no one had put one up she figured it must be the way they do it. I sure hope it doesn't rain while we are here.

She returned to the place in the middle of the temporary camp where armloads of wood had already been placed. She noticed Blue Stone coming with a large branch that she had to drag. Sarah took a hold at the back and they carried it the rest of the way.

"Blue Stone, Moonflower put my weaving in the bundle. Did you bring yours?" Blue Stone was puzzled for a moment then smiled when Sarah pointed at her weaving on the bed furs.

"I have started a basket, but it isn't very good. Mother says it is alright for a first try, but I can't get the handle to stay up straight. Once the fire is going and food is on, we will be able to gather grass and work on our projects. Let's try over there for more wood. The last branch was from there."

"Girls, stop," yelled one of the women. Blue Stone grabbed Sarah's wrist. "There is a large snake there. He is angry. We must not disturb his home further. He is shaking his medicine rattle to let us know that he is there." Blue Stone looked upset.

"I must have pulled that big branch right off from him. I didn't see him. If I don't go tell him that I am sorry he may decide to bite someone and it will be my fault."

"No Blue Stone, you can't go over there. He may bite you if you go back. Stay away," said the woman.

"Let's go tell Moonflower." They hurried to where she was working hard, twirling a stick with concentration to start the fire. She had forgotten to bring a fire horn. It was her responsibility. Now she had to do it the hard way.

"Girls watch the coal drop through the hole in the bottom of the wood to the milk weed fluff." They watched and when it dropped, she blew gently adding a few shreds of wood, then twigs and finally a small branch. Yellow flames bounced along the branch and others were added. "Now what was so important that you had to run like little children, instead of walking like young women?"

Blue Stone explained what had happened and wanted to know if she should return to apologize to the snake.

"You should apologize anytime you disturb an animal's home, but it is not necessary for you to go near grandfather snake. He will know that you are sorry if you whisper it from here. He will hear your words and be pleased. He will sleep and not bother anyone."

"See I told you she would know what to do. She knows everything," said Blue Stone as she walked to a large boulder. "After we get water from the spring then we can probably work on our weaving.

"Let's go," said Sarah, urging her with a motion. She still held the water bag that Moonflower had handed her.

"No not yet. I have to tell him I'm sorry first." Blue Stone climbed on top of the large rock with her arms extended in the direction of the snake's home. Sarah could see her lips moving but couldn't hear what she said. Sarah was puzzled. She knew that this little ceremony of Blue Stone's had something to do with the snake. You can't talk to a snake. Can you? She thought.

"When you return with the water we all will need to help cut green branches to make drying racks," said one of the women as she walked by with another bundle of wood for the fire.

At the spring, Blue Stone bent, catching the water in a pan as it flowed from the rocks.

"We need to help make racks," said Blue Stone. Sarah made a motion with her hands as if she was weaving and then shook her head no.

"Yes I know. My mother said we are here to help. We will have to stay close and help after the hunt, too. Ugh! I hate being around all that blood. The flies come and we have to shoo them away while the meat dries."

"It doesn't seem like we will get much chance to practice our weaving. I wanted to get some done so I could surprise Morning Dove when we go back," said Sarah.

Blue Stone knew that Brave Sparrow was talking about her weaving, just by the mention of Morning Dove's name.

"We will get a chance. Don't worry."

The women cut long branches from the trees and stripped the leaves, placing the branches in the girl's arms. It seemed to Sarah, that they had enough to build a house before the women were satisfied. She watched as the women used short pieces of cord they had brought to tie the branches together into large racks.

"The cords are strong. We have used them many times. We add the hair of the horse's tail. I will show you this winter." The racks were assembled in rows beside the large communal fire.

"After the hunt," said Moonflower, "we will light as many fires as we need to dry all the meat. The fires also help to keep the animals from stealing our meat."

"Fire said Sarah."

"Yes Brave Sparrow, Fire."

As people talked to her she began to learn more words. They spoke to her as if she understood everything. It helped to ease her longing for her family. This was such a foreign environment that it intensified her loneliness. People were close, but she was one of a kind and felt alone.

"Tonight the men will pray that the hunt is successful. They will ask the Great Spirit to protect them so that no one is hurt." Moonflower spoke to Brave Sparrow of anything that came into her mind. "I wonder sometimes if he is God. The Great Spirit, is he a God? He is the most powerful Spirit. It is not for us to think about. That is why we have a shaman.

Talking Mountain will hold a ceremony, just for the men. Don't they think that women pray? Brave Sparrow, I am sure your head is full of questions. So is mine. Women pray. They pray in their hearts that they will have food for their family. They pray that the men will not have to put on war paint, and that a woman will live when she has a baby, and we pray that the men are not hurt or killed when they hunt. A woman's prayers are more like words in her heart. The Great Spirit knows what is in our hearts and answers."

Sarah felt a renewal in her spirit as Moonflower talked. She was not aware of the deep subject of the words but perceived a sense of spiritual bond that had not been there before.

"Heavenly Father, open my ears to their words, open their minds so that I can share your words. Help me Father, to understand them and learn what I must to survive here. Help me to teach them about you, so they will honor Your Son and have eternal life." She spoke silently, but she knew that God heard.

"You may go find Blue Stone." Moonflower pointed at the small piece of weaving as she spoke and smiled.

Sarah was delighted to be temporarily free of duties. When she looked in the direction of Blue Stones camp, Sarah saw that she was on her way toward her.

"There is tall grass by the spring." Blue Stone came hurrying over with a not quite round, basket. "Let's go get some grass before we sit down." Sarah understood the word grass and smiled broadly. They put their work in the shade where Moonflower had indicated and Blue Stone led Brave Sparrow to the backside of the spring, where the grass had not been trampled. Many women fetching water had caused a path to form.

As they started to gather grass for their projects, Blue Stone saw that Brave Sparrow was struggling to break the grass with her bare hands.

"You need a cutting stone like mine. Look at it. It is just a broken stone. Let's make you one." Blue Stone reached into the pool of water and pulled out a round gray flint stone. She smacked it hard with another and it broke into two pieces.

"There, which one do you like?" She asked. Brave Sparrow chose the smaller of the two halves with a smile.

"It is really sharp," she said as she felt the edge. "Now I can cut the grass and not have to try to pull it or break it off with my hands. Thank you, Blue Stone."

"I'm surprised that Morning Dove didn't make one for you. Let's take our grass back and sit down. I'm tired. We have worked hard today and there is more to come."

Sarah was pleased with her new knife. She held it carefully. She realized that it could easily cut her finger or damage her pocket as she tucked it away for safe keeping.

When she picked up her weaving, it was hard to figure out what she had been doing to start it up again in the same pattern. Blue Stone had removed the handle completely and was redoing the top part of her basket. They chatted and laughed as they worked and before they knew it, the rest of the day was gone, and it was starting to grow dark. Without realizing it, Brave Sparrow had started to understand much of what was said.

The men returned only long enough to say something to their wives and then they moved away into the dark, carrying a lit branch. Sarah watched with interest as they lit a fire in a pit that the women had prepared earlier. She had been too busy to notice it there. She could hear occasional sounds as they performed their ceremony, the rattle of the medicine man's gourd and the steady beat of a drum. That's interesting. I wonder what they are doing.

The women drew near the central fire and each filled a bowl and ate portions from the big kettle of stew. The huge amount that Moonflower had prepared still appeared to be a generous supply. They drank mint tea and relaxed for just a few moments before getting comfortable in their sleeping furs. They all knew that after the hunt, they would work long and hard.

Moonflower curled up close to Sarah, being protective. She was always uneasy and felt exposed and defenseless without a tent. Soon they all slept.

Dawn brought a lookout running into camp.

"The herd is on the move," he signaled to the men. They left soon after, moving to the positions they had chosen for the hunt. A feeling of excitement swept over the temporary camp as the men headed out in the direction of the buffalo herd.

As the hunters silently moved to their assigned positions, they remained quiet. The women talked only when necessary and very softly. Nothing disturbed the lovely summer morning. The fire was banked and produced no smoke. Camp seemed peaceful. Blue Stone hurried over to Brave Sparrow but checked her step as she received a frown from Moonflower.

"I found some berries on the other side of the spring. Come pick some with me," she whispered. The two girls could be heard giggling and laughing at a private joke as they gathered the berries. It seemed that the world held its breath as the herd moved imperceptibly nearer.

Moonflower praised Brave Sparrow when she returned with her basket half filled with ripe raspberries.

"These will be a sweet treat to share tonight with our meal," Said Moonflower. Sarah and Blue Stone had eaten enough berries to satisfy their stomachs for quite a while. They decided that since they had no chores to do until the word came that the hunt had been successful, they would go exploring. It felt strange in camp with the restraint on sound and activity. They walked slowly, side by side along the edge of the trees and found that the ground dropped down into a dry wash. The bottom was covered with loose stones.

CHAPTER FIVE
A GIFT OF LOVE AND THE PAIN OF TRUTH

Sarah spotted a stone that was different from all the rest. It was blue with black lines in it. She picked it up and rubbed the dust off. It felt smooth and warm from the morning sun.

"Look, Blue Stone. Isn't this stone beautiful?"

"Oh you have found a stone that is blue, like my name! Let's look, maybe we can find more."

They searched for a long time but found no more. When Sarah pulled it from her pocket to look at it again she noticed the hole that had been drilled all the way through the stone on the narrow end.

"I think someone had this on a necklace. You can see the hole was drilled to put a cord through it." She showed Blue Stone. Sarah held the stone tightly for an instant then opened her palm and extended her hand toward her friend. "This should be yours. It is perfect for you." She said.

"No I can't take a gift of such value, without giving you something of equal value. Let me think about it. I would love to have that stone, but I want to give you something special, too," said Blue Stone. With motions and words the girls were able to communicate quite well. They returned to camp excited and happy.

They found that the women were preparing to process meat. Knives were being sharpened. Large pots were placed near the fires to hold the chunks of fat to be rendered. The hunt had been successful. There were many buffalo to be preserved for winter.

Every hunter had taken at least one buffalo. Dark Wolf and Growling Bear had taken two huge cows each. There would be plenty of rich meat for the people of their village, for widows or families with no hunter in their tent.

All would eat well. The people would not be hungry during the cold months. The animals that were down were not far away. Several men helped to roll an animal onto a large, strong travois and two horses were used to move them to the edge of camp.

Once in camp they helped roll the huge beast over so the hide could be removed in one piece, but after that, it was up to the women to scrape the hides and to cut the meat in thin strips that would be cured by the smoke and dried by the heat until it would be preserved completely.

Many fires were built and large chunks of meat hung near the flames roasting to feed the hungry men. The women worked late into the night all helping until the last strip of meat was hung on the racks. No one acknowledged their painful knees or aching backs. They all felt the same discomforts in varying degrees.

The fires were built up and more had been started. Guards were posted as others rested. No one wanted to lose any of the hard earned meat to the animals that came near the camp. The smell of blood brought large predators. No one walked out into the dark. Blue Stone and Brave Sparrow were instructed to stay in the ring of light from the fires. Moonflower explained to them why. Each time they went to gather more wood; one of the women carried a torch and went with them.

The girls slept long into the morning. They had never been up so late or worked so hard before, dragging wood for the fires and skins of water for the hunters and the women who knelt over the meat as they sliced it. For four days the fires were kept hot and the girls were required to carry wood or stay near the racks to shoo the flies away from the meat.

Finally, the cleaned hides that had been staked out were each piled high with the ready meat and the bundles were secured on a travois or on the back of the horses. The long walk home had begun. The people had been lucky. No one was injured during the hunt and the weather had held warm and dry.

"Brave Sparrow, you are falling behind. Why do you walk so slowly?" asked Moonflower.

"My feet hurt from the rocks and sharp grass." She answered lifting a foot to pick out a sharp thorn. Moonflower inspected the soles of the girl's feet to see small cuts and red spots. She picked her up and plopped her behind the bundle of meat on the horse that she had been leading.

"Hang on to that rope," she gestured, and hurried ahead to match the pace of the other women. Sarah remembered once before riding on the back of a horse with no blanket between her and the horse's hair. Soon her legs would be burning and she knew the pain that would follow if she didn't do something. She struggled to pull her top off without falling off from the slow walking horse. Then she tucked it under her bottom a bit more with each bounce.

There she rode like a queen without a top on until Moonflower looked back and stopped dead. The other women all turned to see what had caught Moonflower's attention. Then they began to laugh.

"You are too big to go without a shirt, but it does show that you learn quickly. Put your shirt back on and you can sit on my blanket. It is too warm today. I don't need it around me anyway," said Moonflower fussing and motioning until the girl was again dressed and settled on the blanket.

Sarah remembered the blue stone and new flint knife in her pockets and checked hastily to make sure that they were still there. She hadn't shown them to Moonflower.

Blue Stone had been too busy working to think of the trade, but now that they were moving slowly along, her mind had time to take inventory of her belongings. What do I have that is worth the blue stone, she wondered? The only thing she could think of that was totally hers was a flute that her older brother, Singing Wind, had made for her. She thought perhaps her parents would be angry if she traded it, but she wanted that stone more than anything. She could ask her brother to make her a new flute. He would understand when he saw the stone on a necklace.

She was excited to get back and make the trade. She didn't look where she put her foot. The pain made her cry out. The snake had been disturbed and angered by the many people in the column, walking ahead of her. It was her misfortune to step in front of him at that moment. He struck her just above the ankle. Immediately the spot was starting to swell. Her father, Sleeping Bear, was not far behind. He scooped her up into his arms and ran to the horse where the medicine man, Talking Mountain, rode.

Everyone gathered around as he knelt beside the child examining the bite. He pulled packs of herbs from pouches fastened on his horse. He called on Singing Lark, his wife, to mix the poultice as he indicated the proper herbs and the right quantities. A small fire was made and Blue Stone was placed beside it on a brightly colored blanket. Talking Mountain held his knife in the fire, while he chanted. Dancing Willow, Blue Stone's mother, cradled her daughter's head on her lap. She knew there was a chance that Blue Stone could die.

The knife was brought down and the flesh sizzled and smoked as he swiftly made two cuts in the swollen area, across the bite mark. The cuts were deep and blood flowed onto the ground. Blue Stone sobbed in pain. Sarah shrieked!

"He is burning her! He is cutting her!" She cried to see her friend in such agony. Moonflower held Sarah close and although she didn't understand the words, she knew that Sarah had never seen such a thing before and couldn't comprehend that Talking Mountain was trying to help her.

The medicine man dipped his fingers in the blood draining from the wound. He raised his hands above his head still chanting. He began to dance in a circle around Blue Stone and the fire.

Singing Lark pulled a small drum from one of the packs on her horse and started to beat out a rhythm as others joined in the dance. Talking Mountain knelt again at Blue Stones side placing his hands near her knee and pulling down hard across her flesh causing the blood to ooze from the wound. He did the same thing again pressing from her toes to the bite, trying to expel the snake's poison. He repeated his motions several times before packing the area with the poultice and wrapping it in soft leather. He secured it there with a strip of leather and then tied it with a piece of yellow yarn.

"The color yellow is a sacred healing color to our people," said Moonflower softly, as she held Sarah's trembling hand.

"Oh, Father, I know that you love Blue Stone and that these people are your children, too. Please heal her. Let her recover. You are the real God and you are above all the strange spirits that they believe have power." Sarah prayed sincerely, squeezing her eyes shut, closing out the scene before her.

Then Talking Mountain turned to Dancing Willow, Blue Stone's mother, and placed a dot of blood on her forehead, as each person danced around the circle; he did the same on their foreheads. A strong tea was brewing and after she drank it, in just a few minutes Blue Stone fell into a deep sleep.

Dancing Willow picked up the sleeping child and began again the long walk home. She carried her as though her weight was nothing.

After a short while Sleeping Bear took her in his arms and walked beside his wife, continuing until nearly dark. More of the sedative was brewed and made ready. When Blue Stone began to wake she was given more and again she slept, lying so still that Sarah feared that Blue Stone was near death. She did not believe in the ceremony and she feared that her only friend would die.

"Father these people don't know to pray to you to ask for a healing for Blue Stone. Please, Father; make her well. I promise that I will not complain anymore and I will wait patiently for my family if you will just make her well again." She prayed attempting to bargain with God.

Sarah knelt on the blanket, close to the sleeping girl. Her eyes glistened with tears as she continued to pray silently.

Then, taking her primitive flint knife from her pocket, she cut a strand of her own long, blond, hair and pulled it out of her braid. After twisting it together, she threaded it through the hole in the blue stone and slipped it around her friend's neck and tried to tie it. The knot kept slipping out. Sarah had never tried to tie hair before. Her hands shook and tears slipped down her cheeks. Dancing Willow pulled a long piece of yellow yarn from the edge of Blue Stone's blanket and threaded it in with the strand of blond hair. Now when Sarah tied it, it stayed tied.

A hush came over the women gathered around, as each saw the large, unusual blue stone lying on the girl's chest. They nodded approval and stood in awe as if something miraculous had just happened. Sarah had no way of knowing that she had done something that everyone would interpret as special and magical, but only if the girl lived. If she died, would they blame her? She did not understand this culture or their ways. She simply wanted to do something nice for Blue Stone.

Sarah's hands were still shaking when she sat down on the blanket beside Moonflower a short distance away. Moonflower put her arms around Sarah and tried to comfort her by explaining what had been done for Blue Stone.

"We each accepted a touch of her blood on our forehead and with it we took a small portion of the poison from the snake. Each person now carries a bit of Blue Stones spirit. As we move and breathe, live and love her, Talking Mountain asks the spirits to strengthen her, and they draw that strength from all of us." Moonflower knew that Brave Sparrow could not understand all she had said, but she hoped that it would somehow comfort her.

"Brave Sparrow, where did you get the blue stone?" she asked.

"I found it and I wanted her to have it."

"To give her such a gift has great medicine," said Moonflower. She handed Brave Sparrow a travel cake and told her to eat it and then rest. Moonflower went to Talking Mountain as soon as Sarah slept.

"Talking Mountain, what does it mean that this girl has given a spirit stone tied with her own hair? Did you see her hands tremble from the power?"

"We must wait and see. I will meditate on this. Do not talk about it with the others. See if you can find out anything from the girl in the morning." Talking Mountain turned and walked away into the darkness. He was very troubled.

Dancing Willow sat beside her sleeping child. She did not eat or drink. She would not say a word. She stared at the stone until it grew too dark to see it as the fire burned down. She reached her fingers hesitantly to touch it and jerked her hand back when she felt the heat in it. The girl's fever had radiated into the stone that lay on bare skin. Dancing Willow didn't realize the simple explanation. She was sure that she had felt power at work in the stone. It frightened her. She stretched out her hand and stroked her daughter's forehead. It was covered in sweat and the breeze made it feel cold.

Dancing Willow had never tried to pray. She had always relied on the medicine man and his ceremonies to take care of the spiritual needs of the people. But now she felt that she needed to reach out to something bigger than the usual spirits of Talking Mountain; a force bigger than the spirit helpers that the medicine man called on.

A quiet whisper inside her, urged her to ask for help. As she sat beside her daughter in the dark, she reached both arms to the sky as she had seen the medicine man do, many times.

Silently her mind and heart sought comfort and help from a Spirit, a God, bigger and more powerful than any other. She prayed to the God that made the sky and the stars, the strongest most powerful God, creator and healer. She asked for forgiveness for her unworthiness to approach Him, as she asked for the life of her daughter. She prayed in the dark for the first time, knowing that He had revealed Himself to her heart. She knew that He was the one true God and that if the other spirits existed at all, they had to be far less powerful. She prayed that this truth be given to the people.

When she lowered her arms Dancing Willow felt at peace. She knew that she had connected to a power greater than all others. She did not feel fear of that power. She felt love. She felt that her anguished prayer would be answered. She snuggled close to Blue Stone and kept vigil through the night.

As the rising sun lightened the sky to a pale glow, Blue Stone woke. She asked for a drink of water. Her fever was gone. Dancing Willow hurried to get fresh water for her. She woke the sleeping camp with a loud and joyous announcement.

"Blue Stone is getting better. She will live." She could hear others repeat the good news as they came fully awake. Sarah ran to her and wrapped her arms around Blue Stone.

"Thank you God, Thank you," prayed Sarah audibly.

Talking Mountain came to examine the wound and told her to wait at least another day before trying to put any weight on it, but that she could sit up. He walked back to his fire with pride, taking credit for the healing. It wasn't until she started to sit up that Blue Stone noticed the stone tied around her neck. She wrapped her hand around it and held it to her lips smiling.

"Thank you Brave Sparrow." Blue Stone smiled broadly at her mother and her friend.

When the walking column of people and burdened horses arrived back in camp it wasn't the boisterous, celebratory people that Falling Stones and Gray Cloud expected. Blue Stone's injury had dimmed the joy of the successful hunt.

Tired and dusty, the people led their horses to their tents where the meat and hides were unloaded. With ropes removed, a swat on the rump was all that was needed to send the horses to the lake for a drink and back to the herd for the comfort and security of familiarity and the sound of the flute played by Singing Wind, the man watching over the herd.

By evening all the meat was stashed and the hides pegged out for further processing. Everyone had, alone or in small groups, made their way to the lake edge to wash and pull on clean garments. Their hunting clothes were scrubbed and laid on the grass to dry. The camp was quiet, and the people rested. Tomorrow would be soon enough for a communal fire and celebration for the achievement of the hunt and Blue Stone's survival.

Blue Stone knew that the necklace had been a gift of love and friendship. She asked her mother when Brave Sparrow had given it to her and Dancing Willow told her. She didn't tell her that she thought that it held a special power or that she had prayed to a most powerful God and He had made her well, for it would not be received well by the people to show doubt in the medicine man's power.

Sleeping Bear came out of their tent and picked up Blue Stone taking her to sit in the shade on a blanket. He had instructed Dancing Willow to allow her to use his woven, willow, back rest. Her father placed her down gently and then stroked her hair back from her eyes.

"You grow strong again. I have joy in my heart," he said, as he walked toward the Chief's tent. Sarah walked over to Blue Stone. She bent and hugged her friend, sitting beside her.

This was the closest thing to a declaration of his love for her that Blue Stone had ever heard. Tears came to her eyes. She brushed them away with the back of her hand, as she watched him walk away. Dancing Willow had waited until Sleeping Bear left and then she came hurrying up with a bowl of cooked grain, smothered in nuts and honey with a cup of strong willow bark tea to ease the pain that still lingered.

"Eat now and drink all the tea. It will make you feel better. Later I will bring your weaving to you so you can work on it, if you want to. Are you comfortable?"

"Yes mother I am fine. Please don't fuss. By tomorrow I will be up and walking again. I don't want to make you extra work. I know that you are tired after the trip with the hunters."

Dancing Willow smiled at her daughter, feeling sure that now she would recover. Blue Stone wondered why her father had gone to the Chief's tent. It wasn't something that was done casually. Usually if her father went to see Chief Rising Eagle, it was because he had been summoned.

Sleeping Bear was no longer a warrior of high rank. He had lost face because of his quick temper. He had been given the name "Sleeping Bear" in a special ceremony, to remind him that a sleeping bear can be roused to fury all too easily. He had to learn to control his emotions. He was an excellent hunter and tracker. Even though he was of lower status now, the Chief appreciated his wisdom and good judgment. He called on him now to help with a decision. Sarah sat still on the edge of the blanket. She knew that Blue Stone was in deep thought and wondered why she had a look of deep concern on her face.

"Brave Sparrow, I need you to do something for me that could get you in a lot of trouble. I want you to take your cutting stone and gather weaving grass from behind the Chief's tent. Listen to see if you can hear what is being said. I have to know why my father was called to the Chief. If anyone sees you and asks what you are doing, just tell them you are gathering long grass for us to use for our weaving. Don't even look in the direction of the Chief's tent. Will you do it for me?"

The look on Blue Stone's face was too compelling to refuse.

"Yes I'll do it, but what are you so worried about?"

"My father is not of high rank anymore. He is seldom called to council. I think he might be in trouble."

"Blue Stone, I think you are wrong. He didn't look upset when he left you. He was smiling and was thinking about the fact that you are getting well. If you promise to eat all your breakfast and drink all that tea, I'll gather enough grass for us to use on both our projects, and I'll do it near the Chief's tent."

When Sarah retrieved her stone knife, she noticed that it was getting quite hot inside. Moonflower had gone to the water's edge with others to cut reeds for making heavy mats for the floor of the tent. Sarah thought she should try to roll up the bottom of the tent to let the air pass through, but it was very difficult alone.

As she struggled with it, Corn Silk came and lifted the weight of the rolled leather so that Sarah could tie it. She was quiet until the job was completed.

"Brave Sparrow, I am sorry for speaking to you the way that I did when we were planting corn. I must have been tired. I hope that you will come to visit the baby sometime." She walked away quickly, before Sarah had a chance to reply. Sarah was amazed! It had been more than a month and the woman had walked past her many times and never said a word to her. She had treated her as if she were invisible. Now today she had helped with a chore and gone out of her way to apologize. Sarah was pleased but totally puzzled.

"Thank you," she managed as Corn Silk slipped away.

She carefully pulled her knife from her pocket and started to cut grass behind the tents. The grass in the shade still carried a small coating of morning dew. Good she thought that gives me an excuse if anyone wants to know why I am close to the tent. I better get a good size bundle in my arms before I go near the Chief's tent, so they can see what I am doing.

Soon she found that she was looking forward to sitting in the shade with Blue Stone and just working on her weaving. Her mind kept wandering back to Corn Silk and she couldn't help wondering what had caused her to change her attitude. Sarah was cutting grass behind Moonflower's tent. It stood closest to the Chief's.

Already she could faintly hear the voices of the men gathered inside. They seemed excited. One was saying that they had less than two days to prepare. Another said it was important that they hit the wagons before they reach a point where they can see the remains of the other attack! Her heart nearly stopped beating! They were planning a wagon train attack. She felt sick to her stomach.

Sarah realized in an instant that these same men had attacked the train that her wagon had left, and that the people she had known on that long journey were probably all dead. She suddenly also felt sure that her family would never be coming for her! Her stomach churned and she immediately vomited. Her legs became so weak that she slid to the ground on her knees.

In an instant, she had gone from innocent little girl, to an anger filled young woman. She thought that she would one day seek revenge, a justice, for the death of her family and the people on the wagon trains. Why hadn't she seen it before? Had she known it all along? She just hadn't wanted to face it.

Now she could no longer deny the fact that the very people she was living with were the ones that had killed her family! Had anyone been watching her face at that moment, they would have seen a mysterious change take place, with a hard set of her jaw, and the cold glaze that covered her eyes.

She was no longer Sarah the frail white child. She was becoming Brave Sparrow, a warrior. These people were at war with her kind. She would become like them! Chief Rising Eagle laughed at me when he gave me the name Brave Sparrow. At the time I didn't understand the laughter, but I remember it and I know now why they all laughed at me. He will find out just how brave a sparrow can be when she fights for her own! I will learn from them and become stronger to do what has to be done.

She suddenly felt much older and a cold stone of pain had settled in her chest. I will do whatever it takes to gain power and respect. They should feel the fear that I felt when they raided my family's wagon, she thought. I will become tough, but well favored and I will fight them in ways that they can't imagine. I will be the enemy in their own camp, and they won't even know it!

Her arms had all the grass they could hold and her mind was on overload. Her emotions were raw and she was just starting to deal with the knowledge that her family would never come for her. She stopped to plan what she would report to Blue Stone. She drifted across the worn grass with her arms loaded, as if she had all the time in the world. She dumped the bundle beside Blue Stone and said she would be right back. She wanted more time to think what she would say. She pulled her patch of weaving from beneath her sleeping furs. It was crooked and pathetic compared to the beautiful mats she had seen in camp. I am Brave Sparrow! I will learn to do everything well. No one will think of me any longer as being different, she thought. An image of a grown and powerful woman was forming in her mind. That woman would be capable of doing what needed to be done.

She flopped down rather hard on the blanket beside Blue Stone and gave a sigh as if she were very tired.

"You are a silly worry wart! I couldn't hear much, but it sounded like they were going hunting again. This time they plan to go a little farther east. They must be melting in there. They still have the tent sides down. I rolled up the sides of our tent when I got my knife. Moonflower has gone down to the water to gather reeds for winter mats, so it wasn't done. Corn Silk came over and held the sides up while I tied them! Can you believe it? She even said she was sorry for snapping at me when we were planting corn. She hasn't said a word to me since that happened."

"That is strange! I don't like her much," said Blue Stone. "She always acts like she is better than everyone else."

"Here, hand me your weaving." Brave Sparrow leaned over and gave the small patch of weaving to Blue Stone. "When it gets crooked like that, all you have to do is pull it like this. See? It straightens right up. There you go. Remember to hold your wrist up when you pass the top ones under. That way it doesn't tangle as much."

"Thanks Blue Stone."

"Good morning girls. Do you mind if I join you? I have been trying to work on new winter mats and don't seem to be getting very far. I always have to stop to do something else."

"There is room for you on the blanket here by the tree if you like. That way you can lean against the trunk and your back won't get tired," offered Blue Stone.

"Thank you, my back does get tired sometimes. It is quiet this morning," Morning Dove said, "Where have the men gone?"

"I saw a couple go into the Chief's tent," said Brave Sparrow.

"Good that will keep them busy for a while. Your mother is by the water gathering reeds. She should be back soon. Maybe she will sit with us, too," said Morning Dove casually using the word "mother".

"That's good," said Brave Sparrow.

This gave her food for thought. If I call her mother it will seem more like I am one of them. Not yet, but maybe I will, at just the right time. She tries hard. I don't think she has any idea what really happens on those raids, or maybe she does... She must know. They all know. The hunters tell their stories at the communal fire. Well I know now. They will all know how horrid they are when I get big enough. Her thoughts hung like a black cloud in her mind.

Moonflower came over to the shade and dropped her burden before sitting down heavily onto the grass.

"I am tired today. Just gathering the reeds has tired me. We all could use a few quiet days in camp. It is quiet right now. Where are the men?"

Blue Stone answered her and both girls continued to work. Brave Sparrow struggled to keep each fold of the grass an even distance from the last. Inside she could feel a whirlwind of feelings brewing. She kept trying to stuff them back inside a small black box in her heart, but with each heartbeat they came closer to erupting.

Before long Morning Dove reached over to her lap and took hold of a long strand that lay unattended on the bottom of Brave Sparrow's work.

"Brave Sparrow, who will weave this piece?" She asked, in a kidding manner. Brave Sparrow's emotions were too raw and too close to the surface to ride the tide of even a gentle criticism. She tried to hold back the tears but they came sliding down her cheeks. Her heart was shattered and she could no longer conceal it.

For the first time she fully realized her mother, father and brother would never come for her. Facing the knowledge that they had been killed, she was starting to mourn. Moonflower's generous lap held her head and shoulders as she wept uncontrollably.

"I am so sorry Brave Sparrow. I didn't mean to hurt your feelings. Please don't cry. Forgive me." Morning Dove was apologetic. She liked the little girl. No one had any idea why Brave Sparrow cried at just that moment.

The mother's heart in Moonflower sensed that it was something much more than the silly comment about the weaving. She held her gently and didn't try to stop the tears. Whatever it was that caused her to weep so, was best allowed to work itself out. If Brave Sparrow wanted to tell her, Moonflower would listen and try to help. Until then she would just try to be a comfort.

Dancing Willow went by the tree and asked if there was anything wrong, could she do anything for anyone? Blue Stone asked if she would bring a water bag and a cloth. Dancing Willow hurried back with them. After a few sips of cool water Brave Sparrow was able to dry her face and stop crying.

She picked up her work and asked Morning Dove quite politely to show her again, how it was supposed to be done.

"I want to learn to do it right," she said. By the next night, Brave Sparrow had finished the small mat and was working on a much larger one.

"You have caught on well, said Morning Dove, as she checked her work. I am proud of you. What will you work on next?"

"I would like to learn to make the heavy winter mats, so I can make them for Moonflower. She does so much. When this is done, will you show me where to gather the reeds, and how to cut them the right length? The pile of reeds that Moonflower brought back has gotten dry and stiff. She hasn't had the time to work on them."

Brave Sparrow's heart was incased in pain as she continually struggled to keep her voice calm and her resolution to do all things exceptionally well.

"Yes, of course I will," said Morning Dove.

It is strange, she thought, as she walked away. She seems changed somehow, almost like she is pretending to be someone else. If Morning Dove had been able to read Brave Sparrow's mind at that moment she would have been shocked, for the girl was looking in the direction of the Chief's tent as he stood outside it.

He is waiting for his warriors to return, from their ugly work, she thought. They will probably have a big fire again and celebrate and tell everyone what they have brought back. What they don't tell is the real bloody story.

The painful stone of anger buried in Brave Sparrow's heart, grew. It was always there. No one knew the way she planned her every smile, her every word and deed until she would be totally accepted by the people and this time she would be invisible to them, by choice. Free to gain their trust and the power that knowledge brings, she continued to learn all she could about what the Chief said or planned.

CHAPTER SIX
DELIBERATE PLANNING

She experimented in weaving mats of intricate patterns. She became an expert, surpassing her teacher. She made strong baskets that held water and were perfect in shape and design, and often her path of gathering her weaving supplies, took her near enough to the Chief's tent that she could hear what was said inside. For the most part the men of the camp ignored her. If she worked near them, they acted as if she didn't exist, because they held her in low regard. She was just a white girl with her head full of strange ideas. Many of them tolerated her presence only because she had been accepted into the Chief's family.

She never shared her knowledge with anyone, not even Blue Stone. She felt that many times the wives of braves were not fully aware of what the warriors did.

She decided that it might be useful to make friends with Singing Lark, the wife of Talking Mountain and with Yellow Bird, the wife of the Chief. Little by little she started a campaign of friendship. She had no way of knowing that her small acts of kindness to the older women would meet with such approval from all the women, especially Moonflower.

One day when she was gathering grass near the Chief's tent; she noted that the basket Yellow Bird carried had a loose handle. When she thought about it, she realized she had never seen Yellow bird doing any weaving.

Brave Sparrow sat down in the shade, not in her usual place but a little ways away. She sat closer to the Chief's tent and started a large carrying basket with a strong handle and wide bottom. She wove the pattern of a bird on all four sides. Her practiced hands worked smoothly and by the time that Yellow Bird returned with a basket of herbs and a few berries, the project was nearing completion.

Yellow Bird noticed the girl working diligently and saw that she had not moved all afternoon. She was curious to see what the girl was making and decided that she would brew a mild mint and clover tea and take two cups to the tree where Brave Sparrow sat. Casually she walked over and sat down in the shade beside Brave Sparrow, placing the cups in the grass. She watched a moment and then offered the cup to Brave Sparrow.

"Thank you Grandmother, It is an honor that you bring tea to me. It is I who should serve the wife of our great Chief." Yellow Bird was very pleased by the manners of the young woman, and the use of the word "Grandmother" was not unnoticed. All though in the conversation of the people, it could be a term of respect to any older woman, Yellow Bird chose to think that the girl was accepting her as family. Moonflower is teaching her well, she thought. She did seem more like one of the people now that her skin had tanned to a dark brown. It had burned painfully many times before it had browned. Her blond hair however had lightened in the sun and was nearly white. Brave Sparrow wore it in a single braid down her back, thinking that it was less noticeable that way.

"The breeze is nice here. I seldom sit under the trees. Usually I stay near the front of the tent so I can hear if Rising Eagle calls me."

"Yes, I haven't seen you outside with the other women. You need someone to help you do some of the chores. If you wish me to come in the mornings for a time to shake the furs and roll up the tent sides to cool it, I will be glad to help do that, but I have never visited you because I feel unworthy to enter the tent of the Chief and his wife without being asked. May I come tomorrow to help?"

Yellow Bird was ashamed of herself. How long had this precious girl been in the family of her son? She had never been to her tent since the day of acceptance.

"I would love for you to come tomorrow, but not to work. Please will you bring Moonflower and come about this time for tea and we will sit and visit?"

"We will be honored to come." Brave Sparrow wondered if it was proper for her to answer for Moonflower, but she knew that it was unheard of to refuse an invitation to the Chief's tent, for any reason.

"Now, I must hurry back to help with preparations for the evening meal. Dark Wolf and the other hunters will return soon.

"Yellow Bird, I would like you to have this gathering basket. I noticed that the handle on yours is weakening. I wish that I knew the secrets of making colors, so that I could have made the birds on the sides yellow." She held up the basket for inspection.

"This is beautiful! I hadn't noticed that you were putting birds on it. This is a unique and useful gift. I will use it often and treasure it, Granddaughter. Thank you. I will look forward to visiting with you and your mother tomorrow." The basket had been the magic touch to form a lasting memory that Yellow Bird would honor by granting any reasonable request that Brave Sparrow might need to make in the future.

A sly smile crept to the lips of Brave Sparrow as she headed back to help Moonflower and tell her of the unusual invitation. Moonflower was more than delighted.

"We will wear our best clothes! You must wear your new shirt that I made for you for winter, and I will put beads in your hair."

"I wish I knew how to make colors", said Brave Sparrow, abruptly changing the subject. "I made a basket for Yellow Bird today and it would have been so much prettier, if I had been able to make the birds on it in yellow."

"You gave Yellow Bird a basket? Why?"

"The handle on her gathering basket was broken, so I gave her the one I was making. That's when she invited us to tea." That sweet innocent face revealed none of the facts that she had planned the whole thing and was learning to manipulate.

Moonflower looked at her and felt pride in her generous and thoughtful daughter.

"Your hands look red and sore. You have worked with the grass all day. Here soak them in the warm water and smear them with this bear grease. I have bear stew simmering and we will have crackers with it tonight. I have the batter ready so that when Dark Wolf wants to eat we can quickly fry them on the flat river rocks. See how they shine. I have them all greased. They are getting hot. When they start to smoke a little then we know they are ready to use."

Dark Wolf and the hunters returned with two deer and several rabbits. Dark Wolf claimed a large roast from one of the deer and a hide, which he handed to Brave Sparrow.

"This is for you to learn to work the hides. Make it soft for winter slippers." She accepted the rolled hide onto her out-stretched arms, not touching it with her greased hands.

"Thank You," was all she said and tipped her face down to appear humble, while gritting her teeth at the memory of the raid on her family.

Whenever he was near, it was more difficult for her. She tried to tell herself that Dark Wolf had not been one of the warriors that had killed her family, because he had been busy pulling her out of the wagon and taking her away, but it didn't help much. How many other wagons had he raided? How many other families had he killed?

"What is the matter with her hands? Did she burn them?"

"No husband, she is not careless enough to do that. She has worked all day with the grass to make a beautiful basket for your mother." He looked puzzled, but pleased.

"Is the food ready?"

"Yes, you can rest. You should sit." She had his willow back rest on the mat near the fire. She dropped a small circle of dough on several of the smoking rocks and quickly turned the browned dough over. By the time she scooped up the stew into his bowl, the crackers were golden and crispy. She handed him several and made more. She filled a smaller bowl for Brave Sparrow and placed several crackers on a smooth wooden plate near her and then fixed her own.

Moonflower sat for several moments without speaking. She ate and enjoyed the family here together. Brave Sparrow's heart grew cold with Dark Wolf near her. She had to force herself to eat.

Moonflower was bursting to tell him that she had been invited by Yellow Bird but wanted just the right moment. Dark Wolf finished his food quickly and stood up.

"I have something I must talk to our Chief about."

"Please tell Yellow Bird, that we will see her tomorrow." He stopped mid-stride. She answered the question written on his face, without him asking it.

"She has invited Brave Sparrow and me to visit tomorrow." He frowned and walked away, wondering what the women were planning. Yellow Bird felt oddly nervous all evening, as the conversation of her husband and son continued.

"Sleeping Bear asked me if I thought it was acceptable and I thought that I would ask you."

"Yes of course, but it is unusual for the people to honor a girl and it wasn't that big of a thing, was it?"

"Father, Blue Stone was bitten deeply by the snake that rattles. Only the strongest medicine could heal such a thing."

"What will Talking Mountain think of this? I fear he will be angry. He believes that his medicine alone cured the girl."

"Perhaps we can get him to have a ceremony and ask him to honor her, and then Sleeping Bear can make the presentation as part of it."

Chief Rising Eagle was troubled. He didn't like things that changed his world. It seemed that the white skinned people were always causing him reason to worry. He had to admit to himself that he didn't like the white skins, and he didn't like it that so many came to his hunting territory. He hated them because they brought the disease that had caused Raven's death, and he resented that a white girl was now his granddaughter. And now Sleeping Bear wanted to honor that white girl. He was sure that this would bring more trouble.

"We will think on this. I will speak with Talking Mountain soon," he said with a dismissive wave.

When Dark Wolf returned to his tent, he noticed that the deer hide was already staked out and scraped clean. She is a good worker, he thought. He did not know that

Moonflower had insisted on scraping the hide, to spare Brave Sparrow's hands.

Blue Stone had no idea that her simple request for permission to give her flute to Brave Sparrow would start such a chain of events. Her ankle was nearly well. The skin pulled when she walked, and caused a slight discomfort but in time that would disappear and only the scar would remain.

She was uneasy about Brave Sparrow lately. Something in her had changed. Blue Stone could not discern the cause but something was definitely different. Brave Sparrow was still warm and friendly, but she didn't seek her out for company as often, and yesterday she sat under a tree on the other side of the Chief's tent and worked all day alone. Blue Stone saw Moonflower and Brave Sparrow come out of their tent; dressed in their best clothes. They looked fancy enough for a special ceremony. They sat in the sun near the banked outside fire and Moonflower braided Brave Sparrow's hair and put in blue and green beads. I wonder what is going on, she thought. She didn't go over to ask. That wouldn't be polite, but she did choose a spot where she could watch, when she worked, grinding the hard roots into flour for her mother.

Her eyes always watched the whole camp. She noticed when the women left to gather reeds for the replacement of winter mats, or throw swift stones to get the ducks on the lake. She couldn't stop a giggle when an old woman slipped and sat down in the water, wading in after the duck she had hit. She noticed when Singing Lark entered the Chief's tent.

Moonflower and Brave Sparrow walked slowly. Moonflower had waited a long time for this invitation and she wanted to make the most of it. She had not been asked, since Raven's death. She carried a small basket containing crackers and honey.

"We can enjoy these with the tea," she said to Brave Sparrow as she carefully arranged the crackers around the bowl in the bottom of the basket.

When they arrived at the tent, they could hear voices inside and just as Moonflower raised her hand to scratch on the closed flap, the Chief stepped out.

"Greetings Moonflower, Brave Sparrow," he said, holding the door flap open for them, as he left.

"Good Afternoon Chief Rising Eagle," was all that Moonflower had a chance to say. He had thought about his conversation with Dark Wolf, long into the night. He was on his way to visit Talking Mountain.

When Singing Lark had arrived a few minutes earlier, he had decided it was a perfect time to be out visiting. He had never liked being around more than one woman at a time.

Singing Lark smiled when Brave Sparrow and Moonflower entered. Yellow Bird offered them cushions of fur, padded with fresh dried grass to sit on. The sides of the tent were rolled up far enough to let the breeze in, but still felt cozy and private.

The tent was large and colorful. The walls of the tent had designs painted inside and out. On the outside entrance was a sun. Inside on the back wall of the tent, a pure white buffalo hide seemed to reflect the light of the fire. Brave Sparrow didn't know the meaning of the symbols but thought they were pretty.

She noted the weapons fastened high on the posts that supported the tent. Strings of dried foods and herbs hung from the support branches above her. Baskets hung in the cooking area as well as setting on the floor in a row, along one wall. Each basket held something different. She saw one that she recognized as being a sewing basket. It contained leather strips in many different colors. Beads strung on a cord, curled in pretty circles, filling another. A large clay pot steamed beside the fire and filled the air with the smell of mint and clover. Black streaks had stained the clay, baked on by many uses near the fire. Yellow Bird chatted happily with her visitors, as she used a small gourd to dip the tea into each wooden cup. In the bottom of the cups she had placed several dried berries. Moonflower had left her basket near the door when she entered. She had temporarily forgotten to give it to Yellow Bird. She reached for it now and each of them enjoyed breaking the crackers and dipping them in the honey, as they sipped the tea and talked.

Brave Sparrow was quiet, as she studied the faces and clothing of the three women. Each was different, and yet each was the same. Then she looked around and her eyes locked on the pure white hide hanging on the back wall. It was the only thing she saw, that was not like them. Earth tones and stains of color filled their world and decorated their clothes and hair. She liked the white hide. Yellow Bird offered her a bit more tea and some more crackers with honey. She thanked her, but declined saying it was delicious but that she had enough.

There was another thing that she liked and wanted to continue. That was being slim. Most of the people in camp were round and not as tall as she knew she would be when she was fully-grown. Both her parents had been tall and slim. Ben was too. She missed them so much.

"Brave Sparrow, you look so far away, what are you thinking about?" asked Singing Lark.

"I was just noticing all the beautiful colors in Yellow Bird's Dress. She has sewn the beads onto pieces of leather that are separate. Each section is a different tone. I would like to learn to color the leather that way."

"Perhaps next time I am using the dyes you could come and watch," offered Singing Lark."

"Could I mother?" She said softly, turning to Moonflower.

Moonflower was so taken by the use of the word mother that she didn't answer her.

"Mother, is something wrong?"

"No of course not, dear. Yes you may learn to dye the leather if Singing Lark wants to teach you." Moonflower felt like dancing! Her little girl was being accepted. The wife of the shaman, the most powerful woman in the village, was willing to be Brave Sparrow's mentor.

Singing Lark was pleased that a young girl would be spending time with her to learn a craft that she felt only she could teach properly.

After all, I am the only one in this camp that knows how to change a piece of leather to pure white, or make it dark red for the holy man, or turn wool to the sacred healing yellow, she thought. There are lots of things that I could teach her if she wants to learn. Her thoughts were filled with pride as she got up to leave.

"I must go now, but it was nice to sit and visit." She thanked Yellow Bird for asking her to join them and smiled at Moonflower and Brave Sparrow as she left.

She wanted to get back to make sure that Talking Mountain had everything that he needed. She was upset when she saw the Chief just about to leave her tent. He was there, and I was not there to serve him. The Chief and the medicine man stood outside and were having a friendly laugh about something.

"Talking Mountain, would you like me to get food, or something to drink for you and Chief Rising Eagle?" She said hurrying to them.

"No, No don't bother yourself, Singing Lark. I am heading back and Yellow Bird will require me to eat, even if I have had my fill elsewhere. She is sure that I am starving to death, at all times." They laughed together congenially and he strolled back to his tent, hoping that Brave Sparrow would still be there.

When he pushed open the flap and entered, Moonflower jumped up as if she had been burned. She no longer wanted to stay. She backed out of the tent as she mumbled a half heard excuse and a Thank you to Yellow Bird.

"That was strange," he said, to Yellow Bird and Brave Sparrow. "Are you going to run away too, or will you stay a few minutes and talk with me?"

"I will be honored to stay Grandfather." She felt a longing as she said the word, picturing her real grandfather that had held her close before her father had lifted her into the wagon. She fought back tears and the bile of resentment came in her throat. Her grief had entered the anger stage and had stuck there. She used all her control, speaking softly.

"If you want me to stay, I will." She blamed him directly for the raids on the wagon trains and death of her family. Even now she sensed his aversion to being near her, as he looked at her.

"I want to ask you an important question. You must answer it truthfully and as completely as you can. Understand?"

"Yes I understand."

"Good. First, please sit down again, here, beside me," as he motioned a place on his fur. She could tell that he had to work at being polite.

CHAPTER SEVEN
THE INQUISITION

"Now then, let us begin. I want to ask you two questions really. First, who gave you the blue magic stone? And how did you know to use it to heal Blue Stone when she was bitten?" His voice was that of authority and his attitude was one of superiority.

"No one gave me the stone. It just appeared. I looked but there were no others like it. Then I noticed that it had a hole in it so I thought it must be for a necklace. I don't think it is magic; at least it doesn't do anything that I can see. It just is pretty, and when Blue Stone was so sick and the medicine man danced, but he didn't pray to the real God. I gave her the stone because I wanted her to get well and I didn't have anything else, and I prayed to God for her and I know that he healed her."

"This God you talk of, how do you know of him?"

"He is every ones God. My father told me about him. He would have told you, too, if you had known him. He is a big, big God and He can make flowers or rain, or make people well."

"So you think your God has power, and you think he made the flowers and the rain. Did he make the blue stone?"

"Yes, He made everything and everybody."

"I see. How do you know all this?"

"It is all in the Bible book my father had. He said everything any person needed to know was in the book."

"Is the book about your God's power?"

"Yes."

"Have you seen that book?"

"Yes."

"What did your father do with the book?"

"He read at night or when he needed God's power to help him."

"Then when he read your God gave him power?"

"Yes, well sort of. It is more like God uses power to help my father. Grandfather, you said only two questions. You are asking me many questions."

"I will ask you one last question."

"Yes Grandfather."

"Do you have God's power?"

"Yes, when I pray, I have God's grace. I am weak, but He is strong." The old Chief furrowed his brow and glanced at his wife. Yellow Bird looked equally concerned and confused.

"Good Night Granddaughter."

"Good night and thank you both for having us to tea." Brave Sparrow left, feeling quite happy with the afternoon. Things had gone even better than she had planned.

Chief Rising Eagle wore a heavy frown as he immediately settled on his sleeping furs. He wanted to close his eyes and think. This had been a day filled with many challenging ideas. Yellow Bird asked if he wanted to eat, but he didn't answer.

Moonflower watched her daughter, as she walked back to the tent.

"Why did you not come back when I did?" She had a tang of anger in her voice.

"The Chief asked me to stay."

"Why? What did he want?"

"He just wanted to talk."

"What did he say?"

"Not much."

"He asked where I got the Blue Stone."

"And I told him."

"If I put on my regular day dress, may I go out for a walk? I would like to find some red grass for a new basket."

"Yes, it will be a while before Dark Wolf returns. Be back before dark."

"Yes mother," she answered.

She changed in an instant and stuffed a huge handful of the crackers in her pocket on top of her cutting stone before she left with her carrying basket over her arm. She headed straight out to the far pasture where the horses were grazing. She could see Gray Cloud perched on a rock, playing his flute. She loved the melancholy sound. He had learned to play from Singing Wind, Blue Stone's brother. Singing Wind was the only one that made the flutes. They were rare and beautiful. Each one was a unique treasure.

Brave Sparrow cut the short red grass that grew near the rocks. He stopped playing and watched her.

"What are you doing out here? You will disturb the horses."

"I need the red grass to decorate a special basket. Please play some more. Don't stop because I am here. She continued to cut a bit here and there as he started to play again. Soon he had totally forgotten that she was there.

She worked her way to the edge of the herd, looking for her father's horses. The big workhorses were easy to spot. The riding horse was not there. They must have Dart Away some other place, she thought. She clacked her tongue at the horses, as she had always done. They came to her and stood waiting for the treat that she would produce. She couldn't reach their ears but she scratched their necks and talked to them, then she gave each one a cracker. She had been lifted onto their backs many times and rode as they worked the fields back home. Father hadn't allowed her to ride on them when they pulled the covered wagon.

"It is too dangerous," he had said. "You could fall off and the wagon might roll over you."

She brushed away a tear, and said "Good bye Daffy, Good bye Duncan, Good Bye Big Joe, Good Bye Sam. I'll come again when I can." She had visited the big horses from time to time, but not as often as she would have liked. They were getting fat. They needed to work. No one used them. They just stood in the field and ate all day. There were many more big workhorses standing together by the backside of the herd. She knew they represented other wagons and other families whose dreams had ended abruptly. She wandered back to camp in a big circle behind Gray Cloud. He was lost in his own world.

Nearly a week went by before Talking Mountain told Singing Lark to instruct the women to prepare the communal fire and a ceremonial feast for the following night.

The hunters left shortly after and were gone all night. They returned in the morning with two deer. Dark wolf returned and tied Dart Away to the tree near the back of the tent. So that's who rides my father's horse. Poor Dart Away, he is used to so much more attention, thought Brave Sparrow, as she observed. She gave him pats and scratches and rubbed his back and sides with dry grass. He was sweating. After walking him to the lake for a long cool drink, she tied him back where Dark Wolf would expect to find him.

Dancing Willow seemed nervous, and Sleeping Bear went in and out of Talking Mountain's tent twice. The second time he carried a package. Blue Stone had some idea about what would take place, but she was not telling anyone. Moonflower cooked grain in huge quantities and added dried grapes and nuts and honey. Each woman made a favorite dish to share. Singing Lark was in charge of the main fire and the cooking of the deer. She didn't have to prepare anything else. She fussed at the young boys and girls to bring more wood. She directed the women how to arrange the food. It always ended up the same but each time she acted as if it was different and new.

Brave Sparrow hated these ceremonies. They always reminded her of the reason for the first one she had attended.

Once again she was dressed in her new winter shirt and with her hair freshly washed and oiled, it was braided with colorful beads. She was restless and with her chores done, she strolled away from the center of the camp.

Blue Stone sat under a tree with a basket of berries, picking the stems and leaves out of them.

"Why are you sitting way over here to do that?" asked Brave Sparrow.

"I wanted to get away from our tent. My mother has gone totally mad! She is very nervous and father acts like he would rather be somewhere else, he is snapping and growling."

"It does get hectic when they prepare for a ceremony. I see that Dancing Willow has made you put on a new shirt, too. It is beautiful. I like the way the beads are in circles across the front."

"She makes pretty things, but I don't like to wear new clothes, they always feel stiff and scratch me under my arms," said Blue Stone. Brave Sparrow noticed that the circles had been sewn with blue beads. They were glass and could not match Blue Stone's necklace.

"I'm glad that your ankle is nearly well now. I know how much you like to dance. It would be sad if you couldn't." Blue Stone reached up and gave Brave Sparrow a hug. This had become a tradition between the two girls. No one else in camp did it openly.

"I will see you later. Now I have to go back and help mother finish up. She will need these berries. This is the third basket I have cleaned today!"

The smell of the many foods cooking was making Brave Sparrow ill. Ceremonies and the stories that she now understood always made her sick. She wondered if when it was served if she would be able to eat. Growling Bear walked toward the fire where the deer was roasting.

"How much longer before I can eat?" He knew the answer. They never tasted the feast until after the Chief and medicine man had finished the ceremony.

"Your name suits you, Growling Bear. Ask my husband," snapped Singing Lark. As wife of the medicine man she had status that outranked even the best of the warriors. She answered to no one but her husband, and the Chief. Even Yellow Bird was careful of what she said to Singing Lark.

The people began to gather just before the sun dropped below the horizon. Everyone chatted and the children poked and jockeyed to get in front of each other so they would be able to see everything. Dark Wolf and Moonflower sat on either side of Brave Sparrow. She would rather have sat beside Blue Stone but knew that she had to sit in her proper place according to family status. They were seated on the left of Chief Rising Eagle. On the right side of the Chief sat Yellow Bird, Talking Mountain and Singing Lark.

The deer had been removed from the fire and now the meat was on great platters, covered to keep it hot.

Chief Rising Eagle stood up and everyone quieted. He began by talking of their great hunters and warriors. Then he was retelling their deeds and successes of the last raid on a wagon train. It seemed to Brave Sparrow that he droned on for hours. She tried not to listen.

Next, Talking Mountain stood. He spoke of his own great power and the power of the spirits and his magic potions. Then he called Blue Stone forward and showed everyone her ankle and said how he had healed her after she was nearly dead. Brave Sparrow was getting angrier at each thing he said. He didn't heal her! God did, she thought. How can he stand there and take all the credit? She was furious and she had not heard the last few sentences. Her thoughts had drowned them out.

Moonflower pushed on her back and told her to stand.

"What?"

"Go to Talking Mountain, and stand beside Blue Stone. Don't be afraid." She rose hesitantly, and when she saw the smile on Blue Stone's face she smiled back and joined her.

"What are we doing," whispered Brave Sparrow?"

"You will see," was all she would say. Talking Mountain raised his hands above his head and spoke to the Great Spirit thanking him for blessings on his people. Then he reached for a long leather wrapped package, with beaded fringe, that Singing Lark had on her lap. He held it high and spoke to the spirits of the night to witness the power, and he pulled a beautifully carved flute from its sleeve. He circled the campfire as he told the story of the blue stone and its magical power. He told how Brave Sparrow had given the blue stone to her friend and so had given it to the entire tribe to increase their power.

"This flute has much medicine and has been made by Singing Wind. It was given to Blue Stone. She now gives it to Brave Sparrow, as a gift of gratitude for friendship and power!" With a flourish he handed the flute to Brave Sparrow.

She stood holding the flute in both hands. She slowly lifted it above her head smiling at Blue Stone and whispered.

"Thank you it's beautiful."

"Talking Mountain, has said that this flute has great medicine." She began in a voice that could be heard by everyone gathered there. "Played by Singing Wind, or Gray Cloud it will make beautiful music. Played by me, now, with no training or practice, it will be shrill and unpleasant. The power of the flute is only in the skill of the one who plays it. Talking Mountain is like this flute. He needs the power of the Greatest Spirit to be able to heal, just as the flute needs the hands of someone who can play, to make beautiful music." Her young voice seemed loud, as it drifted over the silent people, reaching every ear. A gasp was heard when she dared to contradict the medicine man.

"It is the same with the blue stone. It has only the power of love and friendship, but it was given at a time when a great power was called on to save a friend's life. I prayed that God, the Almighty, most powerful God, would heal Blue Stone, and He did."

"God heals, not people, not stones. He is above all other gods! He is my God and yours. He created the heavens and the earth. He created us. He is the One True God and He loves us. He healed Blue Stone, because He loves her, and because I asked Him and He loves me, too. He is all-powerful. He is the power of love." She pointed to the stone on Blue Stone's chest, with the flute. "He is the love that touched my heart to give the blue stone. He is the love in this flute, and I thank you all for it."

She walked slowly to the mat and sat down. She couldn't believe she had said all that. Where did it come from? She thought. Father, am I to forgive these people for the loss of my family and teach them about you? I have a large painful stone in my heart much bigger than the one Blue Stone wears. How can I teach them of you when I want to lash out at them? Help me Father to know and do your will. It will take more strength than I have.

The blood had drained from Moonflower's face. Dark Wolf's lips were a tight, thin, purple line from anger. He jumped up and stalked off into the darkness. No one else moved. They waited to see what would happen next.

The Chief cleared the area of women and children with the sweep of his hand and a command so loud that it bounced off the surrounding tents.

"Leave us!" His command was directed at all the women and children. Quickly they went back to their tents.

The men gathered around to hear what the Chief would say.

"Growling Bear, early tomorrow, you will ride to the wagon where Brave Sparrow was found. Take two men with you. Take Sleeping Bear and Night Hawk. He is our best tracker. You must find a book that the girl's father read from. It is not natural that a woman-child should speak with such power. She has been with us only a short time, yet she spoke our language as if she were an adult, born to it. She has great medicine. Her father's God follows her. He fills her mouth with His words. Leave before first light. Find that book! Now we must not give this thing more power by changing our ways further. Let us eat and dance." The last few words were said slowly and solemnly.

The women, listening at a distance, quickly served the men. Wisely, the women had fed the children and they were now content to run and play in their usual rambunctious way. The youngest ones were hurried off to bed just in case the Chief would allow his temper to explode. The little children couldn't understand what was happening and it would frighten them.

Chief Rising Eagle took a torch and walked out onto the prairie in the direction his son had gone. He found him sitting on the small knoll that over looked the camp.

"Father what does it all mean? These are strange words that come from a small woman not yet grown? She should have been killed, and then we wouldn't have this problem. I should never have brought a white child into this village. What are we to do with her now?"

CHAPTER EIGHT
FIND THAT BOOK!

"Tomorrow, Growling Bear will go to the wagon where she was found. She speaks of a book that her father read each night. He must have been a powerful holy man. I have asked Growling Bear to find that book and bring it to me."

"Father, this is madness! Do you want more of those bizarre teachings in our camp? Father, I will punish her severely and tell her never to speak of her father's God again. I will tell her to apologize to Talking Mountain and the people. We could make her do it right now." He started to rise.

"No," said Rising Eagle. "Do nothing to the girl. Say nothing of this now. Wait until Growling Bear returns. We need to see that book. Now go back to camp. Comfort Moonflower. This has greatly upset her. Do not be harsh with her. This is not something a woman could change. She is training the girl well in a woman's work. I wish to stay here for a time. Tell your mother that I will be back to the tent later. I do not feel like dancing."

Dark Wolf returned to camp, but went straight to his tent. He found Moonflower on her furs. She was awake, but he saw in the firelight that she had been weeping.

"What is to come of her?" she wailed. "Am I to lose another daughter?"

"Nothing will be done; no one pays attention to what a child says. Now dry your eyes woman. Where is Brave Sparrow?"

"I think she is with Blue Stone. They were eating when I left."

"I will be back in a few minutes. I need to give my mother a message from Rising Eagle." He went out and closed the flap.

Yellow Bird sat on a mat near the communal fire. It was growing smaller. No one was tending it. A few people sat around it in small groups talking. The atmosphere of the evening was hushed and felt strange.

Yellow Bird rose as her son approached.

"Where is your father?"

"He says he needs time to think and will come to you at the tent later." He bent and kissed her forehead. This was a tender form of affection. It spoke volumes and revealed how troubled he really was.

"Thank you, son, and good night." She had felt the tension and concern in her son and watched as he moved away.

Growling Bear, Sleeping Bear and Night Hawk left camp on an uncomfortable mission. Everything about the morning seemed wrong. All three felt they had been sent on an impossible assignment. Soon all three men were soaked to the skin. Their oiled leather clothes kept them dry for a while but the continued rain finally made its way through. During the night the rain began. The clouds were dark and heavy as the three warriors headed out. It was later than they would have normally left, because the sun was hidden by the storm. Their horses trudged through the waterlogged grass of the prairie and splashed the puddles up onto the legs of their riders. The low clouds and loud thunder made horses and riders edgy.

At midday they stopped to rest by a grove of trees and could not find enough dry material to start a fire. The wind chilled them in their wet clothes and Growling Bear found many things to complain about. The other men huddled under the branches of the pines trying to find shelter while they ate from the generous supplies left from the feast. Moonflower had made certain that they were well provisioned. Their travel cakes, the usual provision, were left in the wrapper for later.

"Let's go, and get this fool's errand over before we drown," snarled Growling Bear as he swung up on his horse and rode away, leaving the other two to catch up. It was clear that he resented this particular assignment.

The rain stopped and the sky cleared at sunset. The prairie grass was sparkling with the raindrops that coated it. An overhang in a running wash provided a dry spot to rest and they were able to find enough dry wood and grass there to build a small fire.

"We are lucky that the rain came from the other direction," offered Night Hawk as he brought more wood to feed the small fire.

As they got warm and dry, Growling Bear was finally able to behave in a friendly manner.

"Can you believe that we were sent into the rain to find a book, which, if it existed at all was probably ruined long ago. I can't understand why any importance has been given to the words of a child. I think the whole thing is ridiculous, and she should be punished. Why was the Chief even allowing a ceremony over a child's necklace? I think our gray headed Chief is getting old." He laughed.

The other men had heard stories from their wives of that night when the stone had been placed on Blue Stone. They had a feeling that there was something very different about this whole thing. They didn't agree with Growling Bear, but they laughed feebly to appease him. They didn't like hearing him speak disrespectfully about their Chief.

The next day, the three men reached the river and traveled well past the point where they thought they should have found the wagon. They knew this area and couldn't understand how they could have missed it.

Finally they turned their horses around. They could not find a sign of the wagon.

"It is impossible that it is gone," said Night Hawk. "Its wheel was broken. We took the horses. No one would have moved that wagon."

"So where is it?" snapped Growling Bear? He was very brusque again.

"I don't want to go back to camp and try to explain to Chief Rising Eagle that the wagon has just disappeared."

"We must look more closely for tracks," said Night Hawk. He knew that the wagon they looked for had left the train earlier; on the day the wagon train was attacked. Night Hawk was one of the three that had been there waiting.

They went to the burned wagon train, and then headed back along the wagon trail for a short distance. From there, they rode back to the river, investing effort, searching the prairie for a track or sign of the wagon's passing. They headed up river one last time.

"The rain has removed any tracks that we might have found," said Sleeping Bear.

They paused no more than a few yards from the sight where the wagon had stopped and jerked, falling onto its side when its wheels dropped into the deep channel made by runoff. Night Hawk pointed out the tallest oak.

"This is the spot. I know it is." Had they circled the tree, they would have seen the grave and Ben's carved cross on the tree trunk.

They watered their horses and let them feed on the sweet grass growing near the river's edge. They sat in the grass and puzzled about the disappearance, and all the time they were watched by a stallion high on the bluff across the river.

When they finally mounted and rode farther upstream, the stallion went down the precarious path on the other side of the bluff, gathered his herd and headed across the river downstream. He wanted to go far away from the humans. He took them north, farther than he had ever been before. A beautiful cream-colored foal had to run hard to keep up with her brown and white mother.

Finally beyond the normal hunting grounds of the Winahatah they stopped at the edge of a small running creek. There the herd rested.

It was four days before Growling Bear brought his small group back to report that they had failed. They were humbled and embarrassed to tell the Chief that they could not find the wagon. They tried to rationalize that it had been repaired and taken away.

"Did you find tracks where the wagon left?" They had to admit there had been none.

"I think the rain washed away the tracks," suggested Night Hawk rather feebly.

"Talking Mountain stood and waited until he had the full attention of all the men closely pressed into the tent. The Great God of the book has hidden the wagon from your eyes. Perhaps the eyes of the girl can see the wagon and bring back the book."

"No! It is finished! We will not speak of this again!" The Chief seldom raised his voice, but he did this time. He was angry and troubled.

"Nothing is, as it should be, since the white men came to our land. Tomorrow you will plan a large hunt. Growling Bear send the scouts out to find the herds. Night Hawk will have no trouble seeing buffalo or deer I hope." All three men from the party felt the sting of his words and the intended chastisement. Chief Rising Eagle left the meeting, signaling Talking Mountain to follow him.

They walked out of the camp and sat alone on the knoll where Chief Rising Eagle had sat the night of the communal fire. The other men filed out of his tent and returned to their various duties. Growling Bear and Night Hawk talked for a few moments and then within the hour, Night Hawk and two others left camp.

"These are troubling times my friend. Forgive me for speaking to you that way in front of the others. I felt I had to stop this whole thing before it gets too big to handle. Soon it will all be forgotten, if we give it no further importance."

"Are you really going to send the hunters out for more buffalo so soon? If the scouts find a heard close by, I will. Why not? We can always use the provisions. If they are busy doing familiar things then they won't be talking of strange Gods and power stones."

"You are a wise Chief. Perhaps we should go back now and make Yellow Bird happy. She can feed both of us." And they both laughed.

They walked back into camp smiling congenially. Each had privately decided that he wanted everyone to see that he was happy and had no concerns. They saw Brave Sparrow walking under the trees with Blue Stone. Each girl had her arms full of weaving supplies.

"That is good. Keep them busy and quiet," said the Chief with a chuckle.

Singing Lark had been keeping busy and out of sight. She didn't want to mentor a girl that was the center of so much controversial interest. Everywhere people still talked about her. They didn't seem to be criticizing her, but more as if they feared her a little, or were in awe of her. Singing Lark could understand that Brave Sparrow puzzled them. She is so different. There is no telling what other strange things are in her mind, she thought.

Morning Dove made the effort to join the girls whenever they sat under the trees to weave. She liked working with them and was hoping that Brave Sparrow would say more about her God, but Morning Dove didn't dare open the subject.

Sleeping Bear had forbidden Blue Stone to listen to any more talk of her God.

"If she starts it, you tell her you have something to do and come back to our tent right away. Understand?"

"Yes Father."

Blue Stone, like Morning Dove, was curious what other things Brave Sparrow believed.

Brave Sparrow was confused, angry and heavy hearted. She still missed her parents and her brother. She knew that these people were the very ones that had taken them from her. She knew that she was supposed to forgive them. That is going to be the hardest thing I will ever do, she thought.

She finally decided that for now she would continue with her plan to try to do everything to the best of her ability. She also wanted to continue to get information on what the men did. She heard Talking Mountain's suggestion that she be taken to find the Bible. She heard Chief Rising Eagle shout at him.

So the days went by in the same routine. The scouts returned. The men hunted and were gone two nights and returned with only one deer. The women cooked and worked at their crafts. No one mentioned what had taken place. It was quiet in camp.

One day the women went out on a gathering expedition. They brought a lunch and water bags and blankets for the babies to sleep on. They each carried at least two empty baskets when they left camp. Some of the women had digging tools they had made and used for years. Others brought a heavy knife for the same purpose.

They headed across the open grass to the woods in the distance, walking beside the herd of horses.

Once they reached the shade of the trees they stopped to rest and have a light lunch. One of the mothers stayed on the blankets with three young ones while the other mothers started to gather mushrooms. Several went farther into the woods to a damp area where they pulled big meaty roots from the mud. The smell filled the air and identified them as wild onions. One started picking her basket full of coltsfoot, while the rest began to pick up nuts in heavy leathery coverings and they filled their baskets and unfolded large pouches and filled them too.

Brave Sparrow and Moonflower were picking up nuts. Brave Sparrow noticed the dark stains on her hands. She tried to rub the color onto the grass but it wouldn't come off. When no one was watching her, she stepped behind a tree and rubbed a dark casing on the end of her braid. It too, turned brown. When I get back I will see if that washes off, she thought. Her baskets were getting heavy.

One by one, as the baskets were filled, the women wandered back toward the blankets and the sleeping babies. They sat down quietly and soon they were all napping. Brave Sparrow thought that this was very strange and wondered if it was safe. No one was on guard. She leaned against a tree but didn't sleep.

After a little while the babies started to stir and naptime was over. They fed the little ones and then headed back to camp together.

The food that had been gathered was shared and each woman took what was needed for the number of people in her family.

"Next time we go, we will all be gathering nuts," explained Moonflower. "The ones we found today are from late last fall. As the fall comes some of the other things are no longer available but there will be many nuts."

"Singing Lark will be gathering her baskets full of herbs for the medicine man to use for healing during the winter months. She also gathers things for him in the spring."

Brave Sparrow, felt that there had to be a reason this information had been given to her, but she wasn't sure yet what it was.

After they had eaten their evening meal, Brave Sparrow went to the tent of Talking Mountain and Singing Lark. She scratched at the flap and requested entrance.

"You may come in Brave Sparrow," said Singing Lark. She felt annoyed at the girl's presence but determined that she would be polite.

"What is it that we can help you with?" she asked.

"I have come to ask advice. This brown stain is here on my hands from the nuts we gathered. Since you are the best at coloring, I thought you would be good also at removing color. What can I do to make my hands clean again?"

"Sometimes it is more difficult to remove color than to add it. There are several things that will remove certain colors. The stain you have on your hands is a strong one. Come we will take a couple things with us to the backside of the lake and try. Perhaps one will work. We will see."

They walked together until they reached a spot where the edge of the water was clear of reeds and the bank was covered with gravel.

"This smells terrible, but we should try it first." Singing Lark poured the juice pressed from fermented wild apples and grass, onto Brave Sparrows hands.

"That smells terrible, but it makes my mouth water."

"There, leave it on a few minutes." Brave Sparrow held her dripping hands over the water. "Rub them together, and rinse them. Let's see. Well... it looks like the stains are lighter, but still there. Do you want to try this one? It smells even worse."

"Yes, I really want these stains gone."

Singing Lark poured the ammonia made by aging urine over the girl's hands. They both coughed as the fumes came back to them on a light breeze. She rubbed her hands again and rinsed.

"There, you have clean hands. Now all we have to do is figure out how to get rid of the stink," said Singing Lark laughing. Brave Sparrow plunged her hands under the water and rubbed them with sand, over and over. Still they stunk. She ran and grabbed handfuls of grass and rubbed them with that. It didn't work. Finally she happened to grab a handful of wild spearmint and after everything else it seemed to offer a little relief.

"Keep trying, I must go back now."

"Thank you Singing Lark. How did you know to use those things for cleaning the stains?"

"You have much to learn, come in the morning. We will begin."

Talking Mountain was not pleased when he heard that Brave Sparrow was coming to their tent in the morning and that she might be coming regularly. He was not going to stay there while she was there. That girl makes me nervous, he thought. He made a mental note to leave before she came. Brave Sparrow finished her morning chores for Moonflower and then asked permission to go to start her lessons with Singing Lark.

Moonflower was glad to let her go because as long as Singing Lark was training the girl, everyone else would have to accept her whether they liked it or not.

Soon Brave Sparrow was working with Singing Lark daily, as an assistant and a young trainee. She learned well and asked questions that required in depth answers.

She didn't neglect her promise to Yellow Bird. She often slipped to her tent first to help roll up the sides, and shake the furs, or cut fresh grass to pad the sleeping area. She carried water for both women and made herself useful in other ways. She worked hard making sure that Moonflower was not unhappy with her absence. Often she would do the same chores for her, before leaving, and politely asking if there was anything else that she should do before she left.

Bit by bit and day-by-day, she proved her value to the top ranking women in the village. They had all but forgotten about the day she spoke out at the communal fire, but Brave Sparrow knew that the Holy Spirit had used her to plant seeds in their souls.

They were no longer seeing her as the strange white girl. She had become Brave Sparrow, a clever, hardworking member of their family. This was her goal. She never failed to listen when adults were talking nearby. Bits of information were stored away, to be brought back and examined closely in the quiet hours when the camp slept. The rest of summer went by quickly and fall's color faded into cold nights and bare tree branches.

The ripe, dry corn had been picked from the field and stored, along with many wonderful things gathered by the women on their trips to the woods, nearby lake and prairie. The double walled tents had been packed with dried grass between the layers to insulate against the cold. Brave Sparrow found other reasons to be near the Chief's tent since grass for weaving was no longer an acceptable excuse. Most of the grass near the tents had all been cut and used. She asked permission to brush his riding horse that was always tied nearby, or to help Yellow Bird with the cooking. It seemed that all the men gave her no regard and spoke freely near her. It was as if they thought she was unintelligent or was of little importance. What could she do if she knew something anyway? They thought.

She dreaded winter. What if she was made to stay inside Moonflower's tent? How would she endure the confinement? At least now, the tent is a little larger since the women helped Moonflower to add another section of hides. I will have room to store my weaving supplies, she thought.

One morning when she was stirring a batch of dye for Singing Lark, she asked if they would be able to continue to work during the winter.

Singing Lark laughed, saying that winter is a time of rest.

"We will sew and decorate what we have sewn. We tell stories and sometimes eat meals in each other's tents to pass the time more quickly. We all look forward to spring and the passing of the cold months. Hunters work on making bows and more arrows, and some that also know how to carve, have more time to make things in the winter. They craft beautiful things and sometimes they give them as gifts to acknowledge someone that has done something special. Women spin the wool of the buffalo and make blankets. There is much to do if someone wants to be busy. You must be sure to gather a good amount of your weaving supplies, so that when the snow is deep, your hands can be busy."

"Singing Lark, may I dye some of my grass with the colors we have made? Then I will be able to decorate the things I make with color."

"Yes of course. We have made more than will be needed. Which colors do you want to use?" "I like the yellow and red and the green, too."

"If you want to gather three big bundles of grass and bring them here beside the fire, tomorrow we can start dying it. Have Blue Stone help you gather it and then share some of the colored grass with her. She is good at weaving but has never shown much imagination in her work. Perhaps it will inspire her to be more creative, the way you are."

"Thank you Singing Lark. That was nice of you to think of her. I think this bitter berry dye is as dark as it will get. Should we continue to cook it or let it cool and strain it now?"

"Good, Brave Sparrow, you are getting a feel for this. It is done. We will allow it to cool and I will strain it after I feed Talking Mountain. You could go start gathering grass now if you would like to."

"Thank you Singing Lark, I think I will get a start on it." She went to talk to Blue Stone.

CHAPTER NINE
THE MAN OF SNOW

One morning Moonflower opened the tent flap to several inches of snow.

"The winter is truly here now," she said, as she held the flap up for Dark Wolf and Brave Sparrow to look out.

"The sun is warm. The snow will soon melt."

Brave Sparrow pulled on all her new warm clothes that Moonflower had made for her. She had gotten used to the thickness and the feel of leather and furs near her skin and had learned to appreciate them. She stepped out, into the snow laughing. She ran across the center of the camp calling Blue Stone's name.

Blue Stone came out with her new coat and boots on and stomped around making wide tracks.

"Let's make a snowman!" exclaimed Brave Sparrow.

"What are you talking about?"

"Haven't you ever made a snowman?"

"No."

"I used to make them with my brother, Ben, all the time in the winter. We made big ones. It's easy. Just take a bunch of snow and pack it together and start rolling it and it will get bigger and bigger. See? When we can't roll it any more that is the bottom of him, then we will make a middle part, that will be his tummy and then a head. We will have to get someone taller to put the head on for us."

The girl's giggles, as they pushed and strained to move the huge ball of snow, brought others out to walk in the snow.

Adults smiled at the silly girls rolling snow into a big ball, and made excuses to be out. When they had rolled a second ball nearly as big as the first, they discovered they could not lift it to put it on top of the first.

Growling Bear was walking near them so they politely asked if he would aid them and put the ball on top of the first one. He frowned but he did it, before he ducked into a nearby tent. They started a third one and got it rolling. This time they stopped Sleeping Bear and asked him to put the ball on top of the other two. It was smaller and he lifted it easily in place. When he walked away they realized that it was so tall that they would have to stretch to reach the top of it.

They used pinecones for eyes and a rock for the nose and several more for the mouth. He was smiling broadly. They patted extra snow in front to make his tummy even fatter. The girls were having a wonderful time. Two branches became arms, and a loosely woven strip of grass soon became a scarf.

"He needs a hat," said Brave Sparrow. Let's make him one." They wove a rectangle and fastened it into a cone shape. This time they enlisted Singing Wind, to put it on the top with a stone inside to keep it in place.

"There he is. He is done, but I don't think he will last very long. The snow is melting."

"He is marvelous! I love him. I have never seen a man of snow before, Thank you Brave Sparrow," said Blue Stone.

Moonflower came out and circled him completely. Then she started to laugh and laughed so loud and long that others joined her. Soon several people were standing around laughing. Some small boys ran over with sticks and tried to hit it but Growling Bear, who was now standing beside the girls, stopped them. He felt that he had a small investment in its creation.

Before the morning was over, everyone in the village had been out to look at the man of snow. They were delighted with its happy face. Talking Mountain wasn't sure at first if it was a good thing, but when he saw the smiles on the people as they walked by it, he decided that he would join in the fun too, by patting a little more snow on its tummy.

By the next morning the snowman was nothing more than soggy bits of woven grass lying in the mud as a steady rain came down. Sarah noticed right away that in front of the tent flap was a puddle, many feet going in and out had worn the grass and ground away.

She thought about it for just a minute before she pulled her old shirt on and left her slippers in the tent. She ran to the trees and broke off small branches, loading her arms. She carefully placed a layer of the branches in the mud, side by side until the puddle bottom was covered. Then she formed another layer going the opposite way. On top of that, she placed an old, frayed mat. She didn't step into the tent, but stretched in with her arm and pulled out a watertight basket. After it was filled with clean water from the lake, she placed the basket beside the mat, outside the tent.

She asked Moonflower to hand her something to dry her feet and when she stepped inside the tent, they were clean and dry. Moonflower was impressed and pleased.

It was very hard to keep the tent clean during the rain or snow. She looked out at the entryway that Brave Sparrow had created.

"That is a good thing. Now if we can get Dark Wolf to rinse his feet off, it will be useful." Moonflower had placed several old mats in the area of the doorway.

"Your hair is wet and so is your shirt. You are shivering. Pull off your shirt and put this one on, then rub your hair with this."

Brave Sparrow sat by the fire and did what she was told. Moonflower sat down behind her and began to brush her hair. She braided it and added small strips of fur. Brave Sparrow liked it and liked the soft fur near her cheek when she lifted a braid. "Your hair grows darker. It is beautiful in the light of the fire," said Moonflower. She had no idea that Brave Sparrow had been gradually darkening her hair with dye she had made from the husks of the hickory nuts. She had learned to do it without getting stains on her hands. She knew that it would be more difficult to keep it dark in the winter without being detected. She had to figure out a place to do it where she could heat the dye. She had hidden it in gourds among the reeds at the lake. The dye would be frozen in the cold months.

The weather cleared. It stayed cool but to Sarah it was inviting. She tucked her flute in the bottom of one of her biggest baskets with a lid; inside that she put her basket from Morning Dove. In it she put some jerky, crackers and her flint knife. Over her arm draped an oiled hide, and water bag. She told Moonflower that she wanted to go gather whatever she could find.

"I want more weaving supplies for winter."

Moonflower was busy and nodded, not really paying close attention to Brave Sparrow. If she had she would have seen her unhook the fire horn from the wall and carefully roll a live coal into it. She wasn't sure if it would get hot on the outside so she insulated it with wet grass as soon as she got away from the tent. She wanted to try to play the flute but didn't want anyone to hear her.

Heading to the woods where the women had gone on gathering trips, she watched the sky not wanting to get caught off guard by a storm. It stayed clear as she walked across the tall grass of the soggy prairie. She dropped bits of dry twig from her pocket, into the horn to keep the coal alive.

As she moved along, her mind jumped from one thought to another, but always returned to the same message. I must become bigger than life, someone that inspires awe in the people of the village. It is not enough to be like them and good at my work, I need to be different, too. I need to gain power so I can stop the raids and save the people on the wagon trains, but saving the souls of the Winahatah is first.

"Give me the words, Lord, and the courage and opportunity to save them." The intensity of her emotions and the exertion of the long walk were beginning to drain her. She was tired.

It took her a long time to reach the woods and the cove that she had noticed when she had been there before. The backs of the trees were against the start of a rock outcropping. Getting closer to it she realized she was out of the wind completely. Above her head was an overhang that had kept the ground dry. It wasn't a cave, but it did provide some protection. She placed her big basket with the tight fitting lid near a formation of rocks. The cold of the season and the sheltered rocks made a good sleeping den for snakes. It took all of her strength to roll away a stone that revealed a small pit. Inside were two large snakes. Their backs were decorated with tan diamonds. Their silent rattles showed her that they slept, unaware of the girl staring at them.

She knew that if she pressed her hands against the rock for several minutes, they would feel as cold as the stones. It took bravery to reach down and ever so slowly lift the biggest snake out of the pit and put it in the basket. She tied the lid on tightly, wrapping the cord from her waist, first one way and then the other, several times until she was sure that it was secure.

Now, able to breath, she was shaking all over. Not from the cold, but from fear. She rolled the big rock back over the sleeping snake in the pit. She placed the basket out of the wind, against the stones where it would remain cold.

"Sleep warrior snake, rest now. It is this feeling in my chest that you will inspire in others when your skin decorates my shirt."

She gathered sticks and circled them with rocks. In the center she put dry leaves that had been swirled into the rocks. She rolled her coal into the leaves and blew gently. They burst into flame. She added more twigs and small branches and the warmth of the fire felt wonderful against her bare legs. She sat down on the oiled skin close to the fire to enjoy the jerky, and crackers and drank some water.

Remembering how the fingers of Singing Wind, covered the holes in the top, she continued to try the flute until finally she heard a faint wail. She did it again and again, with different fingers lifted and developed skill to make several sweet notes.

She glanced up to realize that the day was nearly gone. The sun will be setting soon. That is good. I do not want to be back to the village before dark. She covered the last of the little fire with dirt and rocks before leaving her cozy camp.

Stepping out away from the bluff, the blast of the icy wind assaulted her bare legs and feet. She was shivering as she pulled bunches of needles from the branches of the stately long needled pines. She quickly filled her carrying basket, covering the flute and the empty fire horn. With the oiled hide wrapped around her shoulders she started the long walk back, worrying that the heavy snake that she carried at arm's length might somehow push his way out of the basket before she got back. She hadn't figured out how to kill him. Although his meat would make a tasty stew, it was the skin she thought she wanted.

As it grew darker she could see the glow of the fires in the camp and she was glad for their guidance as she quietly returned to camp.

Behind Moonflower's tent, she stood listening. The Chief and Yellow Bird were outside their tent talking to Dark Wolf.

Just then she realized that the big snake had loosened the lid and was slowly sliding out of the basket toward the ground. Lowering it slowly, she moved away stifling a scream as it slid across her foot and into the blackness behind the Chief's tent.

"You are awake, my friend. Had you continued to sleep you would have decorated a shirt or coat but I see that you have accepted an assignment to do something else."

After a few more minutes, she was able to enter the camp. She had dabbed at her eyes with spit to create the illusion of tears, and rubbed dirt on her knees and wet grass on her dress, to make it look like she had fallen in the dark. With a rough stone, she scraped across her chin; over and over until she knew that it was marked and bleeding.

As Brave Sparrow entered the ring of light from the fire, she deliberately gave the impression of being a vulnerable little child. Moonflower met her in a strangling hug. She had been very worried.

"Dark Wolf and some of the other hunters have been out looking for you."

"I am sorry mother that I caused you and others to be concerned. I said that I might be gone a long time. Did you not remember?"

"Where have you been, Brave Sparrow? I have searched for you and even now Growling Bear and Night Hawk are out looking for you. Dark Wolf will want to know where you were and what you have been doing."

"Mother it was such a long way and I was not able to see where to go. The prairie is muddy and I tripped. My biggest basket is empty and finally I saw the fires and found my way back."

"Where were you, Brave Sparrow? What was a long way?"

"I went to the woods mother, where the tallest pine trees grow. I wanted to get their needles so that I could try to make a basket the way Corn Silk makes them. The trees around camp all have short needles. I thought that she might show me how, if I asked her politely. She invited me to come see the baby a long time ago, but I forgot. I guess I was learning to make the dyes and that is what I was thinking about."

"You must be cold, and hungry. Were you frightened, alone in the dark?"

"Yes I was, until I saw the camp fires in the distance."

"Don't you know that an animal could have harmed you? You must promise never to do that again. Children should not go so far without an adult. You should always be in camp before dark. Do you understand?"

"Yes I understand, and I will never do this again. I promise." Brave Sparrow managed to stay out of Dark Wolf's line of sight. In front of the Chief's tent where he stood was just a short distance away.

"Here eat this soup quickly and go to bed before Dark Wolf comes back. He will be easier to talk to in the morning."

Brave Sparrow ate the soup and jumped into bed. She curled into a ball with her face turned to the wall. She pretended to be asleep when Dark Wolf returned with a worried sound in his voice.

"Is she here? Did someone find her?"

"Yes she is here. She had gone to the far woods but it got dark before she made it back. She was cold and hungry and frightened. The poor little thing won't do it again. She promised me she would not ever go alone again."

"What was she thinking to try that? She should be punished for causing so many people to worry over her. Even the Chief and Yellow Bird were upset. I talked to them a little while ago. Did she tell you why she went?"

"Yes but I think that there is more to it. She said she wants to make a basket of pine needles the way that Corn Silk does, but I think she just wants to do it to make friends with Corn Silk. I told you how Corn Silk spoke to her when we were planting. I think that still gives her pain. She is a sensitive girl."

"I'll never understand women! I'm going to spread the word that the girl is back safely in her bed. When I come back I will eat."

Moonflower was glad that he had accepted her explanation. She didn't want him to punish Brave Sparrow. She had looked so small and frightened when she came back.

CHAPTER TEN
CHIEF RISING EAGLE IS DEAD

Dark Wolf didn't punish Brave Sparrow. He didn't even think of it. When the morning came, Yellow Bird woke the camp with a scream that sent chills down everyone's back. Chief Rising Eagle lay in his bed with two marks on his neck. The snake was coiled near the back of the tent.

As Yellow Bird moved, its agitated sound could be heard outside. Dark Wolf ran to his mother's side. She stepped, out of their tent shaking.

"Your father is dead! A big snake has killed him! Be careful, the snake is still in there in the back."

Dark Wolf stepped slowly through the flap of the tent, waiting for his eyes to adjust to the dim light of the interior. He looked at his father's face. It was swollen and dark. He reached up to the roof of the tent where a branch held many baskets. He removed them slowly putting each one down on the floor gently. He unhooked the branch from the straps that held it. At the end, a pair of smaller branches formed a fork. He stepped closer to the snake. It watched his every move, responding with a loud distressed rattle. Near his shoulder, a rabbit skin hung. He threw it swiftly, behind the snake's tail to distract it as he brought the fork down hard, jamming the snake's head to the floor. With a quick slash of his hunting knife, the snake was beheaded. Dark Wolf emptied his mother's sewing basket on to the floor and pushed the snake's head into it with the branch. With the basket in one hand and the snake's writhing body in the other he walked to the spot where the communal fires were lit. No stew would be made from this snake. He would burn in the funeral fire that would be lit for Chief Rising Eagle.

Growling Bear warned the people.

"That evil snake can still bite and kill! Do not touch it. See how its body still moves. He poked the head in the basket with a partially blackened stick. The snake's mouth closed hard over the stick when he touched it, and didn't let go." Those that stood near backed up, with wide fear filled eyes.

Others joined Yellow Bird's weeping, as the news of what had happened, spread through the camp. Talking Mountain and Singing Lark would be required to immediately begin to prepare for very special ceremonies. One was to usher Chief Rising Eagle's spirit to the other world; the other to make it official that Dark Wolf was the new Chief.

Brave Sparrow sat up in her furs, with a look of disbelief. Her silent wish that the snake had chosen to kill the Chief had come true.

"Father, I know that your word says not to kill, but people kill in war. My father read about it in the Old Testament. I brought that snake here but I think you sent him to do this. The warriors of this village are killing white people whenever they can. They didn't even know my family, but they killed them and all the people on the wagon train. Father, please forgive me if I have sinned, but somehow I don't feel like I have. I feel like a soldier that has a lot more to do before this war is over. I can't fight the way they do, with guns or bows. I didn't want to harm Yellow Bird. Somehow I think you directed that snake to his throat. I am glad.

She was in the furs beside him and yet it didn't bite her. Chief Rising Eagle hated white people. He really didn't want me in this camp. I could feel it when he looked at me. He directed the warriors to go to the wagon trains. I think he was a wicked man. He would have killed more people by sending his warriors on more raids.

Father please give me strength and show me how to be a good soldier for Christ. I want to teach love, not hate. I want them to know about you and your Son, Jesus."

She whispered her prayer so softly that no one would have heard her, had they been in the tent. Moonflower had swiftly gone to the Chief's tent, when she heard the scream.

Brave Sparrow put her flute back in its sling hanging from the wall. She carefully replaced the fire horn. After putting both the gathering baskets in their proper place she peeked out of the tent. The entire camp of wailing women was gathered outside the Chief's tent; while the men stood near with long, grim faces and questioning eyes. No one seemed to know what should be done. The Chief was not so old that they had expected to lose him anytime soon. Nor was he in bad health.

"This is a very bad omen," said one of the hunters.

"It is bad medicine," said another.

Talking Mountain raised his hands and waited for a hush to fall over the camp.

"Our Chief is dead. Today we will not eat or drink. We prepare ourselves; tomorrow at sun up we will have the ceremony to release his spirit to the other world." Immediately a hush fell over the camp.

All normal activity in the camp had stopped. The movement of the last few leaves on the trees seemed to intrude on the atmosphere.

Only the youngest children were fed. No one else would eat until after the Chief's spirit had left the camp. Some of the families returned to their tents and sat quietly together, feeling the loss of their leader. Some murmured from their thoughts but no real conversations drifted across the camp. All thoughts were punctuated by the sounds of crying and wailing from the area of the Chief's tent.

Brave Sparrow, watched, and absorbed still more of the culture that had assigned no value to the white men's lives. She quietly tried to be helpful, but found that the best thing to do was to do nothing. She sat on her furs behind Dark Wolf and Moonflower. In her mind she practiced the formulas she had learned from Singing Lark.

Suddenly she realized that a great opportunity was passing her by. She quietly pondered if it would be alright if she offered help to Singing Lark today, or perhaps Yellow Bird. Moonflower would say she didn't think there was anything that a child could do. She treats me like a troublesome child sometimes. I could ask Singing Lark. Without another thought, Brave Sparrow slipped out of the tent and went to Yellow Bird. I never bother people, she thought. She scratched on the tent flap, but it was opened by Rising Sun, Yellow Bird's closest friend. Brave Sparrow bolted in the door and knelt, laying her head in Yellow Bird's lap.

"Grandmother, my heart aches for you and me. We will never see my Grandfather alive again." The truth of her words caused tears to form in Brave Sparrows eyes. What the women didn't know was that her mind was fixed on the Grandfather that had kissed her Goodbye when the wagon train pulled out. She missed his gentle hug and the smell of his pipe. She missed his soft wool sweater, when he put his arms around her and the way he patted and stroked her hair and smiled at her. Big tears wet her face as she hugged Yellow Bird and left the tent without saying a word to Rising Sun.

"She is a good girl," said Yellow Bird. "Tell Moonflower that Brave Sparrow is to stand with me at the fire tomorrow morning."

Rising Sun sucked her breath in as a sign of her displeasure at the thought of the white child standing in a place of such high honor at the Chief's spirit ceremony. She was aware of his strong feelings concerning all white people.

*****

The air was cold enough that their breath looked like fog in front of the faces gathered at the pyre. Moonflower delivered Brave Sparrow to Yellow Bird's tent just as she was ready to leave it. Moonflower had been amazed when a young man had been sent to deliver the message.

Yellow Bird was dressed in a beautifully beaded tan leather dress that hung all the way to her ankles. Her gray hair was covered with the blanket that she wrapped around tightly. Brave Sparrow in her long shirt and matching trousers, had slipped into the gray wolf skin coat that Moonflower held for her. She was thinking that it would make her feel too warm, but the chill air crept into her clothing.

Brave Sparrow felt the wrinkled hand of Yellow Bird trembling as it held hers. The drums echoed her heart beat as they drew near.

The body of the Chief was above the heads of his people. The fire beneath the decorated pyre was lit as soon as Talking Mountain saw that Yellow Bird was in her place of honor. It would be kept burning for three days and three nights. The Chief's rifle, his bow and arrows, and his most precious personal possessions had been placed with him on the pyre. His body had been rubbed with oil and coated with red ochre by Singing Lark and Moonflower. They had dressed him in his very best.

Behind the people a second fire was set from the first. The Chief's tent and everything in it would burn until nothing was left. Yellow Bird's personal items had been moved by Moonflower to her own tent and placed in their largest carrying baskets. Since the snake had invaded their bed, Dark Wolf said he wanted his mother to have new furs for sleeping. The only other thing that was removed was the white hide that had hung on the wall. It was sacred to the people. Dark Wolf had carried it respectfully to the tent of their holy man and helped to hang it on the back wall.

Talking Mountain chanted and danced as both fires burned brightly. The drums continued as the hunters followed behind him in a slow shuffle. The women continued to wail. Yellow Bird released Brave Sparrow's hand. She walked slowly toward the sun's first rays.

Moonflower led Brave Sparrow back to their tent. She was rearranging everything, to make room for another set of sleeping furs and the few personal things that belonged to Yellow Bird.

"It will be much better when the new tent is finished. It will be larger and have more room for storage. Yellow Bird will be with us from now on. You must always treat her with respect."

"Yes, of course. I do."

"Your father will be made Chief this evening, just as the sun hides behind the trees. You will put your good clothes back on for that, but for now, put on your regular dress. It is so cold that you may want to leave your trousers on. Just be careful not to mark them. You will soon be daughter of a Chief, my little one. Do you know what that means?"

"I think that it means that he will be the man that tells the warriors and hunters what they must do. He will be responsible. Is that right mother?"

"Yes that is true. But it is much more than that. You will learn more of that when we go to the summer council meeting."

"What is that?"

"It is when many villages get together to talk over problems and make plans. It is fun. People tell stories and make special foods. Some bring beautiful things they have made and sometimes they trade. Sometimes people get married then, or promised for a mate when they are grown."

"Did you marry Dark Wolf at the council meeting?"

"No, we were married here. I will tell you about that another time. Come." Moonflower was sad, but she had tried to give the girl something pleasant to think about.

She walked with Brave Sparrow to the ashes of the Chiefs tent.

In her palm, Moonflower had put a dab of grease. She mixed it with some of the ashes and drew a spiral on her own forehead with the black paste. She did the same on Brave Sparrow's.

"Why did you do that?" She asked.

"It shows that you are family and that part of you goes with the Chief where ever his spirit goes."

"Mother, Yellow Bird needs to have her forehead painted, she is sad. She is sitting alone under the trees. May I take her some tea?"

"Yes. You have a kind heart. We will go to her together, and I will paint her forehead and you can bring her a cup of chamomile and mint tea." Moonflower added two pinches of herbs to the hot mint tea by the fire.

As they approached they could hear the low keening of her voice. It tore at Brave Sparrow. She felt that she had caused the pain in Yellow Bird's heart and wished it wasn't so.

The ceremony for Dark Wolf was held on the spot where Chief Rising Eagle had died. The ashes of their tent had been leveled and covered with clean sand from the area of the small lake. Chief Dark Wolf's new large tent would stand there soon.

*****

Talking Mountain lay on the sand with his face down and his arms straight above his head. He didn't move for what seemed like a long time. Singing Lark stood back and shook a gourd rattle. The sound reminded the people of the snake that had killed the Chief. She came forward still shaking the rattle. As she did he began to rise, slowly and gracefully, like a dancer, until he was standing. Dark Wolf was the only one in the family that had not painted the spiral on his forehead. His face was painted half black and half white. A snake had been drawn on his white cheek and a pair of red dots decorated his black cheek. This would be his war paint from now on.

Talking Mountain placed the headdress of the Chief of the Winahatah, on Dark Wolf. The eagle feathers trailed along a strip of leather nearly to his knees on either side. Brave Sparrow had never seen anything like it. It was beaded with white bone across his forehead and the large eagle feathers at the top and sides made him appear larger than life, an awesome, fearsome figure. Other symbols had been painted on his bare chest. Talking Mountain sang his chant asking the spirits to behold their chosen Chief.

He told the story of Chief Rising Eagle's spirit now leaving the camp. He begged the old Chief to leave his wisdom and knowledge with Dark Wolf and to hover close and direct him when decisions needed to be made. He asked the spirits that watched over the village to accept

Dark Wolf as protector of the people and that they guard the people always.

Incense made from a mixture of special herbs, burned in a large pot and the breeze carried the scent to everyone gathered there.

Brave Sparrow grew chilled and tired of standing still beside Moonflower. She no longer heard the words that were said. The day was growing colder as the sun disappeared. Dark Wolf has no shirt on. I am sure he is cold. I am glad that I have my fur coat on. It feels nice, she thought.

Only the fire of the pyre lighted the camp. It was then that Brave Sparrow realized that all the campfires had been extinguished. It was the first time she had seen it like that. Only Chief Rising Eagle's funeral fire remained.

Finally the rattles and drums ceased. The chanting was finished. Dark Wolf was Chief of the Winahatah.

Brave Sparrow wondered what kind of a Chief he would be.

CHAPTER ELEVEN
IN THE TEETH OF THE STORM

Will winter never end, thought Brave Sparrow, as she finished yet another basket? Yellow Bird sat nearest the fire, for warmth and light. She said little and ate little. She seemed to grow visibly older each day. The glow in her eyes was gone. Her skin seemed gray. Her skinny fingers looked like claws. Brave Sparrow tried to make her smile, or to get her to talk or eat a tasty morsel but usually failed.

The baskets that Brave Sparrow created were nested inside each other. On their sides were intricate designs and pictures, woven in color. She was young, but already the best basket maker in camp. Moonflower encouraged her to make more, knowing that she would be able to trade them at the summer council.

Singing Lark came often to visit; something that never would have happened if the old Chief still lived. She talked with her and brushed Yellow Bird's hair. She brought special treats and tried to get Yellow Bird to try some with her tea. She praised the work in the baskets and brought them forward to discuss the patterns, trying to raise a spark of interest in her old friend. Nothing worked.

One night, near the end of winter, snow pelted the tent, driven by a fierce bitter, cold wind. Brave Sparrow snuggled deep into her sleeping furs. The fire was kept burning higher than usual to ward off the cold. The wind had softened toward morning and deep drifts angled between the tents.

Yellow Bird was not in her furs! When Brave Sparrow looked outside in the early light, there were no tracks leading away from the tent. Brave Sparrow was puzzled. Moonflower sat up as the sharp cold from the open door blew inside.

"Brave Sparrow, close the flap. You are letting the winter cold inside."

"Mother, where is Yellow Bird? She is not in her bed. She has not taken her coat or winter boots. She will get sick."

"What?" Dark Wolf sat up quickly and looked around. He pulled on his boots and winter clothes as fast as he could, grabbing his mother's blanket; he rushed out the door shouting. Others poked their heads out into the cold gray light. He yelled that Yellow Bird was gone. Many rushed out into the cold, half-clad and jumped back into their tents long enough to grab boots, winter coats and hand covers. The search continued for hours but she could not be found. She had not wanted to be found. She had walked away into the teeth of the storm, inviting death to take her to the other world and to her beloved Rising Eagle.

Dark Wolf returned after searching for several hours. His feet and fingers were numb with the cold. They hurt badly as they started to warm. Had he known he would have sat and held her in his arms all night? Her heart was broken, and now, so was his. A tear found its way down his face as he stared into the fire.

Once again the camp was silent all day except for the keening. There would be no ceremony, no funeral pyre. They would not speak her name. It was as if she had never been. Only the quiet and the wind gave tribute to a wandering soul, searching and seeking its way to the other world.

Moonflower rolled up the extra sleeping pad, and arranged the inside of the big tent so that there was no open space where Yellow Bird had slept. Her clothes were carefully folded and put away. Brave Sparrow found it very difficult to understand. She had seen Dark Wolf's tears. She knew that many people cared and yet no one mentioned her. It was the way of the people, when someone chose to leave the living, to be with the dead.

Finally the spring came, and with it, the first signs of greening. Rain fell softly, washing away the last frozen bits of winter. Moonflower gathered a basket of dandelion greens and cooked them for lunch along with fresh rabbit. It was delicious.

Brave Sparrow wanted more than anything, to go out onto the prairie alone but was not sure how to get permission. She asked if she could go out to gather dandelion greens to give to Singing Lark. Moonflower told her the best places to look and warned her to be back by late afternoon.

She knew that the girl liked to get away from camp once in a while, and tried to allow it when she thought that it would be safe enough. Once again Brave Sparrow carried two baskets, one inside the other. She took a piece of jerky and water, her knife and flute. She gathered surviving grain heads into the basket as she walked along toward the herd. The heavy snows had knocked much of the wild grain down but she still was able to gather some among rocks and in sheltered areas. She wondered if Gray Cloud would be the one watching the herd today. She smiled to herself as she heard the sound of his flute in the distance. She walked toward the herd, continuing to gather grain in the small basket and dandelion greens in the larger one.

She was no more than ten feet away, when she crossed her legs and slid silently to the ground. She had learned to sit that way and found it comfortable now that she was used to it. She was to the side of Gray Cloud and could watch his fingering as he changed notes.

She watched intently. He is lucky that I am not an animal sneaking up on the horses. She rose slowly and circled to the edge of the herd before she clacked her tongue. All four, work horses came and so did the sleek riding horse that had been her fathers. She went through the usual routine with scratches and a handful of grain for each. She gave special attention to Dart Away. She hadn't seen him in a long time and was surprised that he had come to her. She wondered who rode him now. Her father said that he was the fastest horse he had ever owned. Dart Away had won races to earn the money for their wagon and supplies. He belonged to Dark Wolf now, but he had many horses and seldom rode Dart Away. He didn't appreciate the sleek thoroughbred as much as he should have.

Brave Sparrow left the herd area undetected. She checked to make sure that the sun was still high in the sky and sat down with her back against a tree, just far enough from camp that she would not be heard. She practiced her flute until she could play a scale.

Her baskets were filled with spring greens as she entered camp. Moonflower had just begun to wonder why she was taking so long. She darted into the tent putting her flute in its sleeve, leaving the baskets by the fire.

"Mother I am back with lots of greens. I will take these over to Singing Lark, so she can use some of them for her meal."

"Hurry, come right back, I have a job for you."

Brave Sparrow seems happy today. Her step is light and she holds her head high, thought Moonflower.

Talking Mountain saw Brave Sparrow coming with the basket of greens and smiled at the girl's energy. She has been good for Singing Lark. She has been happier this winter, even with all the sad events. I wish that we had children. Singing Lark's life would be so different. Brave Sparrow sat the basket down and was turning to leave when Talking Mountain asked her to come in the tent for a moment.

"Brave Sparrow, do you know what these are?" He asked with the wave of his hand, indicating the hanging bundles of drying plants and roots.

"Yes they are herbs for flavoring cooking and some are for healing."

"Would you go with Singing Lark when she gathers the plants this time? She goes far alone. I worry about her. She needs someone to help her."

"Thank you Talking Mountain, for asking me. You honor me. I will be pleased to go and help."

"She will let you know when she plans to go. It will be someday soon. When she returns from the lake, I will tell her that you want to go with her. She does not need to know that I asked you."

"Thank you Talking Mountain."

Brave Sparrow was delighted. That was a turn of events she hadn't hoped for.

"God, I know that you are preparing me for something. Help me to learn all that I can. I want to be worthy to do what you have planned for me. Father I know that I am unworthy. I know that I sin when I rebel inside against the authority you have placed over me here in this village. Please forgive me and help me to see your will clearly. Give me the inner grace and strength to do what I should." She prayed silently.

*****

"Singing Lark, this is fun. I love to wander the woods and see what is there. What are we looking for this time?"

"We need to gather wild apples to make vinegar. That is what I used on your hands first, to remove the stains from the nut casings. Do you remember? I use fermented grass and apples and sometimes a few other things."

"Yes I remember. It had a strong smell, but it made my mouth water at the same time."

"If you add a bit to your hair coloring it will stay on longer."

"How did you know?"

"You have light brows and lashes and sometimes your hair is light where it grows out."

"Does everyone know?"

"No. I think most people notice very little. That is why even a poor medicine woman can help people; they take things at face value, and don't look deeply. People are usually easy to convince. Sometimes when someone is sick, if you give him or her herbs for their tea that are harmless and tell them it will help, they get better right away. It is their Spirit that heals."

"You are very wise, Singing Lark, but I thought Talking Mountain was the medicine man and healer."

"Yes he is. He has the ability to see what is wrong, then we talk it over and he gives them some of what we think will help the most."

"Look here Brave Sparrow. This is a little plant that must be gathered in the spring. It is a strong little vine and difficult to find. It grows only where the ground stays damp. See the hooks under the vine? That is how it climbs. It is used to make a tea for a woman who is starting a baby. It makes her stronger and helps her heart. You must be careful though to use only a little at a time. She carefully cut a length of the vine and coiled it in her basket. It is strong. I never put more than four leaves in a pot of water, along with other herbs."

Singing Lark bent down and started picking a large bouquet of phlox. Their scent filled the air.

"What do you use those for?" asked Brave Sparrow.

"These are for the soul, not the body. I've heard that the blossoms are good in tea, but I gather them because I like the beautiful blue color and the wonderful smell." As they stepped out of the trees, with the edge of camp just ahead, Singing Lark divided the big bouquet in half and gave a bunch to Brave Sparrow.

"Take these to your mother. She will smile. She loves phlox as much as I do."

Brave Sparrow thanked her as she always did, for the many bits of instruction and for the flowers. As she reached the tent Moonflower, was busy cooking and frowning.

"Here mother, I am back to help you, and I have some beautiful flowers for you. Moonflower took the bundle and pressed them to her face.

"They are lovely child. How did you know they are my favorite flower?"

"I didn't but they are pretty and smell nice, too. I'll fill that big brown pot with water for them."

Brave Sparrow dipped the baked clay pot into the lake and as always her ears were open. The women there were talking about the summer council meeting.

"I don't think I will take anything but the most necessary things. The men never help and I get tired of carrying all that stuff and then not using it."

Brave Sparrow carried the dripping jar back and set it on the ground near the doorway to the tent. Moonflower gently lowered the bouquet into the water. She turned and hugged Brave Sparrow tightly.

"You are a very good girl, Brave Sparrow. You are so thoughtful. I am glad you are here to help me tonight. I am a little tired, and my head hurts. The meal is ready. If you will just stay close and occasionally stir the pot, I would like to rest until Dark Wolf returns."

"Yes mother, I will be right here."

She noticed that Moonflower seemed shaky as she entered the tent. Brave Sparrow lifted her weaving onto her lap, after checking the pot of sliced venison and wild onions. She pulled it aside just a bit so it would stay hot without burning. It was done and the meat in it was tender. She gave her full attention to the large backpack she was trying to create. It would be large enough to hold many things and light to carry. She wanted to make it in such a way that it would open up and lay flat, becoming a mat to sit on.

She was so focused on her project that she didn't notice Dark Wolf until he stood beside her.

"Where is your mother?"

"She is resting. I am watching the food for her my Chief." "I have noticed that she is tired a lot lately, I think you are gone too much. Tomorrow you will stay here and do the work so she can rest."

"Yes my Chief," she answered politely. "I think perhaps she should talk to Singing Lark. She seems not well."

"You are wise for a young woman, I will tell her to go. Leave her sleep, and I will eat now. I have something to do right after the meal."

Brave Sparrow filled his bowl generously and handed it and his spoon to him. He devoured the food as if he were starving. Moonflower slept on, not hearing their conversation concerning her. He left quickly.

Soon after, Moonflower came out of the tent wondering why he wasn't back yet.

"He has been here. I fed him and he left again."

"Yes I suppose he has much to do. They are preparing for the summer council. We will be leaving this camp in five days. Our horses will carry most of the things. It is a long journey, many days, and then when it is over, we must travel back again. It makes me tired just thinking about it."

"Before we go, the corn and pumpkins and squash all must be planted. It has been so dry. It will be harder this year. I hope we get rain soon."

"Mother you should rest tomorrow and I will help in the field. Will you eat with me now? I waited for you." Brave Sparrow handed her a bowl. Moonflower ate a small bite and set the bowl down.

"I am not hungry. I am going to go back in and rest." She closed the flap. Brave Sparrow could hear her sigh as she settled back onto her furs.

After washing up the bowls and pulling the covered pot away from the fire, Brave Sparrow went to talk to Singing Lark and Talking Mountain. She scratched on the side of the tent, near the open door way.

"Come in, Brave Sparrow." They listened intently as she described the way Moonflower was acting. Talking Mountain said it was the spring sickness that she would be fine and left the tent.

"Yes she might need tonic after the long winter, or;" Singing Lark hesitated, "She could be pregnant."

"Pregnant?" Brave Sparrow's mouth dropped open as her face became troubled.

"Is she eating well?"

"No she wouldn't eat. She just went back to lie down."

"When she wakes give her tea made with this and some fresh clover and honey in it. It can't hurt and may help. Watch her carefully for any other symptoms."

"Thank You Singing Lark."

Brave Sparrow was stirring a pan of the tea when Dark Wolf returned.

"Is Moonflower still asleep?"

"She was up but went back inside after a few minutes. She didn't eat. I told Singing Lark, and she gave me some herbs to make this tea for her." Moonflower heard them talking and came out. She still looked tired.

"Here mother, Singing Lark sent this tea for you. It will give you strength and make you feel well again."

Moonflower sat down next to Dark Wolf and sipped the tea. The evening air was cool and refreshing. They talked about the coming meeting and that Brave Sparrow would help with the planting of the corn in the morning. Dark Wolf said he and some of the men were going hunting in the morning.

"Moonflower, I want you to stay here and rest. No work for you while I am gone. Do not go to the field at all." Moonflower did stay near her tent all the next day, while Brave Sparrow and some of the others prepared the ground for the corn. The men returned with a large deer, and Moonflower put a large piece of the meat over her fire. Brave Sparrow gathered greens on her way back so their meal was easily prepared.

There was little for Moonflower to do. She sat in the shade leaning against a nearby tree with her eyes closed. Singing Lark sat down beside her.

"How are you feeling today?" she asked.

"I am not ill, just tired all the time."

"I think you need to rest more. Are you eating?"

"I haven't been hungry and I think I must have bruised myself, carrying something. My chest is a little sore."

"Well, did you ever think you might be pregnant?"

"Could it be after all these years of waiting? I don't think so!"

"I think so. How long has it been since you have had your woman's way?"

"I'm not sure. Let me think. It was during the last little snow."

"Two moons have passed since then."

Moonflower started to get excited.

"Oh do you think I dare to hope for another baby? Don't tell anyone. I want to wait to be sure."

"Did you drink all the tea that I sent last night?"

"Yes but I gave one cup to Dark Wolf this morning."

"Good, he will have a strong healthy baby," kidded Singing Lark. Both women laughed.

"Follow me to my tent and I will give you more. Drink two cups a day for a while and you should start feeling better soon."

"Thank you Singing Lark, you are such a good friend."

The corn and pumpkins and squash were planted, but still no rain came. It was the driest summer they had seen in many years. The prairie grass was shorter than usual and many of the foods that the women gathered, did not grow at all, or were small and of little use.

The people enjoyed the summer meeting. It had been fun, but the trip was hot and tiring. Brave Sparrow and Blue Stone had enjoyed watching the games and were awed by the beautifully beaded clothes worn by the young brides and grooms. The girls had plenty of time to talk as they walked along heading home. Moonflower rode one of the horses, part of the time, but preferred to walk with the other women.

The camp was dry and dusty. On the far side of the receding lake, Moonflower pushed her small supply of reserve seeds of corn and pumpkin into the moist dirt on the shore.

"Grow little seeds, to become the promise of food for our people next year." She feared the hunger that would hover near this winter. Their crops had failed. The dry hard ground offered less and less as the weeks went by. Singing Lark still took Brave Sparrow on walks to gather what she could and the women went to the woods for their gathering days, but now they returned with little food to share or store. It was a quiet, frightening time. Moons of starvation loomed ahead.

The older women had seen times of drought before. They dreaded the coming winter.

CHAPTER TWELVE
A REMINDER FROM THE LAKE

The hunters went out more often than in the past. The animals they brought back were lean. The rich fat that the people would need to sustain them in the cold weather was hard to come by. Each family had plenty of dried meat but alone it would not be enough. When Brave Sparrow and Blue Stone, returned to camp one day with a basket of fish, it was more than a delicious meal for their families. It was a reminder to Chief Dark Wolf. His people had used nets to gather fish in the past during the leanest years. It had been forgotten.

Now as he looked down at his hands with greasy fingers from the fish, he decided to resurrect an old tradition that he had enjoyed as a boy. He called for a communal fire the next evening.

Talking Mountain prayed and danced with raised arms, and loud drums. The fire blazed hot against the star filled sky.

Dark Wolf explained the reason for the gathering. He stood and smiled broadly at his people.

"Although our hunters are the best in all the land, they cannot put fat on the animals they bring back. This dry summer has not provided the tall green grass that they need, and it has not encouraged the plants to grow that our women usually gather." He paused. "You must all realize that something must be done to avoid the moons of hunger. We need to make nets to catch lots of fish for the oil we will crave." This met with hearty approval. One old woman stood and told a story of her youth. There was laughter and light hearts as the people listened. "Many of you remember using nets. We will do it again." The people went to their tents to rest with happy hearts filled with hope.

The next morning all the women worked hard to make sections of the new nets and fasten them together. Several would be needed. They had to be long, strong and with no large holes or the fish would slip through. Rocks were tied to the bottom of the nets as weights to keep them down.

When the nets were assembled and stretched out into the lake and tied to poles stuck deep into the mud on the bottom, the people were filled with joy. They laughed and joked as the wet men climbed out of the lake.

"Growling Bear, that is the closest thing to a bath that you have had since this summer started," said an old woman. Everyone laughed at his expense.

They all gathered around the fire sitting close, talking and laughing until their clothes were dry.

The next morning those who were the strongest swimmers approached the nets from the backside and loosened it from its posts. It was slowly crowded toward the shore. The rest of the people waited in the shallow water to scoop the fish into baskets. As the flopping fish were harvested some slipped away but many were seized or trapped and placed in deep baskets.

People fell on slippery rocks on the lake bottom while others laughed and pulled them up. By the time the net was drawn to shore, every basket had at least a few fish in it, and nearly everyone in the entire camp was wet, and smiling.

They were all having a wonderful time, even Growling Bear. To everyone's surprise he proved to be an excellent swimmer. Brave Sparrow had stayed near the shore, but had managed to capture six fish in her basket.

"Tonight we will put the net out again, announced Dark Wolf. Tomorrow we catch fish again." The people applauded and shouted their approval. They had not had this much fun together in years. Besides it was hot and the water felt good.

The fish were cleaned and rubbed inside and out with salt and then strung on long lines above several small, low fires. Songs were sung and stories were told making the work pleasant.

The corn and pumpkins that Moonflower had planted, near the lake, grew and were cherished. It was a temptation to roast the corn and bite into its sweet kernels, but all the seeds were allowed to ripen and carefully stored for the coming spring.

Everyone knew by then that Moonflower was expecting a baby. Chief Dark Wolf was more pleased than he could express. He hoped for a son, that he could train to be the next leader. She was feeling well by the end of summer. Her clothes grew tight and she had to make a dress to wear that rather resembled a tent. She laughed often and hummed as she worked.

Brave Sparrow was glad for her and yet a little sad for herself. She had enjoyed being special. Now she felt a baby born to the tent would somehow push her aside and she would be in second place. She had no idea just how exceptional she had become, not just to Chief Dark Wolf and Moonflower, but to the entire camp.

*****

The tiny baby girl was born on a cold winter night. The new life came during the darkest hours. The air outside was so cold that it hurt to breath. The snow that had fallen a week earlier was banked against the bottom of the tent walls for insulation. So much firewood was needed in each tent that collecting it now was difficult. All the handy trees were stripped of their lower branches.

Brave Sparrow was not allowed back in the tent for two days, but she had enjoyed visiting with Blue Stone's family. Her separation increased her anxiety about being in second place, but that all disappeared when she was allowed back to their tent and the newborn baby was placed in her arms. Brave Sparrow had never held a tiny baby. She gently rocked her and held her close.

"What is her name?" asked Brave Sparrow

"She hasn't got one yet. Dark Wolf will name her on the fifth day. That is naming day usually. Because you were bigger and not born here, you were named as soon as Talking Mountain said that the spirits had accepted you. Can you remember?"

"Yes, I remember. She is so fragile and pretty. She should have a very special name." Brave Sparrow kissed the tiny forehead and returned her carefully to Moonflower.

She brought Moonflower a cup of rich beef broth and then hurried to Singing Lark's tent. She had been working on a baby blanket of rabbit furs for quite a while. She had traded a basket for a fur with many of the women in camp. It was nearly finished. Now she had an idea.

"Singing Lark, will you help me? I need to know how I can put a pattern on the leather on the backside of the blanket so that it is pretty on both sides. What should I use to draw on the pattern?"

"What will you draw?"

"I think I want to put snowflakes all over it."

"You can use a feather to draw with. What color do you want to use?" "Well that's why I need your special help. I want to make them white."

"Brave Sparrow that is very hard to do, but any of these other colors would be nice."

"No. Please, Singing Lark, I really want to try to make them like real snowflakes."

"I don't think you know how much work it is. We have to use the aged urine that we cleaned your hands with. It smells so bad, and in the winter the lake is frozen and you will have to melt snow to clean it. If you use too much, the fur on the other side will fall out."

"I will be careful and do just what you say. This blanket has to be the best ever!" Brave Sparrow's eagerness had convinced Singing Lark, but she wasn't happy about it. She knew how difficult it would be to use the strong ammonia in the wintertime.

With a steady hand, Brave sparrow drew the snowflakes onto the leather, first with charcoal, and then with the rabbit fur blanket outside, on top of the snow, she had to draw them again with the smelly liquid. The lines stayed black and it didn't seem to do anything but wet the lines.

"Here, Brave Sparrow. Place this old hide over the drawings and roll the fur and the hide up together. Now you need to climb up and put it in a tree. Every day take it down and draw the lines again, carefully. Just wet the lines and wait until they dry before you roll it up. When the lines are yellow, bring it back to me."

"Thank you, Singing Lark. I am sorry about the smell, but I didn't spill any of the liquid, so after I take the fur away the smell should leave.

Brave Sparrow hurried to tuck the bundle up in a tree, but found there wasn't any place near camp that she could reach a branch. They had all been pulled down. She walked a long way before finding a safe spot to keep the smelly project. She took the pot of liquid with her. She knew that it would freeze and bust if left outside. She was glad that it had such a good wax seal. Moonflower would not like it if she could smell it. Each morning when she went out to gather wood for the fire, first she would walk to the tree that held the blanket and carefully coated the lines. It did seem to be lightening them, but it took a lot longer than she had thought it would.

The baby's naming day came and went. People visited and brought gifts for the new baby or gifts of food. Brave Sparrow held the baby for a few minutes, when permitted. She loved the name "Snow Star" that Dark Wolf had given her. It was perfect. The ceremony had been held at a communal fire, but had been kept very short due to the bitter cold. The fire was not as large as it should have been because of the difficulty in getting wood.

Many people passed by the bundle in the tree. No one touched it. It was considered very bad medicine to touch something that didn't belong to you without permission. Brave Sparrow thought the smell alone should have been enough to discourage anyone. After several weeks the lines appeared light yellow in color. Gladly, Brave Sparrow carried the bundle back to Singing Lark.

"Now we have to get the smell from the leather," said Singing Lark. "It won't be easy but we will be able to do it." She tossed the wrapper hide outside temporarily. "That will also have to be cleaned," she said. They used melted snow to submerge the fur blanket. Over and Over fresh water had to be made. Finally a rinse of sweet smelling herbs did the trick.

"Now while the skin is wet, we must work chalk into the lines you have made. Painstakingly, Brave Sparrow drew the shapes, over and over with the white mineral. The leather was worked again, as if it were a new hide. Scraped and oiled until it was soft and dry. One last time the lines were drawn with the chalk and rubbed in carefully. The oiled rabbit skins absorbed the chalk and the beautiful, white, snowflake pattern was inside the leather to stay.

Brave Sparrow held her breath as Singing Lark examined it as a whole.

"It is the prettiest baby blanket that I have ever seen, in my whole life!" said Singing Lark. "It will be the nicest gift that the baby receives." Brave Sparrow was speechless. She hugged Singing Lark and hurried out the door of the tent.

Talking Mountain looked at his wife with pleasure.

"She is a very special young woman. No one else in this entire camp has ever made the effort to make leather white. Not even you would do it for yourself in the wintertime, but I would like to suggest that you do it in the warm weather next time. It is easier to breathe in here without those fumes."

"Thank you my husband, I will try to remember that." They both laughed.

Brave Sparrow waited until Dark Wolf came for the evening meal, and then as the cold of night crept into the tent, Brave Sparrow pulled the new blanket from her sleeping furs and gave it to Moonflower.

"This is a gift that I have made for the baby. I am glad that you have named her Snow Star because I decorated the inside of the blanket with snowflakes." She turned the blanket over with a flourish.

Moonflower drew in her breath as if startled.

"It is white! The rabbit skins are white and the snowflakes on the back are white! This is beautiful, Brave Sparrow. It is fitting for a daughter of the Chief," she said smiling broadly.

Chief Dark Wolf looked at her suspiciously.

"How did you make this?" He asked. "It took a long time. Many weeks I had to go to the trees on the far side of the lake to work on it. I put it back in the tree each time until we could finish it. Then it had to be processed like a new hide. Singing Lark helped me. She knows all about colors and removing them remember? I did make it myself and I drew the snowflakes too. You can ask her."

"It is not acceptable for anyone to wear white except a holy man. It is sacred."

"Talking Mountain was there some of the time when we were working on it and he liked the blanket. He didn't say we shouldn't use white."

Dark Wolf turned to Moonflower and said

"Do not put that blanket on Snow Star until I ask Talking Mountain about this. I will be back."

Brave Sparrow burst into tears as he left the tent.

"Moonflower, why didn't he believe me? I just wanted Snow Star to have something beautiful like she is," she wailed. "I wanted to make something different and special."

"Brave Sparrow, let me try to explain. The blanket is too beautiful. He is afraid that it will make the spirits jealous, and perhaps they would make the baby sick."

"He will be back soon. I'm sure that it is going to be all right. Now dry your eyes."

Brave Sparrow couldn't believe what she was hearing. Somehow I will help these people to know the "One True God" she thought. Suddenly she couldn't stand the confines of the tent.

"I must go out. I am fine now." She pulled her coat on as she hurried out the flap. She found herself on the little hill that overlooked their village. The wind was brisk and the temperature was low.

"Father, how can I live with people that do not know you? Their souls are dark and full of fears. Why would they think that a blanket I made with love would be anything harmful? Why do they believe in gods that aren't real? Father, teach me, so that I can teach them." She could see her breath with each word she spoke.

She felt the need for hard work, some exertion to release the tension she felt. Walking swiftly to the other side of the lake helped. She gathered all the wood she could carry and dumped it by the wall of the tent and stepped inside. Her weaving was pulled aside. She took her sleeping furs out in the wind and shook so hard that Moonflower thought she might shake the hair from the leather. She rolled them up and tucked them near the wall so that she could sweep the floor in that area. The crushed grass was traded for fresh dried grass stuffed between the walls. It was spread out and then the furs unrolled on top. It felt soft and clean.

"Moonflower, please move onto my bed to sit; and I will do the same for your bed, and then his." She was just lugging the wood inside when he returned. She kept her head down, not wanting him to see the hurt in her eyes. She didn't want him to know that he had the power to hurt her with just a few words.

"Talking Mountain has said a chant to appease the spirits. We may use the special blanket that Brave Sparrow has made for her sister. I am glad that you are learning such valuable crafts. A cape made like that would trade for many horses. Talking Mountain says that it is big medicine." A scratch at the flap announced a visitor.

When Brave Sparrow saw that it was Corn Silk, she politely asked if there was anything else that needed doing before she left.

"I will put tea on before I go. Perhaps Corn Silk would not mind pouring it for you when it is ready.

She opened the cache that contained some of their food supply and removed five small wrinkled apples. She stuffed them in her coat pockets and put her mitts back on. She headed for the horse herd, walking quickly to keep warm. She had already learned that she could come and go totally unnoticed if she was careful to circle and approach the herd to the side.

She spotted the horses and clacked her tongue. She visited seldom, but they remembered. She was glad that she had brought five apples instead of four, because the riding horse was with the herd. She gave each one some attention and just one of the precious apples. She talked quietly to them and patted each one.

When she went back to the tent, it was time to prepare a meal, but it wasn't necessary. Someone had left food near the door, in a big covered pan. She lifted the lid. It was cold from the ground, but smelled wonderful. It smells like buffalo meat, mushrooms and onions too, she thought as she placed the pan near the small fire inside to heat. Moonflower and the baby were sleeping. Chief Dark Wolf was out so she was alone with her thoughts for the moment.

There was something special about this day and she would remember it all her life. That memory and Dark Wolf's words would serve her well in the future.

"Talking Mountain says it has big medicine," her mind echoed. I can make big medicine? First they thought the blue stone was big medicine, now they think the blanket has big medicine! Both were pretty. Maybe that is what they mean, but I think it means a lot more than that. I will ask Singing Lark sometime when we are working.

The rest of the winter fled by and spring brought all the rain they could want and more. The camp was mud from one end to the other. Brave Sparrow did her best to make a dry step in front of the door as she had before, but there was so much mud that it tracked in anyway.

When Talking Mountain announced that it was time to plant. The ground was so soft that feet sunk in with each step. Each hill of corn was carefully planted with just two precious seeds. Each pumpkin seed was planted in a handful of mulch from beneath the trees, and everything sprouted and grew as if they knew they had to make up for the lack of the year before. There was greenery everywhere. Flowers that had not been seen in the area for years suddenly appeared. The world was a profusion of color. The camp buzzed with activity. Everyone's spirit had been lifted by the cycle of the earth's renewal.

And so with the flow of the seasons, years passed and Brave Sparrow continued to grow, and develop mentally, physically and most importantly, spiritually. The Holy Spirit was her teacher and counselor. She was intelligent and wise beyond her years. Her expert skill in many crafts continued to delight the people of the camp. Young men began to notice a definite difference in her appearance. Her legs grew longer and her body developed into a beautiful woman. She continued to color her hair with the dye she made from the nut casings. The people had forgotten how very blond she was.

Study continued with Singing Lark and Talking Mountain. One morning when Brave Sparrow entered the tent; she found Singing Lark standing in the middle of the tent, mumbling about something. She had forgotten many things lately. Her long white hair and deeply creased face revealed the fleeting years. Her mind was tired and her body bent with aches and pains. The lack of proper nutrition and the cold winters in the tent had taken their toll.

Talking Mountain still tried hard to maintain the aura of vitality he once had, but his dance at the communal fire had changed. The beautiful flow and cadence of steps filled with strength were gone. All that was left was a droning inflection of his voice and a slow shuffle that no longer could stir the inner spirit and enthusiasm of the people.

CHAPTER THIRTEEN
GROWING IN AGE AND GRACE

Chief Dark Wolf was the only one that appeared not to have changed. If anything he seemed to grow stronger and more powerful with time. His word was law. His first concern was the lack of any young man that showed an interest and ability to follow in the steps of Talking Mountain. He knew that before long he would have to make a decision. What would he do to insure the solidarity and loyalty of the people if they had no holy man? His daughters though both clearly bright were not automatically heir to leadership. It was not unheard of for a woman to be in such a position but he did not feel that a woman could ever have enough influence to persuade his people in the direction they should go. He had no son. Talking Mountain had no children. Chief Dark Wolf was troubled. He glanced up to see Moonflower walk slowly toward the lake. She was talking to Snow Star. The girl's energy and animation amused him. If she was a man, in a few years she could lead. She is the treasure of my heart, he thought. She likes to hunt and can ride a horse well, too.

He saw Brave Sparrow duck out of Singing Lark's tent and join Blue Stone. They, too, were heading down to the lake. This one will be a problem to me soon. She is too smart for a woman. She also likes to hunt and rides like the wind. She should have been married long ago. Perhaps I should choose a husband for her, since she rejects the young men that show an interest in her. I will talk to the Chiefs at the summer council about her.

Brave Sparrow walked along with Blue Stone toward the lake. They were not thinking of the cool water. Blue Stone was in love. She had coaxed her father, Sleeping Bear to arrange a marriage for her with Running Deer. He and his brother, Gray Cloud, had always been friends with Blue Stone's brother Singing Wind. The taunting of childhood had changed to friendship and then to love as the years passed. It was a good match and the marriage would take place at the summer council.

Running Deer was not tall, but two inches taller than Blue Stone. He was handsome, strong and a good hunter and tracker. He would provide well for Blue Stone. His black shining hair and copper skin matched those of Blue Stone. She was the same height she had been for the last three years and had to look up to see the face of most of the adults.

Brave Sparrow had to shorten her steps to walk beside Blue Stone. She would soon be as tall as Dark Wolf if she continued to grow. Her blue eyes matched the sky of the spring morning. She wore a well-shaped dress she had made, with long fringe, decorated with beads the color of her eyes forming patterns across the front and down the short sleeves. Her moccasins were decorated with the same beads and pattern. She would be more than an acceptable wife for any high status brave. She was graceful and beautiful. It was the custom with the people that a woman could refuse to marry any suitor. She had gently turned away many. She walked with the self-confidence that only a Chief should carry.

She went freely to the herd now and rode when and where she chose. No one stopped her, and no one asked where she had been. Usually she took Snow Star or Blue Stone with her, but occasionally she chose to be alone.

She would ride away from the camp on one of many horses that were for general use by the hunters. She longed for a horse of her own, a very special horse that was just for her.

When she was out riding, she had seen the herds of wild horses. She watched them from a distance. If I could have any one I wanted, it would be that big all white one that leads the herd. He is so beautiful. Her thoughts were solely for her own entertainment. She told no one.

One day as she watched the wild herd, she spotted a new foal. It was pure white and spectacular. She wished she could stroke its beautiful coat. It pranced and frisked beside its mother, a cream colored mare. She had to have that foal, but how? As she rode slowly back toward camp, she tried to think of a way.

A rider was coming in the distance. He was riding hard. Falling Stones pulled up in front of her in a cloud of dust.

"Come quickly. Singing Lark is very ill. She calls for you." He wheeled around and headed back to camp at the speed he had come. His urgency created a feeling of dread as she swiftly returned and rode directly into camp to Singing Lark's tent. She entered to see Talking Mountain kneeling beside her. The white hair that framed Singing Lark's wrinkled face was wet with sweat. She raised her head slightly as Brave Sparrow entered.

"Grandmother, you are ill. What can I do for you?" Singing Lark's voice was weak, as she feebly pointed at her aged husband.

"He will need you. Promise me that you will marry Talking Mountain now before I am gone." Brave Sparrow was shocked! "You are the only one that knows the ceremonies and medicines. You are the only one that can help our people, to keep the bad spirits away."

Before Brave Sparrow would have felt compelled to answer, Singing Lark's arm dropped to the bed. She was gone. Talking Mountain looked at Brave Sparrow as he prepared his mind to accept the loss of his beloved

Singing Lark. He would have to sing her spirit to the other world. Soon women would be wailing. The entire tribe gathered outside as Falling Stones spread the news of her impending death.

Men would soon solemnly prepare the communal fire, while others built a pyre.

Brave Sparrow panicked. What if they destroyed the tent as they had that of the old Chief? All the medicines that they had worked so hard to gather and preserve, all the dyes that they had made, would be gone.

"Will they burn this tent as they did the tent of Chief Rising Eagle?" He nodded.

"Is there no way to stop it?"

"Only if I had a second wife, then they would not. That is why she asked you to marry me."

"I will, if you want me to, right away. What do we have to do?"

"You must receive a bride's gift, and stand with me beneath the white robe. It is a sacred thing. It would be a real marriage. You would be bound to me and could not take another until I die."

"I understand. We must do it now."

"If you will marry me you will have whatever you name as your bride price. I am old. I no longer need many things that a young man would ask of you, just food and shelter and help with my ceremonies. Help me to help the people."

"It is my wish to do this," she said. He reached up on the wall and removed the large white leather robe.

"Name your bride price."

"There is a beautiful white foal with its cream colored mother, in the herd on the prairie. I was watching them, when Falling Stones came for me. I would have them."

"It is done," he said.

Singing Lark's body had not been moved, nor had it been prepared for the next world. He had not acknowledged her death before the people. Her last wish was being granted. He knew that the people would soon sense that she had died.

"Wait inside until I call you," he said. Talking Mountain stepped out of his tent, with the white robe around his shoulders. He stood perfectly still in front of the gathering until they grew silent. This was not the way they expected it to go. This was not the usual way. He addressed them with a broken heart. Tears slid down his cheeks.

"My beautiful Singing Lark has made a request that I should take a second wife, now, in her presence, before her spirit seeks the other world. Brave Sparrow has consented to be my wife. Come Brave Sparrow; come under my protection until death separates us." As she stepped out of the tent he wrapped the white robe around her, drawing her close to him and enclosing her in the huge, heavy buffalo robe.

"It is done. I would speak alone with Chief Dark Wolf. Thank you, Brave Sparrow, thank you." He paused, as she pressed her hand to his heart. "You and Moonflower may prepare Singing Lark for her journey." He had looked at each in turn as he spoke to them. Chief Dark Wolf and Talking Mountain walked slowly and silently to the knoll overlooking the camp. Talking Mountain's back bent under the weight of sorrow, and his burden of responsibility to his people symbolized by the heavy white hide.

"I have done this thing without asking you my Chief. I had to do it quickly or they would have had to burn the tent, with all the medicines. Brave Sparrow is the only one that has the knowledge to help. Please understand why I did it. She is your daughter. I should have asked you as her father. I am old Dark Wolf. She is like a daughter to me. She has been at our tent every day. I will treat her only as a favored daughter."

"Very well, Talking Mountain, as you have said, it is done. It is necessary that my daughter receive a high bride price. What has she asked of you?"

"She has asked for a pure white foal she has seen in the wild herd, and its mother."

"Do not concern yourself with it, you must prepare for the ceremony tonight. I will send the hunters out tomorrow to find them and bring them back. She has chosen well." As Chief Dark Wolf walked away, Talking Mountain felt that he was on the edge of a precipice. He knew that more than just the life of his wife had ended. The life of the people was changing.

Moonflower and Brave Sparrow entered the tent knowing what they were expected to do. The body of Singing Lark had to be anointed completely from hair to toes with oil and dusted with the sacred yellow ochre, signifying her status as a healer.

"Do you think we should use the dress she wore when Chief Rising Eagle left us, or this yellow one?" Brave Sparrow asked between sobs as she lifted both for Moonflower to see.

"She must be dressed in her finest clothes and jewelry. A pinch of every herb and medicine she has gathered, a bit of every dye she has made should go with her. She will take them with her on her way to the other world." Brave Sparrow did not believe or hear at all, what Moonflower had said.

They chose the new yellow dress. It was the softest leather that Moonflower had ever held. Their search turned up a basket with a cover that held a necklace of shells and beads. It was long and quite heavy from the weight of a large piece of amber as the center pendant. It was slipped on Singing Lark's neck, along with another of white bone beads. Her long white hair was pulled to the left side of her head, into one braid, with strips of yellow leather and white bone beads. The palms of her hands and the souls of her feet were coated with red ochre before they slipped her white moccasins on. Brave Sparrow pulled a sprig of every dried plant hanging in bunches above them and gathered them into a bouquet that was placed in the bend of Singing Lark's arm.

Into a watertight basket, Moonflower had transferred a small amount from every dye container. Brave Sparrow looked into the basket. The liquid was black. She sealed it with beeswax that they had softened near the small fire burning inside the tent. Singing Lark's body was ready. Gently they placed her thin body on her largest sleeping fur, the black fur of a full-grown bear. Four hunters would ceremoniously carry her body slowly to the pyre at the proper time. The volume of the people gathered outside wailing and moaning, was in proportion to the great love the people had for Singing Lark. She would never be forgotten.

It was a solemn people that gathered at the ceremonial fire. They moaned and sobbed in sincere pain for the loss of someone they loved. The wood beneath the pyre that held Singing Lark's body was lit and the wailing that had continued all afternoon was now soft sobs and deep sighs. Some of the women sat with dry eyes rocking and moaning as they watched. Talking Mountain and Brave Sparrow moved, circling the fire. She carried a small drum and set a slow beat for the old feet to follow. Her feet beat a fast rhythm that used the drums sound as the accent step to move forward at the pace of the old shaman. The long fringe on her pale tan dress swayed with the throb of the dance. The chant that was heard was two voices, that of Talking Mountain and Brave Sparrow. She could not hide the silent tears that stained her face and washed two small rivers of paint away. She restrained herself from wiping them. She had loved Singing Lark. She had become much more than a teacher. She watched Talking Mountain and followed close behind in case he faltered. She knew just how frail and tired he really was.

She reached for his arm and led him to sit in the seat of honor, on the right side of Chief Dark Wolf. The white robe was spread out there on top of a blanket so that it did not touch the ground. He looked at her in puzzlement. This was not correct. He had to finish the ceremony. She gracefully lifted the robe and wrapped it around his shoulders. She motioned for him to sit. She knew that he was overcome with exhaustion and grief, drained by age and his emotions.

Once again she beat the drum and motioned for the hunters, one by one to join her as she chanted and danced around the fire. Once they were all up, she led them around the fire three times. She was trying hard to remember the message if not the exact words said at the ceremony after the death of Chief Rising Eagle. She stopped the drum abruptly and directed them to sit down again.

"My people," she began. "Today we have lost a beloved member of our village. One so dear and so filled with knowledge of the earth, that she has helped everyone here, at one time or another. She knew the land and the things growing on it. She knew the sky and the seasons, when to plant and when to harvest. She knew us; our bodies and when we were ill, she knew the medicines to help us become well. Talking Mountain, in his wisdom has used her skill, joined with his prayers to the Great Spirit to keep our people strong. Today she goes to join the Great Spirit in the other world. She believed in His power. She knew that it was the Great Spirit that made the rain fall and the wind blow and now she goes to Him. Our love and a piece of each heart will go with her. We honor you. We will miss you, as you journey, Singing Lark."

She reached down and added a piece of wood to the fire, and then she walked slowly over to Talking Mountain, helping him up. She cleverly adjusted the white robe so that it rested on the shoulders of both of them, sharing the weight, as they walked to their tent, reinforcing the acceptance of their union before the eyes of the people.

Chief Dark wolf rose from his seat and also placed a log on the fire and then walked away. Moonflower followed his example and did the same. Each in turn added a piece of wood before going quietly to their tents.

Once inside the tent, Brave Sparrow helped Talking Mountain to sit on his furs with a willow backrest. She looked around for food she could give him.

The fire was out in their tent. He needed to eat. She went to the funeral fire and lit a stick returning with it. She soon had a small fire going. She was sure that if she offered him something substantial he would refuse it. She decided to make chamomile tea and add ground meat to turn it into a rich broth. In a few minutes it was hot and she poured him a small cup. She poured herself some too, deciding that he was more apt to drink it if she joined him.

She sat quietly for a few minutes and then asked him,

"My husband, are you displeased with me for finishing the ceremony?"

"No my daughter, you did well. I will rest now." He had sipped the broth, but very little was gone from the cup. She made him comfortable before stepping out of the tent.

She carried her flute and went to the herd where she spotted her father's riding horse. She clacked her tongue and he came to her along with two of the workhorses. She scratched them all and said she was sorry that she had no special treats today.

She was wearing a long, lightweight cord around her waist, and she fashioned it into a simple bridal. She swung up onto the bare back of Dart Away and was glad for the long dress that protected her legs.

He was old and wise and easily sensed that she was not in a mood to hurry. He ambled along in the direction of the distant woods, waiting for direction that didn't come. She simply wanted time to think, away from the camp and other people.

When Dart Away stopped at the base of some huge rocks to eat the grass, she slid off beside him and looked at the horse to suddenly realize that he was old.

"You have gray hair on your muzzle. I hope that you have had a good life dear friend. You have certainly had a full one, winning races for my father and then the long trip with the wagon train, and now living with a herd of horses owned by the Winahatah." She scratched his ears and sat with her back against the large boulder. She then started to softly play her flute.

The melancholy sound drifted into the big rock country and her soul. Her sadness was overwhelming, as the tears slid down her cheeks. She longed for her mother, father and brother. Now she grieved for all of them and Singing Lark, her mentor and friend.

Time slipped by and the sun lowered. She returned to find a small fire burning outside the tent, and food prepared and warm near it. She entered quietly but Talking Mountain was not asleep. The white robe was once again high on the wall of the tent. He had been up and changed into a red leather shirt that she had never seen before. White beads of bone clicked together as he moved his arms. They were tied in patterns on the long fringe of the sleeves and around the bottom.

"Your shirt is beautiful, Talking Mountain. I am glad to see that you are feeling well enough to be up."

"Who has brought all the food and made the fire outside our tent?"

"It was there when I got up. I think someone has brought it to Singing Lark, so she won't be hungry on her journey."

"Why do you say this? You know that her spirit left us many hours ago. The food is simply a gift to us from someone who cares. May I brush your hair and braid it for you, my husband?"

"Yes, I tried, but I couldn't do it right."

After removing the leather tie and gently sliding the beads from the braids, she brushed it and rubbed in sweet oil as Moonflower had taught her to do. She brushed it again and after carefully parting it, she worked in white beads and dark brown feathers at the ends of his braids. Then without asking him, she gently smoothed the oil over his face and neck and lastly the backs of his hands, massaging them. She put his backrest, on a blanket outside the tent near the small fire and coaxed him to come out in the cool, early evening air. She knew that his heart was filled with sorrow, but she also knew that she had to give him a reason to live.

She placed a cup in his hands. It contained mint tea and a few crushed berries with honey to sweeten it. She sliced the meat cross grain, so that it would be easy to bite and chew. She placed a small piece directly in his hand. A tiny smile touched his lips for an instant.

"You have learned more than the herbs and how to make dye. You have learned the caring ways of Singing Lark as well."

He ate the small piece of meat and drank his tea, but refused more. Chief Dark Wolf came and sat with him for a long time. They said little. There was comfort in the silent companionship of old friends.

Brave Sparrow greeted him with respect and served him tea and offered him food, and then left.

She went to see moonflower and to gather her things from the tent, but when she found the tent empty, she continued to walk. She found herself sharing with God, her inner most thoughts and feelings. It was very dark when she returned. She passed Moonflower's tent again and she was there, quietly talking to Snow Star.

"Mother, how are you this evening?"

"I am empty inside my chest. Pain tries to fill the space and I am tired, so very, very tired. It will be easier tomorrow. Have you come for your sleeping furs?"

"Yes mother. I will take the rest of my things tomorrow, if that is suitable.

"Yes, we will help you in the morning. I saw that you were able to get Talking Mountain to eat a little. That is good. Babies are weak. They eat little. Then they grow and eat more and get strong. One day, people start to eat less; they get weak again and die. Talking Mountain must eat, that he may live long. Do not allow him to choose to follow Singing Lark."

"Yes, I understand. I will do all that I can to see that he eats."

She carried the furs and stuffed them through the flap. Talking Mountain moved out of the way and then stepped outside. Singing Lark's sleeping pallet had been rolled and pulled to the back wall. Fresh dry grass was spread for a soft base for hers. *I wonder who did that for me. I don't think he would have.* Brave Sparrow spread her furs near his but not touching. She made a mental note to do a thorough cleaning of the tent as soon as she could without seeming to criticize Singing Lark's efforts. *It will seem strange sleeping here. I doubt if I will be able to sleep at all tonight,* she thought.

"Where have you been so long, my daughter?" He asked quietly.

"Not far, just away with my thoughts. Did you need anything before we sleep? Do you think you will need a tea to help you rest?"

"No, Brave Sparrow, my mind and body are tired. I think I will sleep forever."

She did not like the tone of that remark, but decided to ignore it.

"Tomorrow will be easier, and after that, each new day easier yet." She had used Moonflowers words, hoping that it was true. She reached over and stroked his forehead, hoping that it seemed like a small token of affection, but really she was making sure that he had no fever. His head was cool. He sighed, a deep breath and drifted into a deep sleep before she was settled. She was glad that he was able to sleep, but wondered if he had made a potion and drank it before she returned.

In the early light, she could see that he was in the same position that he had been when she put down her head. He had not moved, nor had he slept. He had slipped away to the other world, following Singing Lark.

Brave Sparrow ran from the tent to Chief Dark Wolf. He must be the first to know, she thought. She forgot all tribal etiquette. She burst through the flap but stood there stunned. No one was there. How could this be? It was so early.

She ran back to the side of Talking Mountain, and fell to her knees. A low scream began to form in her innermost core. It built with such force that she could not contain it. The shrill cry was heard throughout the camp. It seemed that every evil they could imagine in their worst dreams must have been visited upon the camp. The screaming continued. It followed so soon after Singing Lark's departure, that to some it seemed that Brave Sparrow must still be overcome with mourning for her, but Dark Wolf knew and Moonflower knew. It was the way. Sometimes couples that had lived together for so many years could not be separated, not even by death. Moonflower had tried to warn Brave Sparrow, but how could she have stopped him?

Chief Dark Wolf had been with a small band of hunters. He was standing beside the mounted group. They had been chosen to find and capture the white foal and its mother and return with them. When he heard the scream, his warriors were alarmed and would have ridden full speed into the center of camp.

"Whatever it is, I will take care of it. Go now and find the bride gift for Talking Mountain." Moonflower had taken Snow Star to the lake to bathe and watch the sunrise over the water. They were listening to the old woman sing the morning song to the sun god.

When she heard the scream, Moonflower nearly fell in the water. She instantly knew that it was Brave Sparrow, and the reason for her scream.

For the second time, in two days death had come to the people. They gathered outside the tent not daring to enter or move the flap. The keening continued as Chief Dark Wolf stepped inside the tent. His worst fears had come to pass.

Now his people had no healer and no holy man. How would he hold their trust? He stepped out and pulled Moonflower inside with him and again closed the tent. Quickly, we must decide what is to be done. She automatically started to join Brave Sparrow in the sounds of mourning, as did others outside. It was now evident what had happened. He talked into Brave Sparrow's ear, telling her to continue to wail but to listen. He spread a blanket on the floor and told her to put all the medicine in it and anything that she would need to help the people and could not easily replace. Brave sparrow understood. She moved silently and efficiently putting the items in a pile in the center, and then motioned to the white robe on the wall.

"Will they burn it?"

"They will burn it." She defiantly pulled the robe down and rolled it in the biggest blanket.

"They will not!" She said. She added her father's rifle gently touching the carved rose on the wood. Her fingers were drawn to it as if it held a promise. She pulled down the wooden containers of dye and added them to the first bundle.

"This is too much. They will know that it has been removed."

"Father, please call the people to the fire immediately. Stand so that their backs are to this tent.

Start with praises for Talking Mountain. Tell stories of his hunts and successes as a healer, anything to hold their attention. We will join you as soon as I have taken all of this and hidden it. Close the flap behind you, and allow Mother to remain with me for now. I alone will bring my husband to the fire. Will you do it?"

"You have never called me Father before. Why now?"

"It is time," she said.

He slid out quickly giving no opportunity for anyone to look inside. He knew it was forbidden. It was against tribal tradition to remove anything from this tent before it was burned, but he also knew that his people might need the medicines that were being spared. He walked slowly to the fire that still burned brightly for Singing Lark. He raised his hands high in invitation.

CHAPTER FOURTEEN
HE FOLLOWS HER

"Come. My people come." He stood silently until everyone had settled on the ground near the fire. He touched the ashes at the edge of the huge fire and drew a line on his forehead. Then he bent and took more ashes and drew a second line above the first.

"She travels alone no longer." Growling Bear stood and did the same. Others stood and marked their foreheads, until everyone wore the symbol of the two bars. He motioned for them to sit down in a half circle facing the fire. This placed their backs toward Talking Mountain's tent.

Behind the seated people and behind the tent, seams were cut, and one at a time, the two large bundles were pushed out through the tent wall and carried through the grass, the distance to the trees. The bundles were tied tightly together and then hoisted into the high thick branches of a pine tree and tied into place. A pair of hides had been slathered with grease and she used them to cover the bundles so they were well protected from weather. They were safe for now.

Moonflower stayed behind while Brave Sparrow made the trip to the trees, young and strong, she quickly did what she had to.

When she returned she slid through the back wall into the tent and helped prepare Talking Mountain's body for burial. They anointed him from head to toe with the sacred oil mixing it, with red ochre. Even his hair was coated. Red ochre symbolized the fire and the spirit world that Talking Mountain had seemed a part of when he was alive. Only red ochre was used on the body of a shaman. They dressed him again in the red leather shirt and dark brown leather pants, knowing now that he had chosen them for this purpose. Moonflower noted that he was incredibly thin. She hadn't noticed it until now. They slid a stunning chest plate over his head made of beautifully carved bone beads and baked colored beads of clay. Over that they placed a necklace of bone beads. The center medallion held a large piece of amber. Moonflower thought it proper that he wear it.

"This looks a lot like the one we put on Singing Lark. I think she must have made both of them," she said. Brave Sparrow then thanked Moonflower for helping her and asked her to join the people, carrying a large basket that contained his possessions including his drum and gourd rattle and mysterious powders. Across her arms rested his empty hunting rifle, bow and quiver of arrows.

Brave Sparrow had to figure out a way to create fear, awe, and respect in the people. It was the only way they would allow her to be what she knew, she must. She had been thinking, and praying about it as they worked preparing Talking Mountain's body.

She had noticed a large piece of cotton fabric folded in the corner. She cut a slit in its center and pulled it over her head. It hung to her feet in front and back forming a cape. She poured rendered oil into her hands, completely coating her hair, face, hands, and the cloth cape with it. She hated spoiling the tan leather dress that she wore but felt it was necessary. Then she rubbed her entire exterior with ashes. The gray ashes turned to black as they clung to the coating of oil. She looked as black as night.

Talking Mountain's body was lying in the center of his favorite blanket. She had seen him sit outside his tent with it wrapped around his shoulders many times. She carefully wrapped the sides of the blanket up over him. Brave Sparrow was shaking as she pulled back the flap of the tent as far as it would go and tied it open. She took a piece of burning wood from the small cooking fire and lit several of the baskets along the back wall.

It took all her strength and adrenalin to pick him up. His body was heavier than she expected it to be. She staggered under the weight. She was as tall as most of the men in the village but not nearly as strong. Brave Sparrow stood still for a moment to become steady holding his weight before she stepped out in front of the burning tent. She felt unstable. I can't drop him! Her mind was screaming, but her blackened face was set in fierce determination. Help me God to do this. She took one step and then another.

Chief Dark Wolf saw her immediately. He stopped speaking. All heads turned to see what he was looking at. The people parted, like the red sea. She walked slowly staggering under the weight. No one spoke, until she had been helped to lay him between the fire and the people. Carefully she spread the blanket so that it appeared that he slept in the middle of it. Four men had been working feverishly to complete a second framework on which to place his body. It was decorated with feathers and strings of bone beads. Yellow and Red dyed gourds swung on cords, clacking together as the pyre was put in place. They stood it behind the fire, as close as they could put it, without themselves getting burned.

The black coating on Brave Sparrows skin and clothing was something the people had never seen before. It frightened them and they sat in awe watching the strange, new ceremony that was taking place before them. The Chief instructed the four men to each take a corner of the blanket and lift it in place. Then his rifle, bow and quiver were placed beside him and the basket that Moonflower had carried was lifted up beside him and placed near his feet.

When it was done, Brave Sparrow circled the fire chanting, "Alleluia, alleluia, alleluia, Holy, Holy, Holy Spirit of God". She asked several to get their drums and for Singing Wind and Gray Cloud to get their flutes. She continued to circle and chant until they returned. Wood was being piled beneath his pyre. With a slow and solemn movement she tossed a gourd filled with oil on the wood directly beneath his pyre where it quickly ignited. The new flames burst into life and the added heat caused some to move farther back.

Brave Sparrow spoke of the last twenty-four hours as if they spanned a lifetime. She told the people of his love for them and his desire, more than anything else, to help them.

"He has gone on the journey of no return. The earth holds its mouth open to receive his dust. Singing Lark and Talking Mountain have no offspring. We cannot see them in the faces of their children. He now stands before the throne of the Great Spirit, with Singing Lark at his side, to be judged."

Just as she said that, the fire ignited the basket and began to burn the many powders he had used to cause special effects in his ceremonies. Whoosh! Pop, Bang! Flurries of color and sparkles of red light flashed over the entire area as a putrid smell of noxious fumes filled the air causing people to cover their noses and cough. She stood silently waiting until the air cleared.

"Is this his legacy? Will they be found worthy to enter the land of the Great Spirit?" She paused. "Will we see them there?" She paused again. "Are you worthy, if you die in your sleep tonight? He said to me that he was so tired that he could sleep forever. Does he? Or will he walk in the beautiful land of the Great Spirit?"

Turning her back to the people, she crumpled to the ground looking strangely like a big black rock. From that rock, came a soulful note, a melancholy sound, joined by two others. The music was hesitant at first, like a spirit seeking its path to the other world. It became stronger and sure as it found its way. The people were puzzled by all of it, and wondered how she could play the flute at all. This music was simple but haunting and sad. No one had ever heard her practice. How can this be? Two flutes continued to play as the drums beat a soft echo in the background, sounding much like a heartbeat. She stood and spoke again. Every eye was on her. Every ear was focused to hear her words.

"Only if you accept Jesus, the Son of God as your Savior, will you be allowed into heaven, the land of the Great Spirit. He is the true God. He sent His Son Jesus to earth as a man. He was born here and grew to be a strong man, but the people killed him. They placed his body in a cave and covered the entrance with a huge rock. But he rose with great power from the dead and walked out of the cave and lives! He lives forever. He took with him all the wrong that we have done or will ever do, and his Father has forgiven us, if we ask for that forgiveness and we accept Jesus as our Savior. If we honor Him, and believe in Him, we will rise again from death to life with God. We will not sleep forever, or be punished for the wrong that we have done. We will not wander alone seeking the spirit world. We will be accepted by God and His Son Jesus into heaven!"

Chief Dark Wolf was more furious than he had ever been in his entire life. How dare she use the death of Talking Mountain as an opportunity to spread her words from that book again? He rose and walked quickly to her. He had intended to slap her face very hard, but when he looked at her eyes, he felt strength in her that he didn't understand and didn't dare to challenge! He lowered his hand.

Instead, he grasped her arm firmly and led her away from the fire and into the dark, thirty yards beyond the ring of light from the fire. He wasn't sure what he could do with her. He had no one that he could talk with for advice.

He had to be careful now. It was a time when his authority and the loyalty of the people could be lost or gained just by a decision. He pushed her to the ground and told her to stay there. She was not to move or speak to anyone until he said she could. He walked away from her and stood before the people. She sat still; surprised to notice that it was night. After a moment she decided that it was good to be away from the fire, its heat and the people. She began to think of the message she had delivered.

She had planned to talk about their need to have a healer and that she would be able to help with some of the simpler things. The Holy Spirit gave her a different message to deliver. She had no idea how she came to say the things she did, but she was sure that Chief Dark Wolf would have more to say to her!

She was far enough away that she could not hear what he was saying to the people, but she could see that he had adopted her little ceremony of each adding wood to the fire as they left. That is interesting. Even he can be influenced, she thought.

It was the darkest part of the night before he decided to come get her and take her back to their tent. Her sleeping furs were gone, lost in the fire. Moonflower had put more dry grass in the back and covered it with a soft fur and over that she had laid a blanket. It would be comfortable. She thanked her. Moonflower had been instructed not to speak to her. Brave Sparrow looked at the nice fur and blanket and knew if she laid on them, they would be ruined by the oil and ash on her and her clothing. She pulled them aside and curled up on the grass. She buried her face in her sleeve and remained quiet.

Moonflower asked if she could offer the girl food and water. He said no.

When the sun peeked over the clouds on the horizon, Brave Sparrow was not in the tent. She had waited only until Dark Wolf and Moonflower slept. She drank from the water bag and ate a large piece of the roast pulled away from the fire. She had not had time or the inclination to eat in the last two days. Now she needed food. She found a pan of greens at one fire, and apples with honey at another. She drank more water. She had quietly sought a fire where the meat dripped grease. She smeared more grease and ashes onto her skin and clothing where some had rubbed off.

She was full and strengthened for her apparent fast. She had to remain strong. She slipped a water bag into her robes and sat down a short distance from the well-fed fire. Two men talked in a low voice, as she approached. They stared at her until she sat before them. For a moment they thought her an evil spirit, beneath her blackened robe that she wore pulled up over her head. Under it, she had placed a woven mat to protect her head and shoulders. This would shade her from the day's sun and allow air to circulate. She sat; head bowed looking eerily like more than the perfect mourning wife or daughter. She was a spine-chilling, powerful presence visible to all.

As the quiet camp observed her and the two crumpled pyres, the people wondered what would become of them with no medicine man or healer.

The spot she had selected could be seen from nearly every part of the camp. When she needed to drink, she pulled the robe further forward, completely shielding herself from view. No one spoke to her or bothered her. They feared her. They didn't know why she sat there in the middle of camp without eating or drinking. As far as they knew, this was the third day that she had done neither. They waited to see what Chief Dark Wolf would do. No one had ever gone into complete isolation right in the middle of camp.

Only the most necessary activity took place. Conversations were short and to the point. No one went to visit at anyone else's tent. The tension in the camp was nearly unbearable. Children were kept quiet and put to bed or kept inside their tents. Adults banked their fires and closed their tents as soon as the evening air had cooled the tents enough to be tolerable.

Different men fed the fire each night. This pair of young hunters seemed less affected by the deaths and duties they attended. Before long the stars were out and they were both asleep. Brave Sparrow got to her feet slowly. She found that she was stiff and her back hurt terribly. She had never sat in one place so long.

She checked in all directions, to be sure that she was not being observed, before she once again made a trip to each campfire to see what was available to eat or drink. She was pleased when she found a large pan nearly half full of tea at, Rising Sun's fire. One small taste told her that it contained mint and willow bark. Someone must have an upset stomach, she thought. Well it will ease the pain in my back and legs, too, she thought as she took a large drink from the warm kettle. She moved on to find stew. She scooped out chunks of meat, onions and roots. A leg of venison was near the coals at Corn Silk's tent. She pulled off a small piece and ate it, too. She went back to the kettle of tea and took another long drink before filling her water bag from a large one hanging outside Morning Dove's tent.

She returned to her spot and sat back down. She curled into a ball and allowed herself to sleep for several hours. She woke suddenly with a jerk of her muscles. She was glad that she had. It was nearly dawn. The two men had slept the entire night. They would soon be waking and scrambling to get a large fire going before the Chief saw that they had been neglectful. She sat facing them as they opened their eyes.

They hurried adding wood and fanning the coals. She said nothing. Late in the day, she heard two women comment as they passed behind her, going to the lake.

"She is not human. No one could sit there that long, not moving, eating, or drinking water."

"She has always been strange. She scares me," said the other.

"Maybe she will die there and we will be rid of her," said the first woman.

"Well I'll tell you this; I am not going to do that if my husband dies. No one does that. Why is she?"

Soon they will all have the answer to that question, she thought.

She slowly stood up looking at the two men; she walked closer before she spoke quietly.

"Tonight you will tend the fire. You will refuse to have anyone change places with you. You will keep the fire going, larger and brighter than it has ever been."

Solemnly and deliberately she walked through camp and on into the trees on the other side of the lake.

Blue Stone shivered as she watched her friend enter the woods. She is so alone now. I want to go talk to her but I'm not sure she would want anyone around. Maybe I can just take her some food, and clean clothes, and soap root. She is going to need that and a water bag and a piece of soft leather to wash with and a soft big one to dry her off. Her mental list grew and she started to gather the items in a bundle. She told Dancing Willow that she was going to find Brave Sparrow and she was taking her small hunting tent and some sleeping furs.

"Mother, may I take one of your dresses? She has nothing."

"Yes, but if you are going into the woods, take your gun child and be very careful. Do not stay with her if she seems not to want you near. She is not the girl you used to play with. She is different in many ways. She frightens me. She is strange."

*****

Brave Sparrow entered the woods and circled around to the herd on the other side of the lake. She wanted to have a horse to use. She spotted the brown horse that she used for hunting. He would do nicely. She gently and quietly led him away from the rest. Gray Cloud was lost in his own world and was unaware of her actions. She led the horse into the woods to a clearing and tied him where he had grass and water from a small trickle from the rocks that formed a puddle before disappearing into the ground.

Just as she was walking out of the trees to the lake's edge, Blue Stone rode up, slowly. She walked her horse toward Brave Sparrow waiting for some sign that her presence would not be rejected. Brave Sparrow pushed back the long piece of fabric that she had worn as a robe and dropped it on the sand. She raised her hands in greeting. Blue Stone rushed forward hugging her.

"Blue Stone you will get all this black ash on you."

"I don't care. I am sad for you, my friend. How can I help you? What can I do for you?"

"You have already done it. I needed a friend more than anything else just now."

"I have brought you cleansing roots and clean clothes and food. You aren't going to continue staying painted black are you?"

"No. Thank you for bringing these. I need you to return with a message. Tell Chief Dark Wolf that I want the people to make a new tent. They must start right away. Everyone must help, every man, woman, and child. The tent must be larger than Chief Dark Wolf's. It must be big enough that all the people can meet inside. It should have a place in the center of the floor for a large fire. It is to have four poles, one in each direction. Tell him that he will gain status from honoring this request. Tell him I will explain more when I see him. It should be on his right side. Tell him I want the ground under it built up so that it is necessary to step up to get inside. Will you do this for me? Can you remember it all?"

"Yes but what makes you think he will listen to me?"

"He will listen."

"Do you want me to leave these things? I brought my hunting tent and some extra furs too."

"Yes leave them. Thank you. Start counting tomorrow morning. Come back in three days to this spot. It must be done by then. Thank you Blue Stone. You are my only friend." Blue Stone hugged her again and with tears in her eyes she turned her horse toward the village.

Dancing Willow saw her daughter coming. She could see that she was upset.

"I am sorry that I let you go. See how upset you are. What has she said to you?"

"Mother she is my friend and she is alone. She mourns. I am sad for her. I need to take a message to Chief Dark Wolf. Have you seen him?"

"He is there by the fire, with some of his hunters. You cannot speak to him when he is having a meeting with the men."

"I must."

Blue Stone approached the group and stood silently behind the hunter of lowest status.

"This meeting does not include women," said Chief Dark Wolf harshly.

"Forgive me, my Chief, but I must speak with you. It is very important." He scowled at her and then at his hunters.

"Go bring back meat. How much talk does it take?"

They hurried away, knowing that now he would be in a foul mood and it would be better to be out of camp.

"What do you have to say that you need to interrupt me when I am busy with my hunters?"

"Brave Sparrow has sent a message. She requests that you build a new tent, on the right side of yours that is big enough for all the people to meet inside. She says that the ground under it must be built up so that it is necessary to step up to go inside. The fire should be in the middle and four posts to hold it up, in the four directions. She says you will gain status from this and that she will explain later. She says that it is important that you have every person in the village; men, women and children help to make it. It has to be done in three days."

"She is in mourning. She fasted in the middle of the camp for three days. Did she see a vision of this?"

"I do not know my Chief but she said it is important that you do it."

"I will think on it," he answered. This was an outrageous request! The only tent that could be placed to the right of the Chief's tent was that of the holy man, the healer. And if it were bigger than his, it would mean that the person living there had more status with the tribe than he did.

He needed to think, to try to figure out why she had asked him to do this. He walked out of the camp and headed to his favorite spot on the little hill. His mind was very troubled. He had no one to advise him. What possible reason could she have for asking this? She must have known that he would have a tent made for her if she wanted one.

She could force him to do it if she wanted to. All she would have to do is threaten to tell the people that he had broken tradition and not burned all of the contents of Talking Mountain's tent. If she decided to tell them when things were not going well, she could say that the spirits were angry and that they had caused the trouble because of it. What should he do? He had to do as she asked! He didn't like being forced. He felt as if his power was slipping away. He would call a meeting when the hunters returned.

When he stood to walk back he could see the group of men returning that he had sent to find and catch the white foal and its mother. They had been successful. They saw him and waved. They were bringing a "bride price," to a white wife that had no husband, and no tent. Things were getting more and more confusing. He raised his hands in greeting, praising their success. Then he said that he wanted two of the men to take the foal and its mother to the other side of a clump of distant trees and wait until they were given further instruction. He warned that they should be extra careful, and not let anything happen to the foal or its mother. The other two men returning to the village were instructed to simply say that they didn't have the foal and that the others were still out there. They were not to give any information.

The men were shocked and saddened to hear of the death of Talking Mountain. The two returned quietly to camp. Those who noticed their return understood their low spirits and didn't ask questions.

Brave Sparrow collected her hair dye from the reeds at the back of the lake. After scrubbing her skin nearly raw, she finally felt and looked clean. She dyed her hair waiting for the color to dry on it. She untangled it first with her fingers and then the ends of grass stems tied in a bundle and cut at an angle. She slid the clothes on that Blue Stone had brought for her. She was glad that she had chosen a dress of Dancing Willow's. It was shorter than she liked but longer than Blue Stone's and it would be comfortable. She tossed one of the soft furs over the horses back and tied everything else into a bundle behind her. She rode straight away from the lake and headed into the deepest part of the woods.

She made her camp at the base of the bluff, clearing the area of leaves and twigs by pushing them into a pile. She ringed it with stones and started a small fire. After setting up the tent and spreading the sleeping furs on the ground near the fire, she ate a bit of the food that Blue Stone had left her.

The horse was restless. He stomped his foot and moved away from the fire to the end of the rope that held him. She talked to him and scratched his ears, coaxing him to the small basin of water. He drank and stood peacefully, feeling protected with her nearby. She took him to a tree where he had plenty of grass and secured him there. Curling up on the furs, she slept.

A rumble of thunder during the night told her that she should have chosen a camp with more shelter. She packed up her few things quickly and put out the fire. The wind was beginning to swirl. She rode farther into the woods, along the bottom of the bluff. It was too dark to be sure of her location, but she knew that somewhere in the far end of this bluff was the narrow opening of a small cave. She couldn't be sure but she thought that it was just above her when she stopped. She waited for the next flash of lightening to show her the face of the bluff for just an instant. Yes! There it was just ahead and up about ten feet. She walked the horse to the base of the bluff where the flash had shown the cave. She waited. Another flash encouraged her to try to take the horse and all up. Between the rocks was a path that, if they were careful they could walk up to the cave. She started up in the light of another flash, just as the rain started to fall. The horse had no problem following her and the fact that it didn't balk at entering, gave her the knowledge that no animal was inside. She said a prayer of thanksgiving.

She crawled on her hands and knees for a few feet and found the ring of stones that she knew was there. She felt the twigs and kindling she had gathered long ago. After spreading her sleeping furs and tying the horse, she found her fire sticks and twirled until she had a small fire going. Inside she was scolding herself for not coming here when she left the lake. She had come to this cave with her flute a few times. The notes echoing from the rock walls sounded like many flutes. In the light of the small fire she could see that all that was left of the nuts she had gathered was scattered shells. She scooped them up and added them to the flames, until the floor of the cave was clean again. The little tent was easy to fashion into a windbreak erected to cover the bottom half of the doorway.

After eating a bit of jerky and having a drink of water, she slept again.

Morning gave no relief in the weather. She wondered what Chief Dark Wolf would do about her request. He couldn't make a big tent in this downpour could he? Then she thought of the bundles up in the pine tree. I hope that the oiled hides that I wrapped them in, is enough to protect all the precious things inside.

The horse was hungry and in the cave, she had no way to feed him, and she was running out of wood. She stripped to her skin and hurried out into the falling, ice-cold rain. She gathered loads of grass, dumping it inside the mouth of the cave. Next she crawled under the huge pines and broke off dead branches and dragged them back.

As the rain poured down, water collected in a depression at the cave opening. The horse decided, on his own that it was a good place to get a drink.

By then she was shivering uncontrollably and the dark brown dye was running down her body in streaks.

Near the fire again she wrung the water from her hair and pushed the water from her skin and dried it with the hide that Blue Stone had provided. The branches were wet but she put a couple pieces on the edge of the fire to dry out. She crawled under the furs and curled up. It continued to rain.

Smoke formed a layer across the ceiling of the cave and slowly slid out the upper part of the doorway. Her self-imposed confinement was wearing on her already.

She was concerned that three days would pass and the people would not have made the big tent. She tried to rehearse what she would say to the Chief when she returned but bits and pieces of memories got in the way. Her mind was ever changing like a kaleidoscope that was being turned. Pieces of life that didn't quite fit together tumbled and reassembled into something different. God will give me the right words when I need them, she thought. He has before.

She thanked Him for helping her with the funeral of Talking Mountain and Singing Lark's, too.

"Finally she understood. Thank you, Holy Spirit for giving me the words to tell the people about Jesus. Please continue to guide me and give me wisdom. Please, Father, open the ears and hearts of the people to the message of the gospel. Lord, give me courage to be what you want me to be."

She prayed that the rain would stop. Then she prayed that the Chief would have the people build the tent in spite of the rain.

Finally she recognized how much she had needed this time apart from the village and alone with God. She began to feel renewed and strong again. She was grateful for Him showing her that she was doing His will. She rested and waited, listening to the rain and God's voice deep inside, refreshing, strengthening and healing her weary spirit.

CHAPTER FIFTEEN
A TENT IN THE RAIN

Chief Dark Wolf hated the weather. His was the biggest tent and it was difficult to have a meeting of more than a few in it. Moonflower did her best to clear away the center of the floor so the men could get inside. He had passed the word that all the men should come to his tent at sundown. One by one they came and crowded in. Finally the rest stood at the doorway holding oiled hides over their heads as the rain ran off the sides. Dark Wolf stood.

"I will keep this brief, since we are all uncomfortable. Tomorrow morning each of you will instruct your wives to help you lace together tightly every unused hide you have, making the biggest piece of leather that you can. When you have that done, bring them here. Bring shovels also."

"Growling Bear take one of the men and go to the woods. Cut four very large poles the same size and drag them back. You will need to take horses to drag them. Be careful that you or the animals are not injured. The poles must be at least as tall as three and a half men and as big around as you are." Running Deer and Gray Cloud, you will collect all the unused strong ropes that you can find in camp and bring them here also. Now you may all go back to your wives. Eat and rest so that you can start early tomorrow. If we must, we will work in the rain."

With grumbling puzzlement the men hurried away.

As soon as they were all gone Moonflower put things back in order.

"We too will sew hides together in the morning."

"Yes my husband, but why do you need so many hides?"

"Is this a time to question me? Go to bed, for you will work hard tomorrow." Moonflower added wood to the dying fire. She pulled her furs up to her chin but still felt cold. The rain chilled the air. She couldn't help but worry over Brave Sparrow. Snow Star had slipped out of the tent before the meeting, and now she dashed back.

"That rain is really coming down hard. Mother, I will put this near the fire. It is raisin cakes. Sweet Water made them and wanted to share with us."

The rain continued to fall, as large rolls of hides were carried and delivered into the Chief's tent. Dark Wolf had been out beside his tent at first light, digging a trench to carry the water away from the front of his tent and the location to his right where they would be working.

Sharp Knife and Falling Stones had brought back a large deer that they cut up and gave to the women to put over their inside fires.

By mid-morning the site of the new tent was built up a foot higher than the area around it. Each scoop of soil taken from the trench was used to build up the area of the new tent. Grass had been cut and a thick layer was placed on top to keep the dirt from eroding. Morning Dove and her husband Roaring Water worked with Moonflower sewing sections together until it all became impossibly large and too heavy to handle inside the tent. She wasn't the only one thinking that this was madness!

"This should be done outside on dry ground with a communal fire burning." What was her husband doing this for, thought moonflower? He had not explained anything. When Growling Bear and Sleeping Bear returned with the four big poles, they were instructed to put them in deep holes and brace them strongly, one in each of the four directions. Digging in the mud with the rain still coming down was almost more than they were willing to endure without an explanation. Water rushed into the holes as they dug them. Chief Dark Wolf sent for Corn Silk.

"Tell me woman, can you make dye?"

"What kind of dye?"

"It doesn't matter what color it is, but it must be strong, to last and not wash away."

"Yes my Chief I can make some dye."

"Good. Make a large pan and make it strong, and dark. Can you do it now?"

"Do I need to do it now, in the rain?" She asked.

"Yes now! Go. Hurry along!"

Her usual sharp tongue was busy as she hurried back to her tent mumbling. It was lucky for her that he did not hear her say that she thought the Chief had lost the little sense that he once had.

By the time the poles were standing in place the rain changed to a mist and then finally stopped mid-afternoon.

Immediately the bundles of hides were pulled out into the wet grass and spread out. Moonflower and Morning Dove were quietly told what it was that they were making and asked to help trim the sections of hides so they would fit together. They were told not to tell others. That he would when the time was right.

Roaring Water, Morning Dove's husband, helped to lift, cut and sew. Finally by evening the grass was starting to dry off and the puddles were disappearing.

On the morning of workday two, the chief called everyone together by the communal fire. The fire had been relit and smoke filled the air more than usual as it warmed the crisp, damp air. The curiosity of the people was so high that they speculated unceasingly about the project and the cause for it.

Once again the Chief simply delegated many jobs to the gathered people, with no explanations offered. He sent hunters out with instructions to bring back meat for a feast. He sent a group of women to gather dry grass, while others were told to remove the wet grass from the raised area. Boys and girls were sent to gather wood for the communal fire and bigger children were told to see that it was kept burning. Old women were told to cook large quantities of their best dishes, while old men took their bows and hunted for smaller game to add to the feast.

The Chief and the rest of the men began to fasten the spliced ropes to the poles. The very center of the leather top of the tent was made to open with flaps so they could be adjusted according to the wind to let smoke out. The covering was too heavy for men to lift but two of the big workhorses were able to pull the ropes that began to raise the tent to the top. The poles began to lean with the weight and pressure. More braces were built to help hold them upright. Once in place it was necessary to take it back down and make patches of tough buffalo hide to strengthen the areas that would be under the most pressure above the poles. Again it was raised. This time it stood proudly in place. The people applauded and cheered.

The morning of the third day was clear and hot by mid-morning. The ground was dry and any mud on the sides of the tent was scrubbed away. Corn Silk had finished the dye and as soon as it had cooled she brought it.

The bottom of hide walls was turned under and stitched, with long decorative stitches of leather strips that had been dipped in the dye. This tent was unlike any the people had ever seen. In the center of the floor a hole was dug and that was ringed with large stones painted white with a paste made of chalkstone and glue from boiled hooves.

The Chief once again asked everyone to assemble at the communal fire. He placed the pot of deep green-brown dye near the new tent. He explained that all the people would help to decorate it by placing their hands in the dye and then placing them along the outside of the tent. He told the women that they were to help the babies to mark the tent, too. As a few hesitant handprints were placed against the new leather, smiles appeared on the faces of the tired people. Soon small giggles, then loud laughter filled the air. A competition was taking place for positions to place handprints nearest the doorway. Still no one had been allowed to go in the tent to sit down or just to stand and look. The flaps were laced shut and the tent stood finished. It was the tallest, largest, tent anyone in the village had ever seen and that included Chief Dark Wolf.

Blue Stone quietly rode out of the camp unnoticed by the people. Only Chief Dark Wolf saw her go. Soon this would be over. Soon he would have an explanation, but already several hunters had commented that this was a wonderful thing. That at last, winter would be a time of getting together. They could already imagine communal meals and games in the big tent while snow piled up outside. He felt that his status had already risen. He smiled and felt quite proud of what had been accomplished. He announced that the feast would start at sundown and that the people were to rest until then.

Blue Stone had heard other comments. Some of them were women saying that now that Brave Sparrow was gone, maybe only good things would happen. They hoped that she was gone for good. She rode slowly to the back of the lake, waiting for Brave Sparrow to come out of the woods and join her. Finally she jumped down and tied her horse to a tree in the shade. She waded into the edge of the water and pulled off her dress. She scrubbed her hair with sand and rinsed her skin again and again. She sat in the grass with her eyes closed, letting the sun and wind dry her. When she heard a small sound beside her she found that Brave Sparrow stood there in silence looking quite sad.

She was afraid to hear what Blue Stone would report. She feared that the pouring rain had prevented the Chief from doing what she had asked. "Don't look so glum! He made the tent just as you asked. It is huge!"

"Wonderful! Did everyone in the village help?"

"Yes," she replied, showing the dye stain on her hands. "They even had the babies involved! But I have to tell you that making a tent that size in the rain and mud sure wasn't any fun!"

"They will appreciate it more because it didn't come easily. Tell Chief Dark Wolf that he is a wise leader. Tell him that I will see him tonight."

"Aren't you coming back now?"

"No. I still have something more that I must do."

"Oh, Brave Sparrow, do you always have to be so mysterious?"

"Hurry back now. Thank you, Blue Stone, I will see you later." Blue Stone returned to camp and gave the Chief the report. He nodded but felt so pleased that he thought that nothing Brave Sparrow did or didn't do could bother him now. He planned to make a big ceremony of opening the tent. He wished that Talking Mountain could have been there to help him. He sent two of the biggest boys around to all the tents to collect one sleeping fur for each person, so that when the tent was opened, the people could enter and sit down comfortably. He had it all planned. No one would ever doubt his wisdom and leadership now.

Brave Sparrow circled around the village keeping out of sight. In the trees, behind the Chief's tent, where the bundles were still safely hidden, high in the pine boughs, she watched until the young hunters had left and laced the big tent shut again. She waited still longer. The village was quiet.

Then she carried the bundles to the back of the big tent and one at a time, she slipped them under the back wall.

When she stood up inside, she was amazed at the room. It took a moment for her eyes, to adjust to the dim light filtering in. It was just as she had imagined it.

She hung her herbs, high across the back wall on the cord that Singing Lark had used for that same purpose. Placing the baskets of dye beneath them, Brave Sparrow had to be sure that no one would recognize them, so she decided that a little color added to the baskets and wooden containers would make them look different enough. She painted each lid with the color inside, using the dye that it held and a brush of dry grass. Next she placed two furs in the back corner, tucking the white leather robe between them and taking care that it would not touch the ground. It could not be seen. With it she slid the rifle. As she touched the rose, she had watched her father carve; she seemed to feel his closeness.

She unrolled a light tan, plain dress with short sleeves that she had stuffed in the bundles at the last moment. Quickly she painted two birds on the front, facing each other with the darkest dye, knowing they would lighten as they dried. A row of triangles across the bottom from the same color dye, just above the fringe would change it enough that the dress would not be recognized, in case someone had seen Singing Lark working on it.

She slipped into it. It fit loosely and was plenty long. She was sure that Singing Lark had been making it for her. No other woman in the camp was as tall. She tied her usual cord around her waist and brushed the dirt from her moccasins.

Her hair still hung loosely drying after she had given it another coat of dark brown dye. Now she brushed it and pulled it back into one large braid that hung down her back. In the end was fastened simple white bone beads and a large brown and white dotted feather from an owl. She had found it on the ground near the bluff. It matched the feathers that she and Moonflower had fastened in Talking Mountain's hair. A chill passed through her as she realized it.

The cooling of the air in the tent signaled the sun lowering in the west. Soon the feast would begin and she was sure that Chief Dark Wolf would hold a ceremony to mark the creation of this tent. Someone was untying the flap. Brave Sparrow dove under the pile of furs in the corner and lay very still. It was the same two young men that had brought the many furs earlier. Now they carried heavy loads of firewood. Several times they entered piling it near the center circle. They put an armload of kindling in the center circle and left after lacing the flap again. The people were gathering around the communal fire waiting for the Chief to start the celebration. The pitch of their voices told Brave Sparrow that they were all excited. The smell of the cooking food and roasting deer drifted in the tent and made her stomach growl. She chewed her last piece of jerky and sipped some water. That will have to do for now. She thought.

As the Chief quieted the people and began to speak, she decided it was time. She pulled a fur away from the back wall and crawled out. She made her way to Moonflower's fire and couldn't resist taking a piece from the remaining venison roast. Then she picked up a branch and lit the end. She carried it, not sure how to get it inside without it scorching a spot on the wall. She blew the little flame out, shoved the branch inside and crawled in behind it quickly; she fed the glowing branch some dry grass and blew gently. Once again it burst into flame. The Chief was fully enjoying the moment saying that like this tent, the people could accomplish anything, as long as they cooperated, under his leadership. He praised their generosity and quality of the hides used. He praised their workmanship.

"Now," he said, "follow us." He took Moonflower's hand and started for the big tent, but as he did, he realized that a fire glowed from within the tent. He had not ordered the fire to be lit. He unlaced the flap and lifted it listening to the happy banter of his people. The Chief entered stepping up onto a thick reed mat, followed by Moonflower and right after them one by one, all the people eagerly stepped up and into the new tent.

On the far side of the fire, with her hands extended, was Brave Sparrow!

"Welcome everyone to our new tent, and your communal meeting tent. Come and sit by the fire." Silently the people shuffled in and sat in circles around the small fire in the center of the room. All eyes were on her. They were no longer smiling. Chief Dark Wolf and Moonflower still stood.

"Thank you for helping with the making of such a fine tent for all of us. You have worked hard and now we can enjoy each other's company in any kind of weather. It is here that you can enjoy games and competitions. Many people can work here together. It is here that celebrations can be held and hunts can be planned in comfort. It is here that you can come if you are ill for I have gathered the plants needed to help you." She pointed at the collection of herbs strung high on the back wall. This tent belongs to you, but I will stay here and I welcome you tonight to our first fire." Dark Wolf was caught off guard.

CHAPTER SIXTEEN
THE CELEBRATION FOR TENT AND HEALER

"You tricked me!" He hissed. "You said I would gain status, but you take it from me by claiming this tent as your home!" She did not reply directly to him.

"Chief Dark Wolf has wisely asked all of you to help in the making of this tent. He has placed it on his right side, to show you that he serves all the people with respect, from the smallest to the oldest. That is why each of you sits here with stained hands, because you have all placed your mark on this tent. That stain marks you, too. It is a pledge to each other to respect and serve the people and our Chief. I said this is my home and it is, but I will live here only to be made more available to all of you when you need me. You may call on me whenever you have need.

I will pray for all of you each day as the sun rises. You may come and join in that prayer. I will pray to the Great Spirit, our Holy God, that you remain a strong people, and that our Chief will be given guidance, that all his decisions are as wise as his decision to create this tent, where you, as a people can be together as one. I will pray that our hunters be successful, and the weather favor our corn so that we will never again know the moon of hunger. Each morning as the sun rises in the east, I invite you to come and pray for God's blessings and protection." Brave Sparrow turned and slowly picked her way between the seated people, to the back of the tent and pointed to the corner where her sleeping furs lay.

"This small corner is all I ask of you. Allow me space for my bed and some personal things and the healing medicines on the wall. I ask that you agree not to touch them and teach your little ones to not touch them." The people nodded in agreement, murmuring and smiling, and in so doing, it was decided that she should stay in the communal tent. It was out of the Chief's hands. The people had decided.

"Now let us all go back to the feast. I am hungry and have been waiting for all that fine food."

As the people moved out to the fire in the center of the camp, Chief Dark Wolf could hear comments that it was good to again have a healer.

"Even though she doesn't honor all the spirits, she does honor the most important one," said one of the hunters. Chief Dark Wolf knew then that he had to accept her and her position for the benefit of the people. He quickly sent word to bring the white foal and its mother. He smiled when he thought that he too, could surprise the people. He walked about the fire nibbling offered samples of the various foods and chatting with first one group and then another, watching in the direction he knew the riders would come. He stood at the opposite side of the fire to draw their attention.

"Tonight we celebrate the first communal tent for our people and we have accepted Brave Sparrow as our healer. She is young, but she has learned much from Talking Mountain and Singing Lark. She was the wife of Talking Mountain, but her marriage was never celebrated, so tonight, let this celebration be also for Brave Sparrow and her new position as healer and let us celebrate her marriage to Talking Mountain. It is time she was given her bride's price." He had timed his speech so that it would end just as the foal was walked into the ring of light. The people gasped and applauded, frightening the young horse and its mother. She backed away, to the end of her rope but the little one reared and pawed the air with his front feet. He was magnificent! This was something that

Brave Sparrow had not expected. This time it was her turn to be caught totally off guard!

"Brave Sparrow will you accept this as your bride's price from the people? It is what Talking Mountain wanted."

"Yes," was all that she could answer?" Tears made rivers down her face as she drew near the beautiful white foal. She took the ropes that the hunters held out to her, and then she reached for the small muzzle and stroked it. He didn't back away from her. It was as if he knew instantly that he belonged to her. Brave Sparrow thanked Chief Dark Wolf and all the people before she led the foal and its mother to the grass behind the big tent and fastened them there away from the fire and the noise of the people. She asked one of the boys to take them a large kettle of fresh water. He immediately hurried to do it for her.

Brave Sparrow sat beside Moonflower at the fire and several women brought her plates with different tempting helpings for her to enjoy. Even the Chief brought her a large piece of the roasted meat. Snow Star smiled at Brave Sparrow and asked her if she ever intended to get married again.

"Today has been rather like a wedding ceremony, don't you think? It was a wedding to the people."

"Perhaps, but that is not what I meant. Is there no one that you favor in our village?"

"I have not thought of such things. I have been too busy, but perhaps now I will."

"Maybe you will meet someone at the summer council." Moonflower knew that this daughter would not choose a husband impulsively. She was sure that Brave Sparrow had a long list of requirements that the young man would have to meet before she said yes.

In the morning the task of moving her things into the new tent took only a few minutes. Snow Star and Moonflower both helped. She didn't realize that she had so many things until they were all placed against the back wall of the big tent. Moonflower gave her a new wolf fur and a deer hide to help replace her sleeping furs that had been lost in the burning of Talking Mountain's tent. She had returned Blue Stones furs and small hunting tent the day she returned to camp.

With additional dry grass piled in the corner, she made her bed, first layering the oiled hides that had covered the bundles in the tree. They will keep moisture from coming from the ground, she thought. Next, a deer hide, and then the white buffalo hide, another deer hide from Moonflower and the quilt her real mother had stitched. Moonflower had kept it in the lining of her tent during the years that Brave Sparrow was growing up. On the top was the wolf fur, thick and soft. It was large and impressive. She stroked it and thought, poor fellow. I hope that he had a full and happy life.

She had a stack of new baskets; her latest weaving project still in progress, extra moccasins, shirts, skirts, trousers and dresses. These she folded and placed in a stack. Her coat and mitts, boots and hat and a few other items went beside them in another stack. She hung her flute on the wall in its case and a fire horn that Moonflower had given her.

A scratch on the wall of the tent near the flap interrupted her efforts to better organize. One of the hunters opened the flap to hold it back while others carried in Falling Stones. He had been trying to ride one of the new horses in the herd and it had bucked him off. His leg was broken and his shoulder dislocated. They laid him on the furs and looked at her hoping that she could help.

Brave Sparrow had never seen such injuries, and had only been told about them and how to help. She told the men to strip him to his breechcloth. She put on water to heat. She could see that his shoulder was out of alignment and felt gently to learn if it was broken.

After examining the shoulder carefully, he was rolled on his other side. She held his upper arm with both hands and placed her bare foot on his ribs for leverage. She instructed one of the men to pull up from his wrist with a firm steady pressure.

Once she felt that the shoulder was in line she slowly allowed the pressure to decrease and the bone popped back in place.

A moan from the man led her to hurry as she rolled him back on his back. She felt the break in the leg. It was starting to swell. She sent one of the men to the lake for cold water, the other for two branches, instructing him to split them so they had a flat side and to use sand to make them smooth.

"Both of you please hurry!" She called to Moonflower to bring her two pans. Moonflower hurried in with them and a water bag but left quickly. Brave Sparrow started strong willow bark tea brewing and added the plant that Singing Lark said would force a deep sleep that lasted several hours. She would need the man to sleep while she set his broken leg.

As soon as the men returned, she wrapped the shoulder in a cold, wet piece of leather and did the same for the leg. She had propped him up a bit so she could give him the strong tea. She continued to make him drink until he had taken the entire cup.

The men watched and waited to see what she would do next. She was waiting for the man to sleep soundly so that his leg muscles would relax.

She knelt and lifted her hands and prayed out loud.

"To the Great God, The Creator and Healer I pray. We ask that you come and help this hunter. Bless our hands, and let them be your hands as we work to help him. Make him heal correctly, so that he will be strong and healthy again. She bowed her head and folded her hands and rocked praying silently. She knew that they expected a ceremony. She gave them the only kind she would.

When the muscles in the man's leg had relaxed enough, once again she had the men gently pulling. This time she needed steady pressure to separate the broken pieces of bone, so that she could align them.

"Pull down steadily and this time I also need two hands pulling up just above the break at the same time. Hold it here. Keep the pressure steady." She felt with her fingers, probing the muscles until finally she could feel the broken bone align.

"Easy now, hold steady. I will quickly pack and wrap it and then we will take the pressure off very slowly". She packed the area with a poultice to reduce the pain and swelling and wrapped it firmly with new leather she had soaked.

"You can both very slowly let the pressure off now. I will be putting the split branches on all sides and wrapping it again." She propped the leg up with furs after having Falling Stones moved to the side of the tent, away from the center fire and away from the doorway. She packed his shoulder with the same poultice and secured it with soft leather close to his body, so that it was supported. The men watched with respect.

"He will sleep until dark or perhaps later, and then he will need food. Send word where he is and have his wife come," She said as the men thanked her profusely and left.

She knelt again this time it was easier to talk to God without someone watching her. She sincerely asked his divine help.

"This man could have other injuries inside that I can't see. Father you see all things. Please look inside him at every bone and muscle and inner part and heal him quickly. Let him be whole and well again, for your glory. The people watch to see if you are a mighty healing God. I have told them that you are. Show them your power and your love."

When she opened her eyes, Red Squirrel was standing just outside the flap, with her head inside, waiting for permission to enter. Brave Sparrow nodded. Red Squirrel hurried to her husband. She took one look at his deep sleep and concluded that he was dead. She began to scream and wail and wouldn't listen when Brave Sparrow tried to tell her that he was sleeping. Finally Brave Sparrow raised her hand and gave her a firm slap!

"He needs your help, to get well. Not this screaming. He sleeps. Be quiet! You must return with two new soft, clean deer hides. Also bring a large pot of stew as soon as you can make it. Bring his sleeping furs, and yours. Leave your little one to his grandmother's care. Now go and return as soon as you have everything needed.

Within a few minutes Growling Bear entered and went to the side of Falling Stones. Concern for his friend and fellow hunter was written on his stern face.

"He will live," said Brave Sparrow, sounding more sure than she really was.

"He must have two good arms and legs that are straight and strong, to hunt. Will he hunt again?"

"I do not know. We will see in time."

"How long will he sleep like that? He looks like he is dead."

"He will sleep a long time. That is a good thing. If you want to help, you can aid Red Squirrel in bringing some things here that are needed." He left the tent quickly and hurried to Red Squirrel's tent.

When he returned he had his arms loaded with Red Squirrel's sleeping pallet. She stepped in bringing two deer hides that had the hair removed. They were soft and expertly processed. Brave Sparrow was surprised that there were any good hides left in camp after the use of so many to make the communal tent.

Sharp Knife stepped in carrying a large pan of stew. He placed it near the fire, rearranging the stones to support the pan.

"What can I do to help you?" He said with a smile. "You have been through so much in such a short time. Are you alright?"

"Yes I am fine. I am tired, but Red Squirrel will be here tonight to help with Falling Stone's care. Thank you."

"If you need anything at all just send for me," he said.

"There is one thing that you could do for me. Would you please make sure that my horses are fed and have fresh water?"

"Yes of course, I will be glad to do it. I want to get a close look at that handsome foal. Caring for them will be a pleasure."

"Thank you." After he stepped out she couldn't help but think how thoughtful he was. She had never paid attention to Sharp Knife. He was seldom around, and when he was, other young men usually surrounded him. She could hear him behind the tent talking to the mare in a soothing voice. A smile came to her face. He wasn't bad to look at, she thought. She liked his quick black eyes and shining black hair. He was the same height as she was but a lot broader. His shoulders were wide and his hands big and strong. When he smiled at her, it lit up his face.

A soft moan from Falling Stones, reminded her that she was responsible for a very seriously injured hunter. She knelt beside his leg and saw that it had swollen so much that the dried wrapping was becoming too tight as it shrunk and hardened. Red Squirrel helped her remove the outer wrapping and adjust the inside wrap without disturbing the leg. She was just tucking more grass under it to lift it higher when he opened his eyes. He looked at Red Squirrel and said that he was thirsty. Brave Sparrow hurried to the fire and brought a cup of the strong medicine and a cup of water. After a few sips of each he was back asleep. They ground meat from the stew and prepared a cup of broth so that it would be ready when he woke again. His shoulder poultice was changed and although it was swollen and showed a dark bruise, his shoulder looked like it would be good in a few days. Brave Sparrow lifted the arm while he slept and pressed on the joint to feel the movement. It was smooth but felt tight.

"He will need to exercise that arm once the swelling is down," she said. Red Squirrel looked around and realized that although the stew was there, Brave Sparrow had no bowls or spoons to eat with. The new tent had many hides and furs but little else in it. She left for just a few minutes and returned with Moonflower and both women had their arms filled with cooking and eating utensils. Red Squirrel put down the things near the fire and left again. She went from tent to tent reminding the people that although Brave Sparrow had received a Bride's Price, she had never had a wedding celebration, so she had not received wedding gifts. Since she was the healer of the people, it was in their best interest to provide her with all that she needed. Soon women started to arrive, bringing pots, bowls, platters, a willow backrest, mats and more blankets. Brave Sparrow was overwhelmed by their generosity. She had intended to make many of the items as soon as time allowed.

Brave Sparrow and Red Squirrel sat near the fire eating the stew when a scratch at the flap announced Chief Dark Wolf. He entered and barely acknowledged Red Squirrel.

"Is he going to be able to hunt?" He asked Brave Sparrow quietly.

"I think he will live. I can't tell how his leg will be yet."

"If you need anything, tell Moonflower. She will come find me."

"Thank you Father." She deliberately said it loud enough for Red Squirrel to hear. "I am honored that you have come to offer help."

"There is one thing that I would mention. In time could you have the people make a liner for the tent? It would be warmer in the winter and cooler in the summer."

He didn't answer, but he knew that she was right. All of the other tents in the village had double walls and the space between them was packed with dry grass and the lower part was often used for storage. He would see to it.

As evening came the hunters drifted into the big tent. Some of them placed a processed hide in a stack near the back. When all of them were present, Chief Dark Wolf entered.

He announced that they would hunt tomorrow and each hunter would be required to put two hides in the stack, before the new moon had passed. He also said that the share of meat that had gone to Talking Mountain would now be brought to Brave Sparrow, as her right as healer. She thanked him and the hunters, and then excused herself saying that she would be with Moonflower, if she were needed. The meeting continued for some time. She went outside and checked the horses. She stroked the foal and slowly and very gently reached up and scratched the mother's ears.

"I asked them to bring you, because I didn't want you to be separated from your baby. A child needs its mother. He would be sad without you and I know that you would miss your handsome son." She talked soothingly and stroked her neck. "Tomorrow I will make crackers and I will bring you some. I hope that you sleep well. Don't be afraid. You are safe here. You are mine. No one will hurt you and you will always eat well." She wanted to hug the foal but was aware that it would probably frighten him. He had been there such a short time. She watched as he nuzzled his mother and began to nurse.

"I must think of names for you," she said as she went to visit with Moonflower.

By noon the next day, she had been given far more meat than she could ever use. She was glad when Red Squirrel hailed a couple of young men and told them that the healer had a need for drying racks. They were gone for quite a while, but when they returned they brought several racks. Complete and strong, they were placed by the outside fire and ready to use. Red Squirrel boldly asked them to return the next day with help to dig two caches. They said they would be glad to do it. While Red Squirrel and Moonflower started slicing the meat to dry it, Brave Sparrow asked Blue Stone and Morning Dove if they would bring her a large quantity of weaving grass. She didn't want to leave Falling Stones yet. They left their work under the tree and went to gather the grass. She suddenly realized that her requests were quickly filled by anyone in the camp. No one had refused or grumbled. She was treated with respect.

After Falling Stones had been fed and his poultice changed on both his shoulder and leg, Brave Sparrow decided that she would continue to give him the willow bark tea, but didn't put the sleep medicine in it. She made a pouch of leather and filled it with sand.

"This will make your arm strong again. Starting tomorrow, each time you wake you must raise it high and out and all around like this, until you are too tired to do more. Do not do so much that it becomes painful again." He smiled and thanked her for all she had done. She smiled back.

"God is healing you, I am only His hands." He looked puzzled but smiled at his wife and accepted the broth she offered him.

Within a week she had a very large, mat lined cache filled with dried venison. The second cache was dug, and she was working on the mats to line it. Several men had worked at making covers for the caches by splitting thick branches and setting a frame down in the dirt far enough that the cover was level with the floor. They attached leather straps for easy entry. The women of the camp had all been busy scraping hides and preparing dried meat. The hunters had been required by the communal work to hunt daily. To store the resulting meat, they had dug another cache under the floor of their own tents.

The men walked with a firm stride, proud of their productivity. They had worked harder than ever, the past few months. It had all been good. They looked forward to the coming cold months when they could enjoy activities in the communal tent together in comfort.

CHAPTER SEVENTEEN
WOMEN GATHER IN THE WOODS

When the summer heat grew strong and the grasses began to dry, Brave sparrow called an early meeting of all the women of the camp. She had prepared crackers and berries mashed with honey to spread on top. She had a large kettle of tea brewed. The word was passed for them to each bring a small plate and cup that they could leave at the big tent, for their use, or their husbands. Some chose to bring more than one. When they were all assembled she asked them if they would all like to go with her the next day to gather some of the grasses and roots for various uses.

"Many of them you will already know, but perhaps we can learn new ones from each other. Should we leave right after you feed your families in the morning? We can take a lunch and be back in time to make the evening meal."

The women were excited to get out of camp for the day. They usually gathered foods in spring and fall, but seldom got to escape the constant heat and work of camp in the summer. She reminded them to bring as many gathering baskets as they thought they could carry filled. It was a time of warm fellowship and even women that were usually not very friendly found themselves enjoying the comfortable big tent and the tasty snack.

Arrangements were made for the story mothers to watch the babies. They would be generously rewarded. They would be given shares of the supplies gathered. Plus meals were made and delivered occasionally. Everyone appreciated the story mothers. Their group included grandmothers or aunts and sometimes a young unmarried woman that enjoyed spending time with the little ones.

When all the women were back assembled the following morning, Brave Sparrow asked them all to sit for a moment.

"I want to remind you that the tent is opened each morning at sunrise for a prayer to God, for thanksgiving and to ask for blessings for the people." She raised her hands and prayed that God would bless their day with success in finding new food sources, with good weather and fun. She asked Him to go with them as they searched for the bounty that she knew He would provide. She asked His protection.

Growling Bear, being surprisingly gentle, had helped Sharp Knife to move Falling Stones to his own tent. There he could be conveniently cared for by Red Squirrel and his mother. Brave Sparrow checked him before she left and promised to share some of the foods that she found with them.

Although all of the women were able to ride a horse they chose to walk. It was easier to see the leaves of the plants if they walked.

"How many of you have walked into the woods in this area?" No one answered. "Has no one? Good that gives us fresh territory to explore without a long hot walk!" They started out at a brisk pace until the older ones grew a little tired. She stopped at the backside of the lake for a drink and to refresh the water bags for their lunch. Once they entered the trees, the women automatically paired off and spread out.

Brave Sparrow walked along slowly watching the ground and checking the trees overhead. Blue Stone came up beside her and asked if she had noticed anything special when she had been here during her days of mourning.

"No I guess I wasn't watching for food then." They heard several voices talking excitedly to their left, so they headed that way. The area ahead was nearly clear of big trees. The trees lay on the ground twisted and stripped of life. Grapevines crawled across some of the trunks and beautiful mushrooms dotted the rotting wood. One of the older women put a small nibble in her mouth and tasted it, holding it under her tongue for several minutes. All the other women waited patiently.

"It is good," she declared.

Immediately many hands began to pick and probe the numerous ferns for more that might go unnoticed.

"We must remember that the grapes are here during the moon of red leaves," said Corn Silk.

"Brave Sparrow, I don't care if I don't find another thing. It is so good to be able to leave the camp for a day. This was a good idea," said one of the young mothers. "It is much cooler here in the woods."

They sat in the grass and ate their lunch not really talking of anything important, but enjoying each other's company and the surroundings. Dancing Willow sniffed the air several times and said she thought she could smell water. Someone else said she could, too. Soon they were all heading in the direction of the bluff.

Large rivulets of water had cut paths down the faces of the rocks, forming a six-foot wide pool at the bottom.

"Mother always finds water if it is around. It is good that she is named for the willow tree. They always like to be near water," said Blue Stone smiling.

Brave Sparrow bent and pulled a cattail root and a few wild onions that grew in a soft area to one side. Then she plucked the new center of several ferns.

Morning Dove stepped onto the edge of the pond to cool her feet and found the rocks too slippery to stand.

She slid into the water and shrieked as her body became totally immersed. Brave Sparrow knelt quickly and grabbed her hand and pulled, while others helped her out. Brave Sparrow noticed that the rock where Morning Dove had slipped was blue under the disturbed moss.

Investigating it was something she wanted to do on her own, not with all the women watching.

She encouraged the group to move to the warm rocks. Stepping in the direction of the village, turned the women's backs to the pool, while Morning Dove dried off a bit.

Now that she was safe and out of the water, Morning Dove felt embarrassed and laughed about wanting to cool off anyway. They circled back the way they had come, knowing that they had to get back to camp soon. Some commented that the day had been so pleasant that they were sad that it was over.

Rising Sun pointed out the hickory nut trees they were passing.

"This fall we will be able to gather baskets full of the nuts. Look how the branches are loaded," commented Moonflower. "This wood is close to camp. We have good things closer to the village. Carrying nuts back can be very tiring. I don't remember why we always go to the far trees. Something must have happened here a long time ago that I don't know about or just can't remember."

As they came out of the shade near the lake, Brave Sparrow suggested that they fill their baskets and arms with weaving supplies. She cut willow branches into a huge pile. It was nearly more than she could carry. Some of the others preferred to pull cattails.

"This way," I have roots to cook for the evening meal, the stems and leaves for weaving and the fuzz from the top to pad something," said Dancing Willow. Blue Stone helped her pull more and soon both women had their baskets and arms loaded.

"Now remember, the most important thing is that you must all look very tired and miserable, when you enter camp. If the men know how much fun we have, they won't want us to go again," said Corn Silk. Everyone laughed and agreed.

When they walked into camp, the women were surprised to see a large shade pavilion. The men had built it near the lake and had cleared the brush around it making a play yard for the children.

"This is wonderful!"

"Marvelous," said another. The men sat under it in the shade, enjoying the praise.

"We will be happy to bring your food here to celebrate," said another.

Chief Dark Wolf sat smiling and admitted that this was something that the young men had built without his suggestion.

"They made the shade for the story mothers and the little ones, but I think it is big enough that we will each get a chance to enjoy it at times."

A few days later Brave Sparrow took one of the horses from the herd and headed into the woods, following the same route that the women had taken. She dismounted at the pool and bent to examine the large rock carefully. It was a beautiful blue-green, with small black lines in it. The rock was bigger than a fat rabbit. She was afraid to try to move it for fear she might drop it into the pool and lose it in the deep water. She looked at the edge of the pool and checked the entire area. She didn't see any others until she looked up where the water ran from the rocks above her. There she could see the same blue with black lines in it and a gold sparkle, beneath the rippling water as it poured down.

It wasn't very difficult to climb up. She used her knife to pry a small rock loose. Another just like it was underneath. She hurried back to camp with her treasure in her pocket, thinking of the day that she and Blue Stone had been together in that wash where the first blue stone had been found.

As she returned the horse to the herd, she saw Sharp Knife walking toward the horses.

"Hello, are you going hunting?" She asked him with a smile.

"Yes. I just wanted to get out of camp for a few hours. It is too hot in the tent to rest well." On impulse she blurted out that she needed someone strong to get something for her.

"Would you mind riding into the woods with me?"

"I'd love to."

"Then if you would get us each a fresh horse and meet me at the big tent, I'll be ready in just a few minutes."

As she entered the camp she saw Falling Stones sitting in the shade of a tree near his tent, carving something. His small son slept beside him on the blanket. His arm is nearly well and I think he will soon be able to start walking a little on that leg, she thought. She walked over and quietly asked him how his leg was feeling. He said he thought it was going to be as good as it ever was. She told him to have patience and that she would check it in a few days.

"You will probably be able to try walking on it when the moon grows small again." He smiled broadly and was pleased that she had confirmed what he thought all along.

He was sure he would be well before the cold weather came.

She hurried into the communal tent and got a hide to wrap the stone. It would make it easier to carry back because it was slippery and it would cover it from being seen. She wasn't sure why but she wasn't ready for others to know about it yet.

She smiled at Sharp Knife as she swung up on the horse and headed for the lake. She circled it without saying a word. He rode beside her pleased that he had been chosen for what was obviously an important task. She seemed lost in thought and he didn't want to interrupt her. She finally turned to him and stopped the horse.

"Will you promise me something? I need you to do this for me, but I also need for you to not tell anyone what we have done or where we went today. Will you promise?"

"Yes I guess so, but not even the Chief?"

"Not even the Chief."

"Well if it's that important, I promise." When she pulled up her horse at the little pool, he thought it was to drink and water her horse until she pointed out the rock and laid the hide on the edge of the pool near it. She said she wanted to take the rock back to the big tent and that she didn't want anyone to know about it yet. He knelt beside it. The amazement showed on his face.

"Do you think it would help if you wet your hands and coat them with sand? I didn't try to get it because I was afraid it would slip and be lost to the bottom of the pool?" He hesitated only a moment before jumping into the pool. He gave a little yell and laughed loudly.

"It's a lot colder than I thought it would be!" he said. He got behind the rock and was able to loosen it with his hunting knife. He boosted it up onto the hide in one motion.

"There that way we won't lose it." She reached down to help him climb out on the slippery edge and he deliberately pulled her into the water.

"She felt the cold water close over her and for just a brief instant she saw a picture of a river nearly hidden by trees. In front of her she saw her father pointing at the biggest tree, an old oak. Her mother was smiling. As she came to the surface of the water she felt arms encircle her.

"There now when we ride back to the camp, they will think we are both crazy, and not just me," he said laughing. He lifted her straight up out of the water and plopped her bottom on the smooth, moss covered rocks that surrounded it.

"That's a fine way to show respect to the healer! You just wait until you get sick! You better not come to me. I'll give you something that will make you turn green!" She furiously sputtered, but at the same time, she had enjoyed it. For once someone had treated her like a person. Not a white person, not an apprentice girl, not a healer, but just a young woman. She felt accepted. She looked back at him struggling to crawl out of the water and couldn't help but laugh and all of a sudden they were both laughing. She couldn't stop laughing. She had tears in her eyes and her side hurt and she still laughed. He sat down beside her on the grass.

"How long has it been since you had a good laugh?" he asked.

"I can't remember the last time I laughed like that." They got up onto a ledge on the bluff. It was out of the sun but still warm. She leaned her head back against the stones and closed her eyes. She was comfortable in his company.

As they rested quietly against the warm rocks, she fell asleep. This was something that had been very hard for her to do for a long time. She was exhausted. The laughter had helped her relax. He watched her face as it displayed the agony of the dream that filled her sleep. She screamed!

"Brave Sparrow wake up! You are safe. Oh I'm so sorry! I scared you so badly that now you are having bad dreams about it. I'm such an idiot. Will you ever forgive me?"

"What? Oh no. I'm fine. I wasn't dreaming about that. It's not your fault. How long have I been asleep?"

"Not long, just a few minutes, but I think we should head back."

"At least the breeze has dried off the surface of our clothes."

"I'm glad that my dress didn't shrink much. I like things loose."

"It doesn't hurt for people to see that you are a beautiful woman. You are you know?"

"I am? I mean, don't concern yourself with that," she said blushing. "How are we going to get that rock back?"

"I'll boost it up onto my horse and if you can steady it there until I get up, then I can hold it on while we ride back."

"Let's make a thick pad of grass so that it doesn't hurt the horse's back," said Brave Sparrow. They rode back slowly with a comfortable silence between them until they had nearly reached the camp.

"What are you going to do with it?"

"I'm not sure yet. Please just help me get it in the corner behind my sleeping furs. I can keep it covered there." He did what she asked and as he took both horses back to the herd, the sound of her laughter echoed in his mind.

Weeks passed before she decided that she could take the time to go back to the pool. She wanted to check further to see how much of the blue stone was really there. She tied the tent flap wide open and said her prayers for the people as she always did. Just as she mounted a horse and headed for the lake, she heard someone calling her name. She turned around to see Sharp Knife coming up beside her.

"You are out early. Are you off to find another mysterious stone?"

"No silly. Sometimes I just need to go off by myself to think, and sometimes I just want to go see if there are any more blue stones by the pool. Would you like to come with me?"

"Sure," he chuckled, "It seems to me all women have trouble admitting when they are just taking a few minutes off for fun. Have you determined what you are going to do with the stone yet?"

"No but if I can figure out how much more there are; it will help me to decide."

"You sound like you are sure there are more."

"I am."

She reached in her pocket and held her hand open to show him the small stone she had pried loose. She had kept it in her pocket ever since. It was as if it held both a secret and promise that she hadn't quite figured out yet.

*****

The old woman that had tested the mushrooms, sat at the edge of the lake and smiled as she saw the handsome couple ride into the trees together. Maybe they will have a wedding at the summer council this year, she thought. She raised her hands to the sun god as she had each morning since she was a little girl and prayed. She didn't know that there was no sun god to hear her prayer.

*****

"When I went back by the pool, I looked up and saw the same color in the rocks. They weren't large, but maybe some are bigger, deeper in."

"This will be another fun adventure. I hope there are lots. How can we tell just by looking?"

"We can't. I brought a strong knife and mallet to free enough stones so we can see if they continue or if no more are behind. We must be careful that we are not being followed. I don't want anyone close enough to hear the tapping. Sound travels in the trees. You didn't forget your promise did you?"

"No, I never even thought about the blue stone until I saw you today, riding into the woods again."

"That's good. Thank you, Sharp Knife. I'm glad I have a friend I can trust."

CHAPTER EIGHTEEN
PREPARING AND HELPING

Blue Stone worked on the beading on her wedding dress. She had made it from the very first stitch. The leather had been dyed a soft cranberry and the beads were yellow and blue. She had a headband with long beaded tassels that matched. Her new moccasins were of the same cranberry colored leather with a yellow flower made entirely of beads. She felt beautiful just looking at the clothes. Dancing Willow told her that she would be the most beautiful bride ever to be married at the summer council.

She knew there would be several couples at the ceremony. Running Deer had told her that his shirt was pale yellow-tan with dark red and blue beads. His mother had worked long and hard on it. Brave Sparrow listened and watched her friend's eyes as she talked about him. She wished that one day she would have someone that she cared for that much.

Dancing Willow smiled up at Brave Sparrow sure that she could read her thoughts.

"Don't fret Brave Sparrow. Someday soon you will be making a wedding dress. It may be sooner than you think."

"Perhaps next year, said Brave Sparrow. I am not in a hurry to wait on a man day and night. My work keeps me busy enough already."

"Yes, said Blue Stone, you work hard gathering in the woods with no basket!" The women laughed.

"You must remember next time you leave camp with a handsome hunter that old tongues wag the fastest."

"He was helping me with something."

"I'm sure he was," said Dancing Willow.

Brave Sparrow suddenly decided that she had enough teasing.

"I am going to the lake for a bath. You may come if you wish, but stop this nonsense!"

"Yes the water will cool your warm face," said Blue Stone. They laughed together as they got what they needed to enjoy the water.

Brave Sparrow spent time every day with the cream colored mare and her pure white foal. She still had not given them names. Nothing that she thought of seemed quite right. Each day she led them down to the lake to eat the sweet grass. She rubbed their coats and scratched in special spots they enjoyed. One day she looked up to see a raiding party returning with a white woman in front of one of the men and a very small boy on a horse with another. The child's face was red from the heat and from crying. She stopped them and simply said,

"Leave them both here. I will bring them to the Chief for you when they are presentable. A screaming child is not pleasant to be near." They were glad to rid themselves of the crying child, and quickly handed him to Brave Sparrow but Growling Bear held tight to the woman.

"Do you think that the child will be quiet without the arms of its mother?" He hesitated for a moment longer and then released her.

Mary sprang down and grabbed Adam from Brave Sparrow.

The men rode boastfully into camp, causing a dusty commotion.

"We will not have long. They will expect me to bring you soon. I can make this easier for you. I was brought here when I was a child. I know the ways of the people. The man that held you on the horse is Growling Bear. He does growl a lot. That's how he got that name. He does not hit or bite, like a bear. No one ever died from noise." Mary smiled a little in spite of her circumstances. Her mouth dropped open when she realized that the woman had spoken in English.

"Now comfort the boy and splash your faces with cool water. Compose yourself. No matter what the Chief says to you, keep your temper. Be humble. It will go better for you if you do. He is a proud man. I am Brave Sparrow. I am the Chief's adopted daughter."

"Thank you for giving me a few minutes before I have to meet him. My name is Mary Parker. This young man is Adam." Adam still sobbed and sucked his thumb at the same time.

"Mary Parker, it is nice to meet you." They walked together toward the village. The beautiful mare and foal followed behind on the long ropes that Brave Sparrow held.

The raiding party had ridden into camp irritating the women by stirring up dust that settled in the open tents or uncovered food. They were shouting with whoops and hollers of victory. They pulled up in front of the Chief's tent as he ducked out and greeted them.

"Come sit and Moonflower will bring water, and food, but first take all the horses to the herd." They brought more big workhorses. What am I to do with them? They eat much and do nothing. He thought, staring at the ground as he walked to the communal tent next door to prepare for the meeting. He had seen the woman and child when they yielded them to Brave Sparrow. He was glad that he had. It gave him a moment to decide what he would do. He knew that Growling Bear had captured them.

The men glanced in the direction of the lake where Brave Sparrow stood talking to the new woman as they rode toward the herd. Singing Wind and Gray Cloud saw them coming and jumped on their horses, trying to look like they were working hard to keep the peaceful herd in the sweet grass between the big rocks and the lake.

Sharp Knife sat with Falling Stones outside his tent.

"I see that the raiders have brought back a woman and child," said Sharp Knife.

"The only way Growling Bear will ever get another wife is to steal someone else's. No woman here would marry him!" laughed Falling Stones. "Who could live with him?" and they laughed again.

Brave Sparrow felt sorry for the woman torn from her home and family. They probably killed the rest of her family, she thought.

"We should go now. Come with me." She circled around behind the Chief's tent and on to the back of the big tent and then to the edge of the trees where she tied the mare in the shade, releasing the foal, knowing that he would stay near his mother.

One of the young boys was throwing stones at a group of girls. As Brave Sparrow walked by, she motioned for him to come to her. She stood still and waited for him.

"You were throwing stones, Bending Grass. You need some work to do that is worthwhile. For three days you will carry fresh water morning and night from the lake and fill that kettle for my horses. If you have done it faithfully, at the end of three days, I will ask the Chief if you are big enough to have a bow and arrows. Now go get water and throw no more stones at anyone."

"Thank you Brave Sparrow," he said as he hurried away to fetch the water."

"You are good with children. He respects you."

"Bending Grass will be a leader of men one day. He is smarter than most his age, but he needs to learn to be caring and responsible.

Brave Sparrow saw Moonflower carry a heavy basket into the big tent. We will sit inside and wait for the Chief and his men. Adam started to whine and wanted to get down out of his mother's arms to investigate the tent and its contents. Brave Sparrow handed him a dried gourd that had loose seeds inside. He shook it and smiled. She gave him a piece of jerky and he dropped the gourd to concentrate on the jerky.

"He is hungry. When did you eat?"

"We had jerky at daybreak, but it is too hard for him to chew."

Moonflower sat beside the fire and said nothing. She left and returned quickly with a bowl of stew and several crackers. She had observed the child's hunger.

"It is too hot for him, but it will fill his tummy when it cools, said Brave Sparrow." She handed him a cracker and gave the bowl and spoon to Mary. She smiled gratefully.

"Mother this is Mary Parker and Adam." Brave Sparrow switched from the language of the people to English as she said, "Mary this is Moonflower, wife of Chief Dark Wolf."

"Welcome to the tent of our people," said Moonflower.

Brave Sparrow noticed the wording of the welcome and altered it as she interpreted. Moonflower had not welcomed Mary Parker to the village, or to the people, only to the tent. How strange, she thought. That was not a slip of the tongue. Does Moonflower not want her here?

Mary took Adam and sat in the back, away from the fire, getting as far away from the door as possible. She watched fearfully as seven men and their Chief filed into the tent and sat down on the furs in a circle near the fire. Mary shuddered when Growling Bear entered and looked her way.

As the meeting progressed, each man in turn told of his part in the raid and what spoils he had brought back. Roaring Water, Morning Dove's husband, a good hunter and warrior, talked expansively of the horses he had caught and brought to strengthen the heard. Running Deer told how he had burned the wagon and cabin.

"What did you find to bring back?" the Chief asked Running Deer.

"Chief Dark Wolf, I brought back a big cooking pot with a lid. With your permission, I would like to give it to Blue Stone." The Chief nodded his consent with a smile at the young warrior and then looked at Growling Bear, his top-ranking warrior. He stood proudly before the others, placing two rifles in front of the Chief.

"I killed the white man and took his wife and child for my own. They are here. Come woman stand before the Chief." Growling Bear motioned for her to come. Mary struggled to stand with the heavy child in her arms. She gritted her teeth and tried to show no emotion.

"I can do all things through Christ who strengthens me," she prayed. A single tear escaped and started down her cheek. She quickly brushed it away.

"You wish to keep her as your woman?"

"Yes, and I would have the boy. They will live in my tent. I have no wife. She can cook, clean and sew for me. I will raise the boy to be a great warrior!"

"Chief Dark Wolf, may I speak?" asked Brave Sparrow.

"This is a meeting for men! You are here only because your mother has brought food. You may help her serve it." What chance will I have here, thought Mary? He doesn't even let the woman speak that he calls daughter. She didn't understand his words but sensed the rebuff in his tone.

"Growling Bear, the woman and child will stay here for now, while you add six hides to your tent and clean it. You must dig a large cache and fill it with meat for winter. Before they can live with you, there must be enough furs for winter sleeping pallets for them and some furs and hides to make winter clothes. If you have done all this at the end of the next full moon, I will consider letting you take her as your wife."

Chief Dark Wolf picked up first one gun and then the other and examined them carefully. Still Growling Bear stood.

"I will do all that you ask, but let me take the woman and child now."

"No. I have spoken."

Brave Sparrow signaled to Mary that she could go back to the place she had been sitting. Mary gratefully backed away from the Chief and sat back down in the far corner. She was shaking all over. Moonflower and Brave Sparrow sought to lighten the mood by quickly passing platters of sliced meat and cooked roots wrapped in large salted leaves. They passed bowls of crackers, shelled nuts and another of dried berries. Each warrior took what he wanted.

Mary was aware that the women were not eating as she spooned the stew into Adams mouth. She had been offered no food or drink since she arrived. When they had finished the warriors excused themselves and one by one they left. The Chief stood and called Brave Sparrow to him. He held out one of the guns to her.

"You may use this to hunt. Hang it high where children cannot reach it. Keep it loaded and ready. Watch that the woman doesn't get it. If the white men bring soldiers looking for her and the child, you may need it. You wanted to speak earlier. Do you still wish to speak?"

"No Father."

He took the second rifle and left. Moonflower stood with her mouth open. Finally she motioned for Mary to join them at the fire. They talked, and Brave Sparrow explained what the Chief had said concerning her and offered Mary food and water. Plenty of everything was left.

"How much time is there, before the end of the full moon?" she asked Brave Sparrow after Moonflower left.

"You have fifteen nights. Do you know the way back to your people?" asked Brave Sparrow.

A look of hope entered her eyes.

"I think I can find the way back, I must go back. I have a son six years old. He took his father's horse and crossed the river and hid in the woods when they came. He is out there somewhere. I must find him before something happens to him."

"Mary, name all the things you saw when they brought you here."

"At first I didn't see much because I was screaming and crying. They camped down in a big crack full of rocks and the next morning we just rode and I knew where I was when they crossed the burned grass, because we had come past it with the wagon when we came out here earlier in the spring. We crossed the wagon trail and headed into the setting sun. I remember riding through more prairie grass, before we stopped again. When we started out we rode toward the big rocks and through them for most of the morning and then we came by the herd and the lake and got here."

"You would make a good hunter. You remember directions well. It is important that you remember all that you saw. Draw pictures with a stick and say them in reverse order so that the trip reverses itself in your mind.

Your son sleeps. You should rest. I will be back in a few minutes with sleeping furs for you." Brave Sparrow walked to Growling Bear's tent. She scratched on the flap. He flung it open angrily. She could see that he was piling everything in the middle of his small tent. The center of the floor was covered with a pile of furs and hides.

"Would you be kind enough to bring sleeping furs for the woman you brought to camp. Perhaps that bearskin would do and several of the deer hides and that wolf pelt. She could see that the bearskin was a new one. It had been worked but needed a lot more care before it would be really nice. She suspected that it was something he had gotten in the raid on Mary's camp. He had deliberately not mentioned it to the Chief.

He eyed her for a moment then scooped up all the hides she had chosen and carried them at once to the big tent. He tossed them in the doorway and turned to leave.

"The only other thing she will need from you is food for the time she stays in here." He hurried back to his small tent acting as if he hadn't heard her.

Mary pulled the heavy furs away from the doorway and toward the back. She looked puzzled when it came time to make a bed with them. There were many furs on the floor of the tent already. Brave Sparrow suggested that it was too warm for the bearskin, but helped her layer the others. Next she took the bearskin out behind the tent and pegged it down in the grass.

"How long had you been working on the bearskin?" Brave Sparrow asked casually.

The New Life Series book 4 by Louise Bouck

"I'm not sure, but not every day. We had so much to do that some days I just couldn't do it."

Brave Sparrow looked around and found just the right round stone. She smashed it on the top of a bigger one and it split in half.

"It is sharp. Take care that it doesn't cut your hand." She got a small basket of bear grease from Moonflower and then Brave Sparrow and Mary Parker worked the skin together.

She picked up the bearskin and moved it farther from the other tents into the shade. She did not want to be overheard.

"I will help you return to your people. You can use a horse from the herd. There are many horses that the hunters use that belong to everyone. One of those would not be missed as quickly, if at all. Tonight we will begin to gather the things you will need. I will take you through the woods when I feel it is safe. It wasn't until the third night.

"Before the sunrises you will be well on your way back."

"Why are you doing this for me? Your Chief will be very angry. He will punish you!"

"I am doing it because it is the right thing to do. He will be angry. If he figures out that I helped you. He may punish me. I know that, but I still want to help you. He can't do anything terrible to me. I am the healer of the people. They would not stand for it."

Growling Bear had left a huge deer meat roast and a basket of six ptarmigan eggs. These will be perfect to boil and take with you for the boy. They cooked the roast in a big pan and soaked the juice up with wild grains. Brave Sparrow put dried, seeded grapes in a small pouch.

"These will make a nice treat for Adam when he gets tired." She walked to the lake and Mary bathed Adam

232

while Brave Sparrow filled two extra water bags, instead of her usual one. She placed them both with the other things Mary would need.

"This big deer hide and your bearskin will be all that you will be able to carry. Now we will eat and sleep until it is time for me to get the horses."

Brave Sparrow had checked her own horses often and was satisfied that Bending Grass was doing what she had asked.

At first light, she quietly circled the camp and headed behind some bushes to the edge of the herd. She needed to find two nondescript horses, but when Dart Away came to her without her calling him, she couldn't resist using him. A handful of grain coaxed the other horse from the herd, where she slipped a soft braided bridle on him. He was a plain brown horse with a small white mark on his face. He was young enough to be sound, but old enough to be responsive and gentle.

Slowly and quietly she led the horses to a spot behind a clump of trees near the big tent. They fastened the bedroll and bundle of supplies on, and a small saddle that would make the trip easier for Mary. Adam had been fed and made comfortable. He was quiet, and still sleepy, sucking his thumb. Brave Sparrow was grateful for that. She added more wood to the fire than usual so that it would appear fresh if anyone looked inside. Although it was still very dark, she tied the flap open wide as she did every morning at prayer time.

She had put a bridle on Dart Away and just a blanket. She usually rode that way. They led the horses away from camp without saying a word.

Once they were far enough away they were able to ride. Dart Away could feel that this ride would be different than the slow ambling walk that she had permitted last time. Brave Sparrow set a moderate, steady pace. The trail was familiar to her, but it was still dark in the woods. Mary was not a good rider, and with the baby tied on in front of her with a big shawl, she had trouble keeping up. Brave Sparrow stopped for a few minutes to let her and the horses rest. She had brought the rifle that Dark Wolf had given her.

"You must take this with you; you may need it. Mary started to object, but realized that she was fighting for her life as she knew it, and the right to raise her son as she chose. Brave Sparrow shoved the rifle into the bundled fur where it could easily be reached. She dropped a handful of extra shells into Mary's pocket. "I hope you won't need to use it. Do you remember the map in your head?"

"Yes."

"Good girl. Be brave and strong. God is with you." Mary was blessed to hear this Indian woman speak of God. She had joined in the morning prayers.

"Follow the bluff. Near the end is a spring with a pond. Water your horse and make sure that both water bags are full. The basket is waterproof; later, you can pour water for the horse in it. Go straight and you will soon be out of the woods. Follow the map in your head. You will be on the left of most of the big rocks when you leave the trees. Just keep going straight. I love you Mary Parker. God bless you. I will pray for you." Mary hugged her tight and didn't want to let go. She was frightened.

"Thank you," was all she said as she rode away. She didn't look back.

Brave Sparrow thought that she would have to be craftier than ever before if she were to escape grave consequences for helping Mary leave. She put her arms around Dart Away's neck and rode back toward camp as fast as the trail would allow.

Before she broke from the trees she checked to see if the old woman was at the edge of the lake. She was. Brave Sparrow went back deeper into the woods and walked Dart Away all the way around the camp to the backside of the herd. She rubbed him with her blanket and scratched his ears before releasing him. Gray Cloud rested with his head against a rock. The camp was quiet.

As the sun came over the horizon, Brave Sparrow heard the old woman begin her song to the sun god.

Brave Sparrow answered the chant echoing across the lake with a hymn to the One True God. She knelt in prayer as the tears ran down her face. She cried for her own loss. Mary will never know how badly I wanted her to stay, to be my friend, to teach me the ways of my real people.

Before Chief Dark Wolf looked into the tent he could hear her sobs. What could make my daughter cry? She sobs like a heartbroken child, he thought. He stepped through the flap, and knelt, cradling her in his arms.

In all the years that she had lived there he had never held her in a fatherly embrace. It was at that instant that he realized that the captives were gone.

"Why are you crying?"

"The woman and child are gone. I thought she would be my friend. I wanted her to be my friend and now she is gone." She continued to allow herself to cry. The sincerity of her tears led him to the wrong conclusion. He thought she had woken for her prayers to her God, to find them gone.

"Stop crying. She can't have gone far. She is carrying that big baby boy. Look around. What else did she take?"

Through her troubled emotions she started to realize that he was being sympathetic.

"Water, she took a water bag and some of the roast I think. She may have taken a sleeping fur. It is hard to tell with so many in here."

"When did you see her last?"

"She was tired and went to bed after we ate."

"Don't cry anymore. I will have the men help me look. She is on foot. She can't have gotten far." He hurried out.

She knelt again.

"Thank You, Father, for shielding his eyes from the truth. Please watch over Mary and Adam and surround them with your Angels of protection. Guide them back to where they belong. Please help her to find her other son. Amen"

CHAPTER NINETEEN
THEY ARE GONE

The next few days were hectic for Chief Dark Wolf. Growling Bear insisted that the hunters continue to search for his woman and child in ever-larger circles. It was two days before they began searching far enough that they found many horse prints around the pond at the far edge of the woods.

The Chief called a meeting, and the warriors gathered in the communal tent. Brave Sparrow walked out to her horses and tied them close enough that she could hear what was said. She brushed the mare and baby and then slid on and off the mare's back.

"Soon you will carry me Pretty Mother, and after that your son Moon Boy will grow strong and he too, will carry me on his back." Without thinking about it or trying, she had finally named both her horses. The foal was so white that it reminded her of the blue white of a full moon.

She listened as the Chief spoke to the men.

"Many horses have entered the woods and stopped at the far spring. We do not know if they are soldiers or men from another tribe but the horses had the iron shoes of the white man. I think that those men found the woman and child and they are forever gone. Growling Bear you will have to find a new woman, perhaps at the summer meeting. We cannot spend more time and energy on this search.

Tomorrow, Sharp Knife and Running Deer, you are to go to the North and search for the buffalo herd. Sleeping Bear and Roaring Water you will go west and do the same. We need a good hunt, before we leave for the summer meeting. You should all tell your wives that it is necessary to carry water to the corn plants. They will die without water. There is no rain. I am not a shaman. I cannot do a rain dance. So you will have them take water from the lake to the corn. This meeting is ended." He stood and walked out.

She continued to brush Pretty Mother until he entered his own tent then she led her down to the lake. Bending Grass ran up to her.

"Did you ask him? Did you?"

"No, not yet, but I will in the morning after prayers when I see that he is up, I will ask him."

"Thank you Brave Sparrow," he yelled over his shoulder, as he trotted toward a group of his friends.

Brave Sparrow detected a change in the direction of the breeze and felt a slight lowering in temperature. Talking Mountain had told her that when she noticed these things, she should look to the North or West and see if a gray line appears low to the ground, far, far away.

"If it does, then you know that rain may come. Then it is good. We beat the drums and have a dance to remind the rain god to finish the job," he had said.

I will not honor your rain god, she thought, but I can have a communal fire and pray to the real God to save the corn. She passed the word to the women that tonight they would have a communal fire and that if they wanted to share food it would be good. She told Moonflower that they were going to have a celebration and that it would be nice if she would encourage the Chief to speak about the old times when the tribe moved from place to place. It would be a new story for the youngest children and those that had not always lived with the village. He liked the idea. It made him feel important and he would point out the wisdom of staying in one place. She invited the oldest woman to tell her best story, and Growling Bear, head of the warriors and hunters, to tell about his best hunt. The entire camp was busy in preparation.

Much to the surprise of many, Growling Bear was also very busy. He continued to follow the Chief's instructions as if the woman and child were still in camp. He enlarged his tent and dug a food cache. He piled the dirt up and packed it before he resurrected the improved tent back in his place, copying what had been done during the building of the communal tent. He traded three good hides for a large cooking pot and hung it near his outside fire pit. He brought Corn Silk three hides, asking her to make him a new shirt and pants before the summer meeting. He told her he didn't want anything fancy but with nice fringe. He promised that he would give her the first heavy winter fur that he got. She agreed.

Red Squirrel told the ladies swimming at the lake that he had suggested that any animal that he brought back to her, she could keep half the meat, if she would dry his half and process the hide for him. This was a good deal for her while Falling Stones was still limping around and not ready to go hunting.

"I think that he is planning to go get a woman at the summer meeting," said an old woman.

Brave Sparrow watched the sky and walked out of camp to the hill, she could faintly smell rain. She knelt and raised her hands.

"Father I praise you and tonight; before these people, I ask that you show them your power. I ask it for your glory. Give us rain tonight. Save the corn, water the grass and forest.

The Chief called the people to the celebration. They ate first just to change the atmosphere of the gathering. The last funeral fires for Singing Lark and then Talking Mountain were recent enough that they were still fresh in people's minds. He hoped they would think of the joy of the completion of the communal tent and its celebration.

When everyone had eaten he voiced regret that his scouts were not there to share in the fun. He began to tell the history of the people as his father had told it many times. The people listened with complete attention. He finished by saying that it was the lake that never went dry that brought their wise grandfathers to decide to stay there and travel no more.

Next the old woman told a story of the seasons and the battle of the sun god and the old man of the cold North. She told them that when it was hot, the sun god was winning the battle, but as it grew colder, they knew that the old man of the North was overpowering the sun god and soon he would be putting the grass and flowers to sleep in his blanket of snow.

Finally Growling Bear stood and cut her story short. He said that the snow was a good thing because it made it easy to track animals. He told a story of a year when the people were running out of food. It was winter and the wind put its icy fingers into every tent. He wiggled his fingers at the children and made them giggle. The hunters went out to find food but returned without any meat, until one day the snow fell and covered the land. The hunters went out again and were able to bring back food because they followed the trail in the snow that the feet of the animals left.

"So the people were saved and grew strong and lived long," he finished.

Brave Sparrow stood. "This night I have heard three wonderful stories. We all thank the storytellers for making this summer celebration fun." She raised her arms to pray, instructing the children to repeat each sentence as she said it. To them it seemed like a game. The adults soon figured out that it was much more.

"We thank you Oh Greatest Spirit, for the good things that we eat."

"We thank you Oh Greatest Spirit, for the good things that we eat."

"We thank you Oh Greatest Spirit, for the fire and its heat."

"We thank you Oh Greatest Spirit, for the fire and its heat."

"We thank you Oh Greatest Spirit, for the wisdom of our Chief."

"We thank you Oh Greatest Spirit, for the wisdom of our Chief."

"We thank you Oh Greatest Spirit, for the corn that grows so sweet."

"We thank you Oh Greatest Spirit, for the corn that grows so sweet."

Someone started a light rhythm on a drum. Brave Sparrow started to dance with her hands raised, moving slowly around the fire while continuing the chant. Soon the children followed her steps mimicking her raised hands and the tones that she sang for each word.

"We thank you Oh Greatest Spirit, for the rain that makes things grow."

"We thank you Oh Greatest Spirit, for the rain that makes things grow."

"You are the Holy Spirit."

"You are the Holy Spirit."

"Now let your people know."

"Now let your people know."

She sang it through several times.

Just as they finished the last line, a loud clap of thunder nearby sent the frightened children hurrying back to their mothers. The adults looked up to see that neither stars nor a moon was visible in the cloud-covered sky. The women scurried to take the food back to their tents, while the men gathered the hides and blankets that had been used to sit on. The rain came, warm and gentle, it fell all night. The morning sun revealed puddles reflecting the bright blue sky.

Brave Sparrow had rushed back to her tent, to thank God for the rain. Then she said and sang the verse over and over until she knew that she would not forget it.

"Father you have helped me to plant seeds this night. Let the knowledge of you grow in the people."

After three days, the scouts returned having seen no buffalo. They said they saw very little game and what they saw was small and skinny. The grass is dry; they have gone where the grass is tall and green.

The sky promised no more rain. Brave Sparrow led by example. She carried water to the corn daily and the rows she tended grew. Others were not as industrious and the short stalks would not produce food for the winter unless cared for diligently. Chief Dark Wolf spoke to Moonflower, as she ground the last of their corn from the previous crop.

"If the women do not carry water to the corn we will have little food this winter. You must encourage them to do it every day."

"I water my rows. They see that my rows grow taller, but they say that Brave Sparrow will make more rain and then it will grow without them having to carry the heavy pots from the lake. Maybe it will rain while we are gone to the summer council, maybe it will not. If it doesn't rain even the rows that I have watered will die while I am gone. We need her to make more rain."

Dark Wolf walked to the small hill and sat there looking down at the orderly camp. He wondered what would happen to his people after he was gone. He felt tired and old.

"My Chief, my father, may I speak with you?" asked Brave Sparrow.

"Yes daughter, sit and see what I see."

"What do you see?"

"Our people are a people of followers. No young men aspire to the position of Chief. They have no holy man and the healer is a white woman that insults the spirits by holding celebrations to her God! The women are lazy, refusing to carry water to feed their bellies this winter. The men return from the hunts time and again with skinny deer and few of them. The drought leaves no food on the prairie for the women to gather. This will be a winter of hunger. Death will walk the camp."

"Father, do not worry. The people will survive. They must.

When will we leave for the summer council?"

"We leave in four days. It is good that the people leave the village now. If the men that were in the woods return, they will find the people gone."

"Do you think they will return Father? I wonder who they were."

"I think they will return. I think that more and more white men will come, until the land has no more of our people!" He stood and looked down at the lovely woman beside him.

"You have been a good daughter. Snow Star is like her mother and will make a good wife, but you? You are so different. What will your life hold when you are my age?"

Chief Dark Wolf didn't expect an answer. He walked slowly to the village and entered his tent to rest. He told Moonflower to pass the word that he would have a short meeting tonight in the communal tent after the evening meal. Then he turned his face to the tent wall and lay very still.

Moonflower did pass the message to each tent, and then she watered her rows of corn. She was getting very concerned. She sat in front of the tent wondering if the people were going to have enough food for winter.

Brave Sparrow made two, deep, large, watertight baskets and braided wide straps to hold them on. She went to the herd and brought back her favorite of her father's old workhorses.

"I have need of your strength, old friend. Will you help me water the corn?" With her baskets in place, she led him to the lake and with a pot she filled the baskets until they were sagging. Slowly she led him to the field. All day she made trips to the lake, until every stalk of corn had been well watered.

That night she asked Blue Stone and Morning Dove to help her and they sat together by firelight and made more baskets and more straps. In the morning she searched the herd for the gentlest workhorses and found that four she had not noticed before stood together at the side. She walked to them slowly and scratched their ears as she slipped a lead rope on each. With the baskets in place the women began to fill them from the lake. The men watched as the slow parade of women and huge horses went to the field. Each day the field was generously watered. The corn would live if watered faithfully.

The night before they were all to leave, Brave Sparrow called a meeting and told the people she would stay behind to continue watering the corn. She would miss them while they were gone, but they would not come back to a field of dead stalks.

They didn't want to make a long trip without their healer with them. They argued that she had to go.

"Then you must pick someone that can handle the horses to do the job. That person must be someone who loves the people and is responsible enough to know how important this job is."

"I will," said Sharp Knife. "I will stay to water the corn."

"I will stay also," said Falling Stones. "I can't hunt for meat, but I can pour water on a stalk of corn. I wasn't looking forward to that long trip this year, with my leg still sore. This will give me something useful to do." Red Squirrel, Falling Stone's wife, started to object, but Chief Dark Wolf stopped her.

"It has been decided that Sharp Knife and Falling Stones will stay and water the corn. Everyone else except Gray Cloud will leave in the morning, when the sky grows light. We will stop to sing to the sun god on the trail. Gray Cloud will care for the horses that we leave behind." Chief Dark Wolf turned and walked out of the tent. The meeting was over. Brave Sparrow was happy. It had gone well, just as she had wanted.

Brave Sparrow had never been in the tent of Red Squirrel and was hesitant as she scratched at the flap.

"Who comes?" asked Red Squirrel.

"I am Brave Sparrow. I must speak with Falling Stones before he sleeps." Falling Stones stuck his head out of the tent and stood there looking like a turtle sticking its head out of its shell.

"What do you need Brave Sparrow?"

"I would ask a favor of you."

"Anything that I can do, I will do for you."

"Will you guard and care for my horses, as I have? Will you see that they have fresh water twice a day and move them to shade and fresh grass to eat? They will miss me."

"Brave Sparrow I will care for them better than if they were my own. They will be fat and happy when you return. I give you my word."

"Thank you Falling Stones."

She walked away knowing that he would keep his word. It wasn't that she didn't trust Gray Cloud; it just seemed to her that he often slipped into a world of his own where only he and his flute existed. She would feel comfortable knowing that Falling Stones was giving her mare and foal special care.

The path they took was the same path that Mary Parker had described to her before she left. Brave Sparrow prayed that the people would not find her again. She must have people near here, she thought as they drew near the trees along the river. A tiny hint of smoke was lingering in the air. She jumped down off from the hunting pony and immediately started a small fire. At least this would stop anyone else from noticing the scent of smoke. She quickly helped an old woman to light a second with a burning stick.

"This will protect you while you sleep Grandmother," said Brave Sparrow. Soon others were doing the same. Good, thought Brave Sparrow. If they are near surely they are wise enough to have a sentry. They will see the fires and stay hidden until we move on in the morning. Dark Wolf thought it strange that the people had started fires that night. They seldom did when they traveled. They ate jerky or travel cakes. No one cooked and it wasn't cold, yet he could count seven small fires.

Moonflower woke with a start. She listened to the night. It held sounds from her past. She pulled on her traveling shoes and walked quietly through the camp and then the trees, to the river's edge. She sat on the gravel bank enjoying the serenity of the scene before her. The moving water mirrored the color of the full moon in every little ripple. She watched a small branch bobbing on the surface, making its way along, and carried by the current.

Chief Dark Wolf knew when she got up, but when she didn't return after a few minutes, he wondered what could be keeping her. He found her sitting quietly near the river.

"You are as lovely now as when I first saw you sitting near the river. Your parents slept then as our camp does now. Moonflower you have been a good wife to me all these years." He kissed the top of her hair tenderly and turned to leave.

"Do not go yet, my husband. Stay here with me for a while and enjoy the night."

As the sky lightened, Chief Dark Wolf walked in the midst of his sleeping people.

"Come, come. Get up. It is time we move on," he said. "Pour water on the fires. Fill your water bags. Water the horses. We soon leave the river." It was just light enough to do what he asked. The people moved out within minutes of being rousted from their sleep.

They continued on straight, as the river gently curved away and disappeared into a beautiful, dense virgin forest.

Soon the people moved through grass as tall as a man. They hurried feeling apprehensive. It enclosed them and formed a wall that seemed to conceal a threat. Every sound was muffled and absorbed. The people had always lived in the open. They hated this part of the journey. If they could have, they would have taken a different route to avoid it.

Chief Dark Wolf looked at the tall grass and had to admit to himself that soil that would grow grass this tall could certainly grow corn.

They didn't stop until they were out of the tall grass. Soon they would camp by a small stream that wandered across their path. There the children could play in the water and the adults could sit and soak their tired feet. This was the most pleasant stop of the trip for most of the women. The water was shallow and the children were safe to play with a minimum of supervision. They could rest and relax. The camp was set up on the other side of the little stream so they would start out with dry feet in the morning.

Blue Stone became more nervous each day.

"I will be glad when it is over and Running Deer and I are married. Mother, Running Deer wants to stay with the Omati until late fall. His father's brother married one of their women and lives with them. He wants to visit with them. I have never been away from you and Father. What will I do?"

"You will do whatever you must. You will be with your new husband. The time will go quickly, and if you choose to stay with the Omati, I will see you at the next summer council and we will be together again."

Dancing Willow could see that her daughter was having a difficult time resigning herself to the fact that she must go wherever Running Deer chose.

"I will miss you, my daughter. I have hoped that you would stay with our people, but so often the young couples go to live with other people in search of a better life. The Omati remove shiny silver metal from the ground and the white men give them valuable things for it."

"Yes Mother, Running Deer said that if I wanted to trade my necklace, the white men would give me many things for it. I told him that I would never part with it even if we were starving. This piece of blue stone will tie me to Brave Sparrow forever."

Dancing Willow sighed as she walked along.

"I will be glad to get there, just so I can rest. This has been a difficult year. I miss Singing Lark and Talking Mountain, too. I am very tired, Blue Stone."

"I know Mother. It is your spirit that is tired."

CHAPTER TWENTY
THE SUMMER COUNCIL

Many leaders brought their people to the summer council each year. Others came greater distances and attended only the special councils, that took place every seventh year. It was a time of dedication to the spirits. Men held serious competitions and fun games. The women visited and shared their skills with each other. The boys practiced to be men, imitating what they saw. The girls told stories, giggled and watched the boys. The leaders held many long talks trying to decide about things out of their control. What could they do about the drought? How could they stop the white men from moving onto their hunting ground? There were no real answers, only opinions on how to survive with the conditions.

Chief Dark Wolf proudly told of the unique way the Winahatah were keeping their corn alive and growing.

"At first when I saw them I thought that the work horses of the white men were big and ugly, but now I see them as beautiful, strong, gentle beasts that work willingly even under a woman's hand. I'm sure that we will find many uses for them now that we appreciate their good qualities and willingness to work. Others made comments saying that they had turned the big horses into their herds but hadn't tried to use them for anything. A discussion broke out on the many ways the strength of the big horses could be used.

Moonflower and the other women of the Winahatah renewed old ties and shed tears as they learned of the loss of loved ones in other villages. They talked for long hours in the shade of the ancient trees. Most had brought crafts to keep their hands busy as they visited. Others took the opportunity to learn new skills.

As the news spread throughout the summer camp that the Winahatah had lost both Talking Mountain and Singing Lark, a young shaman apprentice offered his services to Chief Dark Wolf. The chief detected a conceited attitude that was abrasive. He declined the offer, but it gave him food for thought. Maybe one of our young men will consider training with a Shaman here, he thought. I must find time to think further on this.

Brave Sparrow stayed near Blue Stone and helped her prepare for the wedding ceremony. She knew that Blue Stone was afraid to leave the only people she had known.

"I will always be your friend Blue Stone. If you and Running Deer stay with the Omati all winter we will see each other at the Summer Council. You must promise me that you will continue to take time in the mornings, when others pray to their sun god, that you will listen to the voice of the Great Spirit. You can tell Him anything, or ask Him for his help with anything. He will answer, not in words like people, but you will know when He answers you. As long as you know Him you are not alone."

"Peek out. It looks like they are ready for you. Most of the people are gathered."

Dancing Willow brushed the tears from her cheeks and stepped back into the tent where Blue Stone and Brave Sparrow had been talking.

"Blue Stone we must go."

"Yes mother" she said.

"You look very beautiful," was all that Brave Sparrow could say as she watched her friend walk toward the spot where Running Deer nervously waited. Other handsome couples stood nearby, each shuffling their feet or fidgeting in some way. Each couple was as excited as the next and equally eager to have the ceremony completed and the feasting begun.

The week went quickly and when the summer council was over, Blue Stone, now Running Deer's wife, said Good-bye to her family and friends and followed a people new to her. Brave Sparrow was sad. She had been a friend with Blue Stone since the very beginning of her life with the people. She would miss her dreadfully.

In her thoughts she replayed recent conversations. Fire Grass had said she was Sharp Knife's mother. She was disappointed that he had not come. She was beautiful. Her hair and eyes were dark but something about her was very different from the other women she had met. She liked her well enough but there was something troubling about her. Then she realized that it was because she looked like Sharp Knife. He was different too, not like the other young men. If he is her son, why does she not live with our people? She wondered. When we stop to rest, perhaps I will ask Moonflower.

Brave Sparrow noticed on the way back that the ground beneath the tall grass was damp. The heads of the wild grains hung down; bent with the moisture they held. She hurried the horse along until she rode beside Dark Wolf.

"Father, may I speak?"

"You may speak," he said with a smile.

"The ground here has had rain. The grass hangs heavy with it."

"Yes it is a good sign. Perhaps we have had rain at the village."

"I think not Father. It is the many rains here that make the grass grow to such height."

A rider came up swiftly interrupting their conversation.

"My Chief, there is buffalo ahead. Should we lead the people around? Do you wish to hunt here? We are so far from home."

"What direction do they travel?"

"They come to meet us."

"Lead the people to the east to the edge of the tall grass. Have the women set up camp there. We will hunt and dry the meat."

"Yes my Chief."

The men were happy to help with the preparations. It had been a long time since they had seen enough game to know that they would have a good hunt. The camp was quickly established. Areas were cleared of grass and brush. Stones were placed in rings to contain the fires that would be needed to dry the meat. The women made racks hastily. If all went well, there would be much meat to dry and this would not be a winter of hunger.

Just as the men were gathered with the Chief ready to leave the temporary camp, Brave Sparrow entered their circle and asked if they had asked God to protect them from harm. They looked at her with solemn faces.

"We will pray now," she said, raising her hands. "Father God, You are the God above all Gods. You have sent the buffalo so that the people will not go hungry this winter. We thank you. We ask your protection for our hunters. Please keep them safe. We ask that you guide their shots so that the animals do not suffer. We ask that the hunt be successful in the name of Your Holy Son, Jesus. Amen." She quickly walked away toward the women, feeling the disapproving eyes of Chief Dark Wolf burning on her back.

"Wait until the buffalo are close so the meat does not have to be moved far to the camp. Growling Bear, as always you will lead and give the signal. He nodded in response to the acknowledgement. It was amazing that so many people could be that quiet as the herd moved slowly closer. Even the young children seemed to understand. Some of the hunters were strung out in a line in front of the camp, to prevent any animal running through and harming the women or children. They waited. Finally the rifles sounded and the pounding hooves sent clouds of dust flying into the air. The small herd raced past the camp and through the tall grass crushing it to the ground as they ran. Although their numbers were hundreds instead of thousands as in years past, the buffalo had once again given their lives as provision for the people.

After hours of hard work, all the meat was sliced and on the racks, drying, and the women rested. Soon they became bored and experimented with cooking the wild grain heads that abounded in that area. It didn't take long to realize that here was another food source that they had never taken advantage of. Baskets were made and filled and the lids tied shut for the trip home. The long stems of the wild grain provided supplies for making new baskets that took on a different appearance from those made with the darker, shorter grass that grew near their home camp.

When the long overdue and weary column entered the camp of the people, most of them were walking. The horses carried heavy bundles and pulled travois with the dried meat and heavy hides. Baskets of grain hung on the hips of the women and bounced with every step. Backs were bent with additional burdens.

Brave Sparrow was pleased to see how God had answered her prayer. Not one person had been injured in the hunt. They came home with more food than they had ever brought from one hunt.

"My Chief, we will certainly have a joyous celebration in camp, when the people have rested! Remember all your worries for the winter food supply? God has been generous." She left him with that thought and returned to walk beside Moonflower, as they entered camp.

Sharp knife and Falling Stones had kept their word. The corn was alive and growing. Brave Sparrow was eager to see Pretty Mother and Moon Boy. They stood in the shade of the trees at the edge of the woods. Pretty Mother blew a greeting and Moon Boy trotted over to her to rub his muzzle on her back until she turned around and scratched and hugged him.

"I missed both of you." She said.

The next evening the communal fire was lit and food was brought by every family. Spirits were high and once again the hunters strutted and told stories of their part in the successful hunt.

After the people had eaten and enjoyed the food and talked of the security that it offered, Brave Sparrow stood. First she honored the Chief for his decision to hunt and dry the meat on the way home from the summer council. It had never been done before, but now the people would have a good winter. She praised the wisdom of the women who had recognized that the grain was a good food source and praised their hard work to provide the baskets and hands to pick the grain.

Then she asked all the people to stand. She raised her hands.

"Father God. You answered our prayer for a good hunt. You have given us the buffalo into the hands of our hunters. We Thank You. Father God you gave us the grain to keep our bodies strong during the cold of winter. We Thank You. Father God. You brought all of us home safely and showed us the abundance of the lands around us. We thank you and honor you through Your Son, Jesus Christ. Amen."

The people played the drums and flutes and sang songs that told stories of great hunters and good times. Late into the night they celebrated.

Before the cold weather settled in, the big tent lining was completed with deer hides that the thicker buffalo hides had replaced. The chamber between the layers was filled with the dry grass from the floor and a thick new layer of fresh grass created a soft sweet smelling carpet beneath the furs.

Brave Sparrow and several others, hauled enough grass inside to cover the floor many inches deep. Young men carried in stones to increase the ring of stones in the center enough to allow the larger fires needed for winter.

With the aid of the young people of the camp, a very large supply of firewood was stacked inside the big tent and more outside. They built a cover to keep it dry from rain or snow.

A third cache had to be dug, for the dried buffalo meat along the far wall where the ground would stay cold.

A brave effort provided the camp with honey for their cooked grain. Sharp Knife and Falling Stones found the bee tree while hunting and decided to surprise everyone with the sweet treat. They had returned only long enough to get several large waterproof baskets from Brave Sparrow. When they returned the second time they were suffering painful welts from many stings on their necks and hands. She was puzzled that the only sting on either face was near Falling Stones' left eye. It was nearly swollen shut. The brave honey hunters explained that they had caked mud all over their faces and hair before they disturbed the bees.

"The mud was a good idea but we should have used a lot more said Sharp Knife." Brave Sparrow applied an herbal wash concentrate to the stings and patiently repeated the applications until the men felt relief. When she looked into the baskets she was amazed at the quantity of honey they had collected.

"We still could have gotten more but we left that for the bees to eat during winter," said Falling Stones.

That night a special celebration was held and each family was given a share of the honey. When it was time for Red Squirrel to take her share, the Chief said she should have an extra measure since Growling Bear seemed to eat most of his meals at her campfire. Everyone laughed and Growling Bear nodded.

"Falling Stones better treat her well. Red Squirrel is the best cook in this camp," he said. The Chief gave a hearty laugh.

"You say that because you know that none of the other women will feed you." Everyone laughed again at Growling Bear's expense.

He stood and waited for everyone's attention.

"Well next winter you will all miss me. I have a promise from Big Flower to wed at the next summer council. I just may choose to go live with her people. Then I won't have to put up with your disrespect!" He stomped away pretending to be angry. Actually he was fully enjoying the attention. He knew that he would never choose to leave Chief Dark Wolf and his hunters. He would never admit it out loud, but he loved all of them and a strong bond existed.

Brave Sparrow worked with Pretty Mother until she could ride and direct her with ease. She trained her with gentle kindness. The cream colored mare was a good horse, strong and fast and she loved Brave Sparrow. Often when she would ride, Moon Boy would run alongside and pass his mother. He was as fast as Dart Away had been when he was young. Now the racehorse wasn't as fast. He still came when Brave Sparrow went to the herd, but after scratches and a treat she would choose a younger horse to carry her.

The women gathered often in the big tent to sew or weave or just to drink tea and talk when the winter was cold and unpleasant for outside work. The men would hold their meetings there too, but seldom hunted in the cold weather. Most of the meetings were for entertainment. Games of skill and dexterity were developed that could be played in the confines of the tent. The people liked the big tent and told the Chief on many occasions. The winter passed quickly. With the coming of spring, the old worries returned.

The first wagon train crossed the prairie earlier than ever before. It was spotted by Falling Stones and Night Hawk when they were out hunting. Many wagons in a long column were making their way down the trail. They reported it to Chief Dark Wolf. He called a meeting of the warriors immediately.

Brave Sparrow remained in her back corner of the tent. She had created a separation of her personal area by hanging several hides across the back corner. She had become adept at slipping in and out of it under the back wall unnoticed. She sat on her bed, quietly sewing and listening as the men talked.

"We must stop them now. We cannot allow anymore entering our hunting grounds."

"They drive away the herds. They take the land and call it their own."

"I say attack! We should stop them before more come." Growling Bear was standing before the Chief with his fists clenched. He wanted action.

"We should kill them all but one. Send that one back on a horse to tell the others that if they come to our land, they too will die!"

Night Hawk stood.

"Chief Dark Wolf, all my brothers, it was not always our way to kill others that did not attack us. Should we not first go to the wagon train and talk with them? We could tell them they must turn back."

"It is not possible to talk to the white men. They shoot their rifle and do not wait for talk. When they do talk it is best not to listen. They are not honorable. They do not tell the truth. They will promise to leave our land and then return with many soldiers. It has been so in the lands of our brothers. This is what they told me at the council," Chief Dark Wolf was angry. His hand shook as he reached for his cup of water. He sipped it and then continued.

"The many riders that were at the watering hole when Mary Parker fled from us, do you think they will not return?" I am not young, but with old age, I have been given a measure of wisdom. One does not stand and talk to the animal that stalks him. We are at war! Soon their soldiers will be in our camp. They will kill our wives and children. We must stop them now!"

"Yes, stop them!" The warriors stood as one, shaking their fists and shouting in unison. Brave Sparrow trembled and wished she had not heard what was said at that meeting.

"Father God, is there something that I can do? Show me what I can do. They will kill and be killed until death walks through every tent in our camp and the camp of the white men. Must it be so?"

I must go to the river where Mary Parker's people are. They can send word to stop the wagon trains, before it is too late. I will go tonight. When the men left the meeting, Brave Sparrow packed bundles of supplies and included the white robe that she had kept hidden. She took her father's rifle with the rose carved on it and wrapped it in a blanket. With two water bags, and food, she was ready. The last items she added to the bundle were her strongest mix of color remover and several pieces of the white natural chalk, and a heavy necklace made from several very large pieces of turquoise.

She waited in prayer asking God's help with this journey. She wanted to save the lives of the people.

"God I cannot do this alone. Be with me. Guide me and fill my mouth with words that will convince the white people to stop the wagon trains."

She rested until the camp had been quiet for several hours. She walked silently to the herd. Once again Dart Away came to her without being called.

"Am I the only one that gives you a scratch my friend?" she said quietly. She scratched his ears but then fastened a lead rope to a younger horse, taking him slowly and silently back behind the big tent.

She saddled the brown hunting horse and put the bundles on Pretty Mother and a lead on her and Moon Boy. She looked up to see that Dart Away stood only a few feet away. He wanted to go with her.

"You may come, my old friend, but this will not be an easy journey for you." She patted him and slid up onto the saddle on the brown horse. Slowly she walked the horses away from camp. She rode through the woods, circling to the path that she had taken with Mary. She directed every step that the horses took, not wanting to have them injured in the dark.

She stopped at the pond to fill the water bags and give the horses a chance to drink. She thought that Dart Away would have stopped by now, but he was there with the others. She smiled at him and patted his rump.

Once the horses had rested a bit she slid back up and headed in the direction that Mary had taken. It was the same path the people had started out on when they went to the summer council.

She left the woods and bluff behind. As it grew lighter, the trip was easier. She stopped again to switch her bundles to the hunting horse and put her saddle on Pretty Mother. She let them eat a little grass. The bundles are a lot lighter and that will give him a rest so that I can keep going, she thought. She gave all the horses water from one of the barrels placed in the edge of the big rocks by the hunters and realized with Dart Away along, it would be necessary to ration water closely as she crossed the prairie. She took a small drink from one of her water bags and decided against eating any jerky because it would make her thirsty. They continued on until afternoon. She was making good time. She had crossed the wagon trail and rode through new green grass.

Here and there she could see the blackened stump of a burned bush.

"There must have been a wildfire here," she said to her companions. She stopped to rest and let the horses feed. She felt here in the wide-open prairie that the world was hers for the taking. She could see for miles and there was not another person. She relaxed and was able to doze for a couple hours. The horses did not wander more than a short distance. They had all they could eat right in front of them. Once again she switched to the hunting horse and headed in the direction of the river.

When I get there I wonder how I will find Mary or her friends. She did say they were on the other side.

She was thinking that she should stop to give the horses water when she spotted the line of trees far in the distance.

"That has to be the river!" She announced to the horses happily as she slid off and poured water into a basket offering it first to one horse and then another. Each gratefully had a small share.

"Dart Away you look so tired. The journey is nearly over, at least for now. When we reach the trees I don't know which way to turn but maybe by then we will be able to tell."

She continued on in a straight line until she reached the river. To the left was the direction that the people had moved and finally camped at a big bend. Perhaps to the right she could see something. She walked the horses along outside the trees looking up. She remembered that Mary had told her about a crossing near the biggest tree. It was a huge old oak with a cross on it. There was a very big tree up ahead. She entered the shade. There it was. She could see the cross and some writing. I wonder what it says, she thought. I wish I knew how to read.

She dropped her bundles in the grass and tied all but the hunting pony near the water where they could eat and drink. The river felt cold as it splashed against her legs.

After crossing, she looked around for something to guide her. Stepping down she walked up the bank and headed for a bluff just a short distance ahead.

There before her was a hill with a door in it. That is a house! How strange to live inside a hill, she thought. No smoke rose from the hole in the roof, but she could smell smoke in the air. The fire had recently been extinguished. A path led to a clearing and there she saw a large ring of stones that had been used many times for fires to dry meat. The racks were still standing nearby. The path to the lake passed the corner of the corral. She didn't notice it.

Her attention was on the path and the orderly garden ahead. She followed the path around the lake and saw the wonderful house sitting on the hill.

As she neared it, she called out. No one answered. She called out again, and again. Where could they be? Who lived there? Did they know Mary Parker? It was then that she noticed the big barn placed behind the willows. She walked to the corral gate and let herself in. When she swung open the barn and saw the horses in their stalls, she was puzzled. Why do these people keep their horses in a barn in the daytime? Where have they gone without their horses?

She whirled around when she heard the sound of the rifle being cocked. The man was a bit taller than she, with brown hair and dark eyes. He wore trousers made of leather and a shirt of tan cotton with rolled up sleeves. His feet were bare. His rifle was pointed at her middle as if his intention was to stop her at any cost. He didn't look fierce, but he did look serious, and a little frightening.

"What are you doing here? What do you want? Who are you?" Jed asked. Suddenly Brave Sparrow realized how foolish she had been. She had entered the camp of a white man without her gun or any means of protection at hand.

"I am Brave Sparrow. I am looking for a woman called Mary Parker. Do you know her?"

"What do you want with her?" He asked.

"I must speak with her. It is a matter of life or death. Is she here?"

"How many have come with you?"

"I came alone. Tell me. Is she here? Do you know where she is? There isn't time for this! I must speak with her now!"

Jed wasn't sure what to do. After all that Mary had been through. He thought the last thing she would want to do was to speak to an Indian. Brave Sparrow turned her back to him and yelled as loud as she could.

"Mary Parker, are you here?" Mary heard her then and knew instantly that it was Brave Sparrow. She hurried out the front door of the house, leaving Adam with Beth inside.

"Brave Sparrow, I am coming. What are you doing here?" She entered the corral running and wrapped her arms around the woman that had saved her.

"I have missed you Mary Parker and prayed for you daily."

"I have missed you too, Brave Sparrow, and prayed for you."

Jed finally lowered his gun.

"Jed this is Brave Sparrow. She is the woman I told you about. She helped me escape from the Indian camp."

"It is nice to meet you, Brave Sparrow. We are grateful to you." Ben had remained in the house to protect the rest of his family if need be.

Now he came out and the others followed. They stood on the grass near the house, still hesitant to get any closer. Mary wrapped her arm around Brave Sparrow's shoulders and led her toward the waiting group of people.

"Ben, Beth, this is Brave Sparrow. She is the woman that gave me the horse and helped me leave the Indian camp. I will always be grateful to her." They all greeted her then and Joshua came running out the front door. He had been in the escape tunnel nearly to the woods.

"Brave Sparrow this is my son Joshua, and you already met Adam."

"They are good strong boys. They will be men to be proud of when they are grown. I am glad that you are here and have found Joshua."

"Now that you know who I am, is it alright if I sit down? I have been on the trail a long time."

"Oh forgive me," said Beth.

"Come in please. Sit here and I will bring you some tea." Mary sat in the other willow chair near her, and the men sat on a bearskin. Joshua volunteered to bring her horses and bundles across the river. He put the horses in Jed's corral and added several bundles of hay. Brave Sparrow could see him through the window, rubbing down the horses with dry grass. She told her reason for being there, more to the men than to Mary. She needed someone to stop the wagon trains. She wanted them to warn the leaders of the white men.

"They must not come! You see, I have lived with the people since I was little. I have learned their ways. They rely on the animals to survive. The white men drive the animals away. They have entered the camps of our brothers with soldiers and killed everyone, even the women and children. Our warriors are brave and they are angry. They will fight and kill the people on the wagon trains. They will not let more white men come to the hunting grounds of the people."

Now that her message was delivered, exhaustion began to show. Her hands shook and she felt sick. She hadn't eaten. Joshua came in and reported that he had her bundles outside. She thanked him.

"Is the old horse alright? He was my father's horse. I have kept him as a friend all these years. Poor Dart Away, he insisted on following me even though he was so tired."

Ben let her words soak in for a moment before he realized what meaning they really held for him.

"Did you say that the horse's name is Dart Away?" asked Ben.

"Yes, my father gave him that name, because he was so fast. He won many races when I was a young child." Ben's stomach started to flutter. What was your father's name?" She had a mental image of a tall man that she called Daddy. She had to search deeply into her memory. It had been many years since that day when she had been grabbed from the wagon and taken by Dark Wolf.

"My father was killed when they raided the wagon, my mother and brother, too. They were Josiah and Mary Slater and my brother's name was Benjamin." Ben's face turned white and then red.

"I am Benjamin Slater! Sarah?" She had not heard her name spoken in many years. She couldn't instantly respond. Could this be true? Was this real? Beth and Jed were stunned! Even Joshua understood what was happening.

"I am Sarah." She said. She started to stand and collapsed to the floor. Ben scooped her up and cradled her in his arms as if she were the small child that he had lost. His tears wet her face and hair as he held her close.

"Sarah. Oh Sarah. I didn't find you, so you found me! Thank you God! Oh thank you." Beth and Mary were both crying. Even Jed and Joshua had tears in their eyes.

CHAPTER TWENTY ONE
HER BROTHER

Sarah woke to find herself in a bed with sheets and blankets. She looked around the room to see the sunshine streaming in the open window. She could hear the birds in the trees behind the house and then she heard Adam jabbering to his mother and Beth and Mary laughing at his comment.

"No Adam, you can't ride the white horsey. It belongs to Sarah."

"Sarah looked at herself as she swung her feet out of bed. She was wearing a long white gown. Her skin felt clean. Someone had helped her bathe and change her clothes. Her braids were out and her hair had been brushed. It hung long and loosely. She couldn't remember much after the realization that she had found her brother. She wondered how long she had slept.

Beth heard the rustle of the bed as Sarah got out.

"Sarah the men are gone, you can come out in your nightgown." She stepped into the main room and for the first time, she began to see the comfortable, cozy room.

When her bare feet touched the bear rug she looked down to see Adam playing with a wooden horse.

"Hello young man. I see that you like horses." He nodded shyly and then mustered his courage.

"I want to ride the white horsey."

"Well we will have to see about that, won't we?" Mary held her hand out toward Sarah, and asked her to sit with them at the table. Beth poured her a cup of tea and gave her a thick slice of fresh bread with jam.

"Sarah you were so tired when you arrived. I don't know how much you remember. I am Beth. I am Jed's wife. We are all glad that you are back with your family. Sarah you are welcome here."

"Thank you Beth and thank you God for bringing me to a home filled with warmth and love." She bit the bread and sipped the tea. Before long she was eating eggs and fried potatoes. She had not eaten a good meal for several days. They had offered her food, but she was in shock. She couldn't eat.

"How long did I sleep?" she asked.

"Jed made you a tea with a sleeping potion in it. We tucked you in at dark last night," answered Mary. "It was apparent that you were exhausted."

"Jed and Ben have gone to the Fort to see if they can warn the wagon trains. Sarah, they will not stop coming. They will simply carry more arms and be more on guard. There will be war and there is nothing that any of us can do to stop it."

"I had to try," she said sadly. They sat together getting acquainted.

Sarah pulled her clothes on. They had been scrubbed and were soft and dry. She walked out to see her horses. She was surprised at how well Dart Away looked.

"He likes the barn," said Joshua, "We didn't even have to tell him. He went in by himself last night. I put him in the first stall. He seemed like he thought that was his place."

"He probably remembered being in a barn when he was young," she said.

"I like the white horse. What is his name?" asked Joshua.

"He is Moon Boy and his mother is Pretty Mother. The brown one doesn't really have a name. He is a hunting pony that many people can use."

*****

Sarah had been there more than a week, when she took the color remover to the river and with great resolve, used it to scrub every bit of the dye from her pale blond hair. The fumes had been so bad that it had made her ill. She was grateful that the river carried that away with the scent as she continued to scrub and rinse. Beth had given her soap to use to try to remove the smell, once the color of the nut casing dye was gone. Sarah could feel the awful tangled mess that once was long silky hair.

She poured the rendered bear fat onto her hair and gently began to smooth it down with her fingers. Bit by bit the hair relaxed and hung in long limp greasy strands. She stood in the flowing water for a few minutes, letting the oil soak into the damaged hair. Then ever so gently she washed it with the lilac soap. This time the hair hung in soft strands beyond her waist.

Both Mary and Beth helped her to comb it until every tangle was gone. Sarah pulled it back into a single braid and tied it with a strip of leather.

"You look so different with that dye gone. Now your hair matches your light brows and lashes."

"Sarah, do you have any idea how beautiful you are?"

"A friend told me that I am a beautiful woman once but I have never thought of such things. God has kept me healthy and strong. I pray each dawn that I remain beautiful in His sight and that is all that is really important."

Sarah worked for days on the dress she was making from the pure white, buffalo hide. If the people knew that she had Talking Mountain's sacred hide they would be angry. They would be even angrier if they knew that she had dared to cut it to make this dress. She finished the dress and moccasins and tried them on. The thick leather felt heavy. She practiced parting her hair in the middle and pulled both sections forward letting the hair tumble down on either side of her face. She held it there with strips of white leather braided in only at the very top. She looked at the folded clothes and knew that she was as ready as she would ever be.

Wearing her regular clothes she said good-bye to everyone, saying that she had a duty to the people. She tried to explain to Ben and her newfound family why she had to go back, but now that she was there, Ben didn't want her to go. He refused to understand and he feared he would lose her again. Perhaps this time it would be forever.

"I must tell Chief Dark Wolf that the trains will be heavily guarded, or many of the people that have cared for me all these years will die. Ben, can't you see? Please try to understand. I am standing with my feet in two worlds. One is the world that you know. The other is a world of people that wanted a daughter so badly, they were willing to steal and kill to get her. They have been kind to me and have treated me with love and respect."

She lifted the rifle from the blanket as she prepared to leave.

"Ben I brought this. I have kept it all this time. Do you recognize it?"

"Yes," he said as he turned his own rifle over to show her that he had carved a small rose on his also.

"Take it Ben. Keep it here where it will be safe. I won't need it." Ben looked at her and wondered if he would ever understand.

"I remember it. I remember the day that it was taken! They killed our parents! Sarah, how can you go back there?"

"I must. If it is God's will, I will return. I am leaving Dart Away. Maybe he and Blaze will have beautiful thoroughbred babies. He loves it here. He likes being in the barn at night. Will you keep Moon Boy for me, too? He is very special. He is my most valuable possession. One day I would like to ride on him. Now my sweet brother, I must go."

"Wait, don't leave until we have prayed with you," said Ben. Everyone joined hands. Each one asked a different blessing for her. Ben's prayer was that she be able to be God's instrument, to open the eyes and ears of the people she returned to, that through her they would come to know the one true God. She gave him a quick hug and swung up on the same brown horse that had brought her. She led Pretty Mother. Her saddlebags held the treasured white clothes and she still carried the pieces of white natural chalk as she crossed the Hickory River and headed out of the trees onto the prairie.

She didn't hurry on her way back. The time became a continuing time of prayer. She knew that God would provide a way for her to return to her people that would give her the power of persuasion she needed. She asked wisdom and guidance.

Beth had given her a simple white shawl she had made. Sarah pulled it up over her hair and knotted it under her chin, just as the answer came in the form of Sharp Knife. He had been out alone hunting and was returning as he saw her stop at the edge of the woods. He rode to her at once.

"Where have you been? We have all been worried about you. Do you know that you have been gone fifteen days?"

"Yes, I know. Sharp Knife, tell me, did they attack a wagon train while I was gone?"

"Yes they did, and two of our warriors were killed. Sleeping Bear is wounded. We need you here. You are our healer. Aren't you? You should have been here!" She didn't respond.

"I must ask you to do something for me. Tell my father that I have a message for him. I will give it to him tonight at the communal fire. Tell him I will come then. Tell him that God is not pleased with the people."

Sharp Knife looked at her with awe. How can she know the mind of God? He wondered.

"I will tell him, but you should know that Chief Dark Wolf is angry with you for leaving."

"Oh and Sharp Knife, I need one more thing if you are willing. I need you to bring the big blue stone out to me at the communal fire, when I signal you. Will you do it?"

"Yes, but why?"

"You will hear tonight." She slid from the hunting pony and pulled off her saddle and bridle.

"You have served me well horse, now return to the herd so that Gray Cloud can be happy when he counts tonight."

"Where is the white yearling?"

"He is safe." Sharp Knife was irritated. She never gives me a straight answer, he thought. He rode toward the village without glancing back.

Brave Sparrow, bent low behind the screen of willow branches that shielded her from the bathers on the other side of the small lake. She washed her hair again with the precious soap and rinsed it. She picked up a small basket that contained a white paste she had made by mixing just a tiny bit of oil with the ground white stone. While her hair dried she worked the paste into her hair and brushed it out, over and over again. Finally when she was satisfied with the color reflected in the lake, she took the basket into the woods and did the same to Pretty Mother's coat.

Little by little the cream colored mare became snow white.

Dusk filtered through the trees of the woods as Brave Sparrow put on the dress she had made from the sacred robe. It felt stiff. The buffalo leather was thick. She pulled on the white moccasins, and slipped the necklace of large blue stones over her head. She spread the piece of white cotton that Beth had gladly given her, over her saddle. The last thing was to use some of the ground white stones as powder on her skin. She patted it on her face and neck, her arms and legs. Her skin took on a white ghostly tone, and yet her humanity had never been more visible, as her bottom lip quivered, knowing how important it was that she must deliver her message just right. She raised her arms and prayed again with all her heart.

"Father, help me to help them."

She sat patiently beside Pretty Mother, waiting until it was totally dark and all the people would be assembled, she knew that if she could not convince them, that the people would soon all die.

She could see Chief Dark Wolf talking on the side of the gathering with Growling Bear and some others. She wondered which warriors had died. From this distance she could not see who was missing.

The fire was burning brightly and the Chief had seated himself in his usual position. It was then that Brave Sparrow rode slowly up to the light of the fire on Pretty Mother. The dark of the night made a perfect backdrop for the fire lit image of the woman and horse in white. All conversation stopped. No one made a sound. The people were stunned.

"I am Sarah, of the Blue Stone People," she said. She paused for effect. Brave Sparrow is no more. The Book of the Great Spirit says, "I am the Lord your God! You are not to have other gods before me! You are not to kill. You are not to steal. You are not to say what is not true. The one true God is a jealous God. He angers because we do not follow his rules that he has written in our hearts. Chief Dark Wolf, what are the names of our dead warriors?" He was startled. He stood and looked at her with trepidation.

"Fire has consumed the bodies of Night Owl and Crying Fox. Sleeping Bear is wounded."

"You sought the white men to kill them. Two of our men found death!"

"The wagon trains come with families of men, women and children. They come not to make war, but to find a place where they can make a home. They come to plant corn and raise their families. Do we have more right to live than they do? Did God tell us that all the land is ours? No, He did not. He said, do not kill and do not steal. Our warriors kill and then steal from the white man's wagon. I am one of the children they took from a wagon after killing my family. I am white! I have lived here with the people for many years. I have learned your ways and have learned to love my adopted parents. Moonflower and Chief Dark Wolf have treated me well.

Times are changing. The people must change with them. The white man comes to this land as many as the raindrops that make the rivers and lakes. We cannot stop them anymore than we can stop the rain."

Still astride the white horse, Sarah made an awesome figure. She paused again to allow the people to think about what she had just said. She continued.

"There is a way that we can become more than we are today. There is a way that we can grow and prosper. God has shown me the way. God has given us the way! We can become a new people. We must not forget our heritage, but we can add something to it that is new and exciting!"

"Can all of you remember the day that Dancing Willow's daughter was bitten by the snake that rattles? Can you remember Talking Mountain your holy man? Can you remember what he said, when I gave the necklace to Blue Stone? He said the stone has great medicine. We can be a people of Great Medicine if we live by the laws of the Great Spirit. We can be the people of the Blue Stone!"

She motioned for Sharp Knife to come. He brought the stone in its bundle from the big tent. Brave Sparrow had spent parts of many days polishing it. She dismounted and walked to a spot in front of Chief Dark Wolf. Sharp Knife laid the bundle at her feet and smiled. She smiled back, thinking he was very handsome.

"I give the medicine of the Blue Stone People to Chief Dark Wolf," she said. She lifted the heavy necklace over her head, and slowly placed it over his and adjusted it so that it lay smoothly on his chest. The people had quietly shifted so that they could all see what was happening in front of the Chief. A hushed murmur could be heard, as his hand touched the stones resting near his heart.

He hesitantly started to remove the hide. She placed her hand on top of his so that he would stop.

"Before you all see what is inside this, I want you to know that its only medicine is in the desire of the white man to possess such stones. There is no magic here."

The stone had taken a long time to clean and polish. It would shine and reflect the light of the fire. She lifted her hand and he pushed aside the hide, revealing the huge piece of turquoise marbled with black lines and small rivers of gold.

"Oooo's and Ah's," went through the assembly.

"God has shown me where there is more of this stone. The white man will treat us well. They will pay a great price for even a small amount of this from the Blue Stone People. We are the Blue Stone People!"

The Chief stood and picked up the heavy stone, lifting it far above his head. He felt suddenly young. He could feel the power and strength of his youth in his limbs. His spirit was filled with joy and hope for the future!

He began to dance, strutting and stomping, around the fire. Someone started a drumbeat in time to the Chief's steps. Sarah began to dance, too, whirling and laughing. Soon others joined and more drums sounded. The people cheered singing and dancing far into the night.

Sarah slipped away long enough to take a clean dress and Pretty Mother to the lake. She dove in and swam back and forth, rinsing the chalk from her hair and body. She took a piece of soft leather and washed Pretty Mother's coat free of chalk too. After slipping the dress and her regular moccasins on, she tied Pretty Mother to the back of the big tent. The all-white outfit was put away. The saddle and bridle were stored before she walked to the tent of Dancing Willow.

Sarah scratched near the open flap and stepped in slowly as Dancing Willow motioned for her to enter.

"Sleeping Bear is much better than he was, but he is still in great pain," she said.

Sarah's wet hair appeared tan in the glow of the fire. Dancing Willow wondered about the change, but didn't mention it.

"What have you been doing for him?" She asked. "They shot his upper leg, but the bullet went out. Sweet Grass packed a poultice on both sides, using the infection fighting plants that you showed us when we went for the walks. I had some dried and she added it to a willow bark tea for him to drink."

"You have done well. He must stay off that leg for several more days, until all the swelling is gone. Change the poultice every day. You can add clover to the poultice. He will walk and hunt again. Do not look so worried. Come have tea with me in the big tent tomorrow. We will talk."

Sarah slipped out and returned to the dance. Growling Bear now carried the stone as he danced around. Others danced and sang loudly. Moonflower motioned for Sarah to sit beside her.

"I am so glad that you returned. I feared that you had gone and would not come back. I missed you Brave Sparrow."

"Mother, you must call me Sarah now. We are a new people with new ways. I missed you, too."

"Sarah." She tried it out rather uncomfortably but didn't challenge the change. "Sarah, where did you go?"

"I traveled far out on the prairie, mother. I needed to spend a quiet time alone with the Great Spirit. I went to warn the white men to stay away from our hunting ground, but they will not listen. More will come."

"What are we to do?"

"We will make it known that only the Blue Stone People have the blue rocks. They will take care not to make enemies of us so that we will trade with them."

As the months of summer sped by, Sharp Knife came to visit at the big tent often. He went with Sarah to gather the blue stones. Only a select few had been shown where they were. Chief Dark Wolf posted a sentry at the far edge of the woods to protect the village and the blue stones from discovery. The people of the camp were told not to enter the woods behind the lake.

Sharp Knife surprised Sarah one day by giving her a new necklace. It was every bit as impressive as the one she had given to the Chief. She was delighted, knowing the time and effort that had gone into its creation.

When everyone in the village arrived at the summer council wearing a necklace made of the blue stones, it became widely known that they would trade for only the best goods. Chiefs of other tribes wanted the stones and offered high value for even a small stone. It was as Sarah had predicted. The Blue Stone People became well known.

White men came. First only a few came cautiously, to the place on the wagon trail that the Blue Stone People had chosen and marked as their trading place.

They covered a large boulder beside the wagon trail with white crushed chalkstone and grease. It could be seen for a great distance.

People brought wagons of trade goods and left with small pouches of stones. At the summer meeting, young men and new couples were eager to join the Blue Stone People. The village grew.

Sharp Knife and Sarah hunted together and fished the lake side by side. One day when the weather turned cool he told her that he would not stay in the village during the winter months.

"Singing Wind and I are planning to head south to find a more pleasant place to spend the winter months. I want to follow the wagon trails, South and West.

"There is so much that we have never seen and never will if we sit here in a tent each winter. We follow the same trails in the summer. I want to see more and learn more. I have been told that there are large settlements in the West where a man can learn to be anything he wants to be. Where we can learn to read and write the white man's words and learn the white man's medicine."

Sarah was shocked that she had not anticipated this. She waited for him to finish speaking.

"I will come back Sarah, and when I do, I want you to marry me."

"I will not be here when you come back. I have a dream to follow also. I will be leaving soon to go to my people. I don't think that I will be back. Sweet Grass has learned well, the ways of healing. She has worked with me for many months. Snow Star has learned to make the dyes to color the leather. I have done all that I can for the people. I too, long to learn the white man's ways. I want to read God's words and worship the God of my white father with others that believe as I do. I want to be able to read the Holy Bible for myself."

"We have been the best of friends for a long time. I will miss you," he said.

"I will miss you, Sharp Knife."

"When do you plan to leave?"

"Singing Wind and I will be heading out after the sun comes up tomorrow."

"It is so soon."

"We will say Good-bye to everyone then."

"I will leave then, too. We can ride out together." He wrapped his arms around her for just a moment. Come with us. We will have our adventure together." He could feel her resolve to follow a different plan.

"I will see you in the morning," was all she said, as she slowly turned and walked back to her tent.

*****

The old woman had finished her song to her sun god and the sun was high when they each said Good-bye to their family and friends and tied the last bundle to their packhorses. Sleeping Bear and Dancing Willow didn't want Singing Wind to leave.

"First Blue Stone left me, and now you. A woman should not be alone in her old age she wailed."

"Mother, I will return in the spring. Do not carry on this way."

Moonflower and Chief Dark Wolf stood close to Sarah as she swung up on Pretty Mother. They had talked far into the night trying to dissuade her.

The three friends headed out of camp, around the lake and into the woods. Stopping, they each broke loose several pieces of turquoise and tucked them into their saddlebags. After filing their water bags with the fresh spring water they headed through the edge of the big rock country, past the big white trading rock.

When their horses stood on the wagon trail, Sharp Knife and Singing Wind headed toward the Silver River on the wagon trail. Sarah crossed it and directed her horses toward the open prairie.

"I will see you again," called Sharp Knife. "You will be my wife!"

She waved back as a tear escaped her eye. "I love you," she whispered softly as they rode away. God, I wonder if I will ever see him again. Must I always be separated from the people I love? Will we ever be **"Together"**?

AN INVITATION

If you do not know Jesus, as your savior but you would like Him to be, please pray the following prayer. Invite Him into your heart. Commit your "New Life" to Him. He will be your constant companion, counselor, comforter, and protector. The Holy Bible tells us that He will never leave you or forsake you.

"Dear Jesus, please forgive my sins. Give me grace, Lord, so that I will not commit them again. Come into my heart and strengthen me, so that I can start a "New Life" with you as my companion. I want to live according to your will and commandments. Bless me Lord and lead me in a life that is pleasing to you. In Jesus' Holy name I pray. Amen"

If you prayed that prayer, you are saved. You are born again. Your soul is whiter than snow. The angels in heaven are rejoicing as they write your name in The Lamb's Book of Life.

Get a Holy Bible and begin to read it. Sign it and date it as an outward sign that you have committed your life to Christ. Find a good bible believing church and start attending, so that you can learn more about Your Heavenly Father. Be Baptized. What a wonderful God we have!

I will pray for you. God Bless You.
Louise Bouck

ABOUT THE AUTHOR

Louise Bouck is a follower of Jesus Christ. She and her husband, Dale, live in Arizona. Together they have raised six children.

Until an early retirement from her fulltime job in 2000, not much time was available to allocate to writing or art. With many interests, Louise enjoys painting on location. The lush greenery of Michigan, her home state and the abundant flowers in her grandmother's greenhouses and flower shop all encouraged her eye to appreciate the colors and beauty of nature.

Later after moving to Arizona, the rugged landscape of the mountains and desert stole her heart and took her artistic soul in a new direction.

Paintings in many media cover the walls of her studio as she has deliberately turned her creative side more to the discipline of writing.

Hesitantly she withdrew from the art gallery where her work was sold and left the position of resident artist at the local Historical Society Museum. Louise has written a series of Christian; Bible based stories that she is now starting to release for the first time as she works on still another story and another painting.

She hopes that you will enjoy her work and be blessed.

Books titles in

The New Life Series

More than Survival

Life's Many Journeys

The Land's Heritage

The Story of Sarah

Together

The Blue Stone People

Teewahpanee the Boy, Two Feathers the Man

The People of the Lion

The Lion's Den

Just the Beginning